Galactic Illusions

Book Two of the Talus 3 Series

Peter Sandor

Galactic Illusions, 1st Edition.

06-05-25, Rev. 8

ISBN 978-1-7772782-3-6

Copyright 2020 by Peter Sandor

Read other books by Peter Sandor

<u>The Wyld Wynd Trilogy</u>

Book 1 – Wyld Wynd The Rising

Book 2 – Wyld Wynd The Unrest

Book 3 – Wyld Wynd Unleashed

<u>The Wall Plug Boys</u> – a hilarious adult comedy.

The Talus 3 Trilogy

Book 1 – Arctic EMP

Book 3 – Forsaken Drifter

Book 4 – Time Undone

Paperbacks, hardcovers and ebooks are available from Amazon.

Contents

Prologue

7:00 a.m. September 23rd in the year 2084.

The day began with ease and less than remarkable expectations. I awoke early after a restful night, pulling on shorts, a thin short-sleeved shirt and sneakers, before setting out from my Zurich home. Although, for the last two weeks, I hadn't run along the jogging path, bordered on one side by rows of century-old, renovated, luxurious homes, and on the other by the Limmat River, my five years living within the beautiful Swiss city kept the route familiar to me.

Running through the trees, the sun, still low on the horizon, warmed the ground, creating a low fog across the dew-covered grass. Birds chirped as they began their day from the protection of the oak and maple trees, dotting the parkette surrounding the pathway. The warmth on my face brought back memories of my youth when one could actually see the sun. Now, after more than a century of burned carbon gases being pumped into the atmosphere, there was a perpetual, thin layer of muting haze covering the sky.

After working at the European Space Agency moon base for the past two weeks, the effects of lower gravity on my body were still evident. I was a veteran of missions to the moon with 18 under my belt. As such, I knew, after two weeks of exercise, my muscle mass and cardiovascular function would return to normal. Since my muscles ached, it didn't take long for my stride to slow, and my breaths were more labored than they usually would be. I worked through the aches and continued down the winding path. Having been through this recovery phase many times before, I forced my mind to other thoughts, purposely distracting the weariness I felt.

Five years ago, I moved to Zurich from Moscow. Ten years before, in 2069, Russia joined the European Union, propelling the EU to become the dominating economic and military power of the world. Not long after, a European Space Agency launch site was built in the foothills of the Alps, 50 kilometres east of Zurich. It was an identical sister site to one built northeast of Moscow. I was one of a team of 20 Russian nationals sent to the Nurigbach launch site. With missions to the moon base becoming a weekly event, and with some of these trips becoming only the first leg of the recently-enacted, exploratory trips to Mars, my medical degree with a specialization in human, zero gravity interaction put me at the forefront of needs at the Space Agency.

Notwithstanding the perpetual haze in the sky, there were days such as today when the haze was thinner, and the sun worked seemingly harder to break through the obstructive layer. I wiped the sweat from my brow with my forearm—at least the beads not evaporated by the cool, morning breeze from the west. I found it harder to distract from the muscle aches, especially those in my calf muscles. I moved my thoughts to my wife and two children, still in bed at our townhouse, where, in hindsight, I should have still been. Grimacing, I continued on, no longer noticing the lapping sound of the river, nor now showing any concern for the architectural qualities of the houses I passed. My mind was in a zone—almost a meditative state.

Consequently, it should've come as no surprise, when, from behind, a sack was adeptly thrown over my head. I was caught utterly off guard. Before I could react, a needle was pressed into my arm, and my need to cry out was replaced by a lethargic effort to maintain my feet. Failing miserably, a rough hand under each arm supported me just as I fell into unconsciousness.

When I awoke and forced my eyes open, it was to see only darkness. Since the sack was still over my head, heightening my other senses, I could hear the lapping of water and the slight rock of what, obviously, was the motion of a boat. It was silly since the sack was quite effective, but still, instinctively, I turned my head from side to side. From close by, I heard a voice say, "He's awake."

A moment later, the sack was removed. I raised my forearm over my eyes due to the irritation from the daylight, but as my eyes adjusted, I lowered it to see I was indeed on a boat—but not just a boat; rather, it was a large, luxury yacht, at least 20 metres long. The sleek yacht was white with red trim. The doors to the main cabin were open wide, revealing an interior living area, matching the expensive look of the exterior.

I found myself on a cushioned bench seat along one side of the open-air, rear deck area. Looking up and to my left, a young man was peering down from the elevated cockpit area of the vessel. A second man was standing in front of the entry to the main cabin of the cruiser. He was easily six-foot-tall with a stout build. His frame fit well into a pair of khaki slacks and a long sleeved, dark-blue polo shirt. This man looked 40 years old, mainly from the wisps of grey interlaced in his light-brown hair, neatly swept back at a length to cover his ears. I thought it odd since the length hadn't been fashionable for quite a few years. If not for the grey in his hair, I would've thought him younger due to the smooth, wrinkle-free skin of his chiselled face.

This man was holding a drink containing ice and a straw. Peering over it, he offered, "My apologies for the less than cordial invitation." He tipped his glass towards me and asked, "Can I get you one?"

I took a few moments to take an accounting of my surroundings before responding. Looking to my right, out the stern of the yacht, Zurich was 300 metres distant and receding quickly as the yacht plowed through the calm water of Lake Zurich. Swivelling my gaze out the starboard side of the vessel, I observed the wind farm on the far shoreline, consisting of 500 wind turbines providing most of the power for the city. I rubbed my chin and my eyes darted furtively as I saw the distance to shore was only 200 metres. Since I was not bound in any way, I considered jumping, then swimming for safety, but thought better of it. My muscle mass was compromised from my recent space trip. My hesitation was also heightened by the recent drug injection, leaving me less than fully alert.

There was a mini bar just inside the main living compartment where the man retrieved a bottle of spring water. Still somewhat dumbfounded from the events of the morning, I accepted the water from him as he clarified, "The water will help flush the drug from your system. Do not be worried. You were given only a mild dose, so you were unconscious for less than 40 minutes. You will feel perfectly normal in no time."

My mouth was dry, so I took the opportunity to drink deeply from the bottle. My senses were coming back to me, and my state of shock was drifting away along with the effects of the drug. If my abductor's aim was to kill me, they would've already done so. They wanted something, likely having to do with my function at the Space Agency. The obvious question finally came. "Why am I here?" I asked.

The man casually sat down on the bench seat across from me, crossing one leg over the other. He pointed beside me and indicated, "There are long pants and a long-sleeved shirt beside you. It's a bit cool on the water today, so I suggest you take a moment to change before I answer your first of, what I am sure are, many questions."

I hadn't noticed it before, but at the far end of the bench beside me were the described clothes, neatly folded. My confusion was beginning to irritate me more than the abduction. First, I was accosted and drugged, then whisked away on a boat. Yet, granted, the boat was a luxury yacht, and my abductor appeared to be calm, polite, with a general concern for my well being. I was given water, clothing for my comfort, along with what appeared to be the freedom to move about the vessel—or so I thought.

"I'll go into the main cabin to change," I offered as a test of the freedom I assumed was there.

The man nodded and smiled. "Of course."

Rising to my feet I made my way inside. Once out of sight from my abductor, I found a well-appointed kitchen area just beyond the lounge. There, it didn't take me long to find a long, sharp kitchen knife. I changed quickly into the clothes provided and was surprised to find they fit my 6-foot-5-inch frame perfectly. They were similar to what the man outside wore except the slacks were black, and the shirt red.

As I made my way back out onto the rear deck, I made no effort to hide the knife I grasped. The man across from me took no notice of it while calmly taking another drink from his glass. I returned to the bench across from him and suggested, "My wife will be frantic by now. She would have called the police."

The man replied, "No, she received a call from the Space Agency a short time ago, indicating you had been brought into work due to an emergency. She was told you would not be back until late tonight."

My first thought was one of relief. At least I was expected to be back home later tonight. My second thought was more concerning. The man had an extensive knowledge of me: where I worked, the exact size of the clothes I wore, and exactly what to tell my wife. It wasn't difficult to determine he was a foreigner, evident from the slight, but unique, accent his words carried. It wasn't from the official languages of Switzerland: German, French or Italian. He wasn't Russian, and, suddenly, I almost spit out a mouthful of water. It was only now I realized the man was speaking to me in English. My English was excellent, but I hadn't used it in some time. "I'm asking again, why am I here?"

The man grinned as he saw the dribble of water from the corner of my mouth. He squinted, then looked up towards the sky as if somehow the answer was there. Once his gaze returned to me, he simply said, "I am here to fulfill a vow and give you a message, or more accurately, to tell you a story."

I held my hand out, palm up. "All this, to tell me a story?"

There was a vein just above his temple, swelling slightly as the tone in his voice became more urgent. "Are you not Yevgeni Ivanov?"

"Well, yes…"

"The son of Vlas Ivanov and the grandson of Luca Ivanov?"

Hopefully, the shock I felt was not so evident on my face. I just nodded my chin up and down.

The man continued. "The same Luca Ivanov who some knew, at least for a short period of time during a mission to Canada, as Nick Anderson?"

Now, there was no hiding my shock as my jaw dropped, and my eyes opened wide. Nick Anderson was a name I heard many times through my youth. It was a name from a story my grandfather told me, sometimes with my father present. When my grandfather died, my father continued to repeat the story, although with less zeal and bravado than my grandfather did.

Even though my abductor could see I was in shock, he was expecting an answer. I tried my best but still fumbled my words. "Well—yes. Nick Anderson is a name my grandfather told us he used on a mission a long time ago. But—but, we were sworn to secrecy. No one else knows his association with that name, so how could you?" I realized, at that time, I didn't know who this man was. My lips tightened and my eyebrows lowered. "Just who are you to know all this?"

He grinned again, slouching back against the cushion of the bench. The protruding vein relaxed and calm came over his face once again. "You ask the wrong question. My name, or *who* I am, is not as important as *what* I am."

Creases appeared across my brow as the man spoke in riddles while appearing to be quite a conundrum. An unusual accent, his knowledge of me and even his carefree attitude towards my abduction, added to his mystery—one I wanted an answer to. So I followed his advice and asked, "*What* are you?"

He took another long drink from his glass and placed it on the table before he responded. "My descendants are from the planet Kor. I am a Korian, here to fulfill an obligation to an oath and tell you the fate of the Korian people on the asteroid known as Talus 3."

In that moment, I wasn't sure what to think, but the entire story my grandfather told me flashed before me in a matter of moments. My grandfather, in his prime, had been an agent in the Russian secret service, and in 2020 was assigned a mission taking him to Canada. Another Russian under the operative name, Logan Russell, was to co-lead the mission with him. It wasn't long before Logan told Nick a fantastical yarn about another world called Kor having been decimated in an interstellar war several thousand years earlier. And for the thousands of years since, survivors of Kor travelled across the universe in an asteroid called Talus 3, looking for a new world to populate.

However, their unrelenting adversary in the long war was from a nearby world called Shol, and it was just as ravaged as Kor. The Sholites were perpetual, mortal enemies of the Korians and followed them through many galaxies.

After thousands of years of space travel, Talus 3 was on a path coming in close proximity to Earth. A Sholite group, preceding Talus 3, arrived on Earth and set about building a machine to deflect the asteroid from what the Sholites falsely foretold as being on a direct collision course with the planet. But the electromagnetic device was, in fact, being made with the help of duped Earth scientists, in an effort to *destroy* Talus 3. Although the Sholites told the Earthers Talus 3 was a Sholite world, in actuality, it was filled with eight million Korians; it was a deception within a deception.

Finally, there was a battle on the outskirts of Fort Nelson, a small, long-forgotten town in Northern Canada. The battle wasn't epic, but it was decisive in that the device built by the Sholites was destroyed by a joint force of Korians and Russians. Both Talus 3 and millions of lives on Earth were saved. My grandfather, Nick Anderson, and Logan Russell, led the attack on the Sholites. On Earth, their efforts were completely unknown, but on Kor they became famed heroes.

However, they were not as famous as another man, Josh Harris, who was a Korian infiltrator within the Sholite group. He was the brother of Logan, and the real hero of that day as he sacrificed his life to stop the ignition of the device.

The last piece of the unbelievable story, as told by my grandfather, was the involvement of Natalie Lowe, a Canadian secret service agent. She was one of those duped by the Sholites, and while working with them, she and Josh fell deeply in love. After Josh died, heartbroken, with little to look forward to on Earth and pregnant with Josh's child, she left with Logan to live her life out in Talus 3.

This was the story my father told me several times before his untimely death, but never with as much emotion and conviction as my grandfather had. After all, it was quite unbelievable. I hadn't yet told my own son the story as my conviction was even more diluted. Yet here in front of me was a man who just said, "He's a Korian." I couldn't help but stare at him, and he sensed this as my desperate need for more information—my need to know what happened to Talus 3 after it left, if, in fact, the tale was real.

My abductor explained, "There are four critical players in the story. The man you know as Josh Harris is immortalized as a hero in Talus 3. He gave his life to save our world. His brother, Logan Russell and your grandfather Luca, were also heroes as was Natalie Lowe. Between their efforts, eight million Korians were saved."

I mumbled, "That's the way I remember the story."

"Then, you also know of the oath made between Logan and your grandfather?"

One eyebrow raised as I asked, "You know of that as well?"

The man rubbed his chin as I think he was starting to become frustrated. It seemed he was trying to get to something bigger, and I was delaying him. He sighed and said, "Your grandfather and Logan were more than comrades on that mission. They respected each other, knowing without the skills of each of them, it was unlikely the mission would have been successful." His voice lowered. "They became good friends, so when they were about to part ways forever, it was difficult for both of them.

Logan made a suggestion, one that would maintain their link, so your grandfather readily agreed. Talus 3 was once again hurtling through space in their search to find a planet they could call home. Logan pledged, one day, when their search was over, even though such technology was not yet available, the Korians would find a way to send a message back to the man they knew as Nick Anderson. If it did not come in their lifetimes, then the story and the oath would be passed down through their future generations."

"So you're a messenger."

He nodded and waited as if he knew I was not so easily led on, or more specifically, so easily led to believe such a story at face value. The story, as told to me, I thought of as more of a fairy tale. It's one thing to give more belief to it, but completely another to blindly believe in alien species, not to speak of these aliens fighting a battle on my world. I wanted to understand his conviction, so I prodded him on. "Your message has been sent. Can I leave now?"

He slapped his thigh, and he threw his head back in laughter. When his gaze returned to me, he said, "The story I am about to tell you is not so simple. It begins over four light years from Earth, and having travelled that far, it deserves more than a momentary, fleeting dismissal."

"What would you suggest?"

There was a hidden drawer under the table top, and from it, he pulled a tablet, placing it on the table. "Many, many years ago, the Korian people in Talus 3 learned of the oath between Logan Russell and Nick Anderson. Since then, scholars have painstakingly recorded critical historic events." He pointed to the cockpit above him as he continued. "Pascoe is considered Korian, but he was born here on Earth, descended from a small group of Korians who decided to stay instead of returning to Talus 3. They have taken the time to translate the lengthy story of Talus 3 into English, so you can hear it in its entirety, thereby fulfilling your part of the oath between two friends from different worlds, 64 years ago."

I recalled my grandfather Luca telling me much about the Korians was quite different from our Earth lifestyle. With that in mind I asked, "I understand the Korian system of math and time is very different from Earth. Will I be able to understand these aspects of the story?"

My abductor tilted his head slightly. I think he was impressed by the question. "I see your grandfather told you the story with quite a bit of detail. You are correct in that our measurement of time, distance, geometry, and speed are all based on the number 5 and multiples of it: 5, 25, 125, 625 and so on. I am sure it sounds awkward to you, but think about your own metric system with a base of ten. Then your time is based on 60 and 24. Your circular geometry is based on 60. Throw in the many bastard units still used: inches, feet, miles and knots, and we Korians wonder, with such inconsistencies, how people of Earth can function at all, not to mention achieving space travel."

I was silent, thinking of his words, slowly coming to the conclusion, he was right.

"Fear not," he said. "For the sake of your understanding, during the translation to English, the units of measure you are familiar with have been kept, in most cases."

I paused, thinking of my grandfather, Luca, who I loved dearly and missed even more. He would want me to take the time to listen to the rest of the story. My eyes became moist as I recalled the many times, as a boy, he took me out onto his balcony to look at the stars. He would tell me their names, but often his words changed to those reminiscent of his friend, Logan. I wiped my eyes and whispered, "I would like to hear what happened to Talus 3."

A wide smile came across his face as he was about to pick up the tablet. I interrupted him with a raised finger. I still held a scruple of skepticism, and it had to be put to bed before I would listen. "I have one request before you begin," I told him.

He paused and his eyes turned up to me. "What do you need?"

"I'm sorry, but the events of this day are surreal and unnerving." I was careful in choosing my words. "If you're a Korian sent here to deliver the story, then you know the story in great detail," I surmised.

"Of course," he replied as his hand still hovered over the tablet.

I explained, "There's a point in the story when Logan tells my grandfather he was an alien. My grandfather laughed and didn't believe it. Then, Logan did something to prove, irrefutably, he was a Korian. What was it?"

My abductor rose to his feet while slowly shaking his head from side to side. At the same time, he mumbled words from some foreign language unknown to me. However, from the curt tone and the look on his face, I was quite sure he was cursing. He came to my side and picked up the knife I had previously retrieved and forgotten about. He ran the side of his finger along the sharp edge before holding his cut finger over the glass tabletop. Drips of blood fell, creating a small pool. Although my grandfather, in his story, told me of the expectation, still my eyes opened wide in surprise. Involuntarily, I yelled out, "Your blood is blue!" Indeed, it was light-blue in colour—just as Logan's was 64 years ago—just as it is the colour of every true Korian's blood.

He returned to his bench after retrieving a napkin to wrap around his finger. He lifted up the tablet, crossed one leg over the other and calmly asked, "Are you ready?"

I was embarrassed at having him cut himself, but it needed to be done, just as my grandfather needed Logan to do the same. I nodded. In response, he pressed a finger to the screen of the tablet and cleared his throat.

This is the story he told me on that warm day—September 23rd, 2084— a day I naïvely thought would be less than remarkable.

Chapter 1: Playing in the Garden

Ryder and Gaylin squatted on their haunches, leaning back against the stone fence bordering the far side of the large estate. The two boys were evaluating the expansive yard as they had done many times during their numerous visits to the home of their grandmother—vidame of the Gunn family. Gaylin, Ryder's cousin, pointed at a short, stout tree with large, yellow and green leaves, near the fence some 60 metres distant. Ryder nodded, then pointed at a large, red rock with silver streaks through it, half the distance between the tree and the house. Finally, Gaylin pointed at a thin, tree with dark-brown bark and a burst of white leaves only at the very tip, 30 metres in the air.

Ryder gave a determined nod of his chin. The course was set. Both twelve-year-old Ryder and ten-year-old Gaylin, shifted their stance to a pounce, their bent legs like coil springs ready to release their pent-up energy. When Gaylin's whispered countdown was complete, both boys shot out across the dark-green, artificial grass. Gaylin was tall for his age, but thin and gangly. Ryder was more compact and shot out to an early lead in the race. However, after 20 seconds, Gaylin's longer stride put him ahead of his older cousin.

Gaylin reached the first tree, and his long legs made an awkward turn around it before propelling him towards the large rock. Ryder, being more agile, caught the tree trunk with his hand and, with his feet skirting the ground, swung around the tree, shooting out after Gaylin. By the time Gaylin was circling around the rock, Ryder had made up half the deficit.

Although he was young, Ryder had an overabundance of competitive spirit. He liked having fun, but it was always about winning. It didn't matter that it was his cousin and friend; he needed to beat him. Ryder didn't run around the rock; rather, he ran into it, arms bent, before shooting off it as his arms extended. He almost lost his footing, but his quick steps kept his balance. His eyes were half closed, and his mouth was set in a determined, stern line. *He was the hunter and Gaylin was the prey.* Typically, Gaylin's younger and thinner legs would not maintain the pace, and today was no different. Ryder's arms moved in perfect unison to his legs. He passed his cousin only a few metres away from the thin tree by the house. He touched it first, just seconds before Gaylin.

Gaylin thrust back his head and cursed, "Shit! I lost again!"

Ryder smiled widely from under his mop of dark-brown hair. His blue eyes were alight with the exultation of victory as he slapped Gaylin on the back and offered, "It was really close, Gaylin. I was lucky to win."

Gaylin's eyes, also blue but darker than Ryder's, narrowed as he slapped his cousin's hand away. "You always win. Luck never seems to be on my side."

In an effort to cheer up his cousin, Ryder exclaimed, "Let's play cards!"

At first, Gaylin didn't respond. He just looked at his feet while Ryder continued to urge him towards the new game. After the fourth such effort, Gaylin's frown began to break. Gaylin knew he was good at cards, and this was a game where he would have an excellent chance of beating Ryder. Gaylin's tilted smile came just before he agreed, "Cards it is."

The two boys walked up onto the huge, polished-stone deck, supporting two large, rectangular tables. The adults had finished their lunch, and now, Vidame Natalie Gunn was seated in a cozy lounge chair alongside the wall of the house. Ryder's parents were seated on a couch opposite Natalie, while Gaylin's parents were standing, cold drinks in hand, having a conversation with Arlo Gunn, long ago known as Logan Russell.

Arlo left Earth with Natalie after the Battle of Fort Nelson. Natalie was pregnant with Rowan Gunn's child. At that time, on Earth, Rowan was known as Josh Harris. With the assistance of the Korian doctors, a son, Pateer was born. When he came of age, he married Nola, and the two became the proud parents of Ryder.

On Earth, just before Rowan died, he gave Natalie a betrothal ring. The bond never came to fruition, and as quickly as Rowan heroically died, Arlo was there to support her in her grief. As they say, "One thing led to another," and Natalie was drawn to the similarities between the two brothers, Rowan and Arlo. Arlo and Natalie became good friends, and it wasn't a surprise to others when they fell deeply in love.

In addition to consummating the deep love they had for each other, when they bonded, it solved a huge problem they had in Talus 3 society. The problem arose from the betrothal ring, which Natalie only then learned, was the ring belonging to the matriarch of the Gunn family.

For the most part, Korian society on Talus 3 was matriarchal. There were over three thousand extended families, the lines descending from the planet Kor, thousands of years before. Of these, there were 79 larger families, and within this group were nine primary families that formed the government of the people. The Gunn family was one of the nine, and arguably, the most powerful in the group.

The manner in which the matriarchal leadership was passed down is interesting. The son of a presiding matriarch was called a primor, or first in line. The primor would choose a wife, usually with irritating interference from the family, along with negotiation from other prospective families. The partner could be from within the extended family, but typically, she was arranged from another family with the intent to improve standing and power of both families within Talus 3's society.

Natalie didn't know, but Rowan was the primor of the Gunn family at the time he gave her the betrothal ring. She also didn't know the ring marked her as the next matriarch when her predecessor would pass; each family had such a ring, and each was of great importance.

A year after they were bonded, Natalie had another son from Arlo, and in honour of Arlo's friend from Earth, they named him Nick. Nick married when he came of age and his wife bore a son, Gaylin.

Natalie easily grew into her leadership role to honour the memory of Rowan, her life with Arlo and the acceptance of the Korian people. She had honed many skills, including multitasking and observation. She put them to use now as she listened to the conversation around her, but also watched her two grandsons on the far side of the patio.

Gaylin opened the squeaky drawer of the tall cabinet leaning against the wall of the house. There were several games inside, including the playing cards in a painted, ceramic box. The two boys sat cross-legged on the polished-stone surface and put the cards between them. They played several hands; the exact Korian name or type of game was not important. Each game lasted about one quarter hour, with one boy or the other throwing their arms up in exultation at the end of each hand. For the first two hands, it was obvious Gaylin was victorious. Of course, it was important for him to gloat greatly in Ryder's face, so Ryder took the same opportunity, with great satisfaction, when he won the following two hands. It was the best of five. The air temperature was computer controlled to a cool 20 degrees Celsius, yet both boys had sweat on their brow as the final hand played out. Each time they picked up a card, before they threw one down, there was hesitation. Finally, Gaylin threw down a card Ryder immediately snatched up, and he laid out his hand; his face tilted slightly upwards with a huge, smart-assed grin.

There were six cards left in Gaylin's hand; he threw them into his cousin's face. Bouncing to his feet, Gaylin kicked the laid down cards, scattering them across the deck. He crossed his arms, and with his chin pressed firmly against his chest, he stomped a path towards his grandmother. Natalie saw him coming and rose to her feet. Before Gaylin could say anything, she put her arm around his shoulder and led him to a quiet spot, just off the edge of the patio.

Gaylin looked up and tears were streaming down his face. His voice was shaky and muffled as he blurted, "He always wins! It makes me so angry."

Natalie bent over and wiped the tears from her grandson's eyes. She kept her voice low, not wanting the discussion to carry to the other adults. "He's older than you, so he'll win more often. You should play for fun. As you get older, things will even out, and you'll win as many times as Ryder does." She smiled lovingly to him as only a grandmother could do.

Gaylin's arms uncrossed, only for his hands to be placed obstinately on his hips. "But he always wins. It's not just most of the time. It's always."

Natalie knew better than to patronize him with a tap on the head or a stroke of his cheek. She knew her grandson, and he appreciated being treated as a man, although he was still just a little one. She put her finger under Gaylin's chin, lifting his gaze to hers. "You can come to me with any problem, but first you should try and take care of it yourself, or with Ryder. That's what a great man would do."

There was some sting in his grandmother's words, but he knew she loved him as much as he loved her. She was the vidame of the Gunn family, the most important family in all of Talus 3. Gaylin wiped his eyes and thrust his chest out while pulling himself up to a height impressive for a ten-year-old. "You're right. Thank you, Nana Natalie."

Not being able to resist, she now gave Gaylin a huge kiss on the cheek, just before her grandson wiped it away while uttering out a huge, "yuck!" Gaylin ran off, searching for his cousin, the next contest and, hopefully, a win.

He found Ryder as he just finished putting the cards away. Gaylin poked him in the shoulder as if nothing was wrong. It was a sequence seen many times as the competitive contests between them had been going on from the time they learned to walk. Gaylin pointed to another tree, wide with many leaves covering the branches. Many times, the two boys had climbed the wide, gnarled branches, twisting their way to a height 20 metres above the ground.

They both ran to the tree and took a set position at the base of the trunk. Again, there was a countdown, after which they both reached up for a branch, one on either side of the tree. They were like little animals as they scampered up the tree, striving for a spot near the top where they both could sit. The upper branches were a bit thinner, the leaves on them shaking with a few falling to the ground. To Gaylin's chagrin, Ryder reached their little nest before him. Ryder sat on a curved section of branch, looking back and down at the house. Just behind him, Gaylin sat on a second, similar branch, once again defeated.

Ryder half turned and patted his cousin on the knee. "You climb really well. It was so close."

If Ryder would've turned, he would've seen the amount of anger in Gaylin's face from the red tinge to his skin and his clenched teeth through slightly open lips. Gaylin was staring at the back of Ryder's head. He was fuming, having lost again. He was sick of it, just as it appeared his grandmother was sick of him coming to her every time he lost. *She was right.* As a young man in a great family, he needed to take care of issues as a great man would.

Without another thought, he gave Ryder a huge push in the back, thrusting him off the branch. Ryder deflected off a lower limb; then, he took a hard bounce off a second branch before twisting off, falling the last two metres to the ground with a loud thud.

Gaylin, through narrow eyes, looked down at his cousin, unconscious, with one arm twisted at an impossible angle. He thought, *so much for your winning streak.*

Chapter 2: The Birthday Party

The official name of the asteroid was Talus 3. Initially, thousands of years ago, there were five Talus asteroids built by their forefathers. All of them were destroyed except for Talus 3, the only remaining vessel of the Korian people. Since there was only one Talus asteroid left, there was no longer a need for the designation, *3*. Almost all Korians now referred to their home simply as—Talus.

The Gunn Spire, built only 10 years ago, was one of the newest, ultra-modern and magnificent buildings in Talus. Spires were buildings extending from the floor of the cavern to its roof. It was a distance of 300 metres; as such, since they tended to block out the artificial light, city bylaws limited how many spires were allowed and where they could be located.

The Gunn Spire was in the tail section of a 20-kilometre-long by 9-kilometre-wide chamber, dominated by many buildings owned and run by the Gunn family. Most of these, since they were smaller and older than the spire, were made of courser, dark stone either mined from the Talus asteroid itself, or farmed from the many meteors the mining ships found randomly hurtling through space. Using more recent technology to polish stone to a smooth hue, and also using rare, metallic materials collected over many years, the Gunn Spire's granite-like, silver colour, with light-blue, interlaced streaks, made it the class and envy of their world.

Ryder Gunn was in a massive banquet room on the 28th floor of the Gunn Spire. Since this was the 22nd hour of the 25-hour Talus day, there was little light from outside the building, and this allowed the ornate, gem-covered chandeliers to be at their peak of beauty. The subtle streaks of light filled the room with the colours of the rainbow. At least, these were the thoughts going through Ryder's head as he took a long drink of alcohol-spiked fruit punch from his glass. Inside, he laughed at himself. No one in Talus had ever seen a rainbow, other than those in history books.

As Ryder looked across the room, he considered the artificial world created inside the asteroid. The builders did their best to simulate the world they knew on their home world, Kor. Consequently, the Talus day began at the 6th hour, when the city's computers set the artificial light to 100 per cent. This was maintained until the 18th hour, when the light was reverted back to 60 per cent. At the 21st hour, the light levels were reduced to 30 per cent, starting the nighttime cycle.

Twisting from the waist, Ryder put his empty glass on the bar behind him. He felt a twinge of pain in his shoulder as he stretched his arm out. He was now 40 years old, and even though it had been 28 years since his fall from the tree in his grandmother's yard, his joint never did fully recover.

A young woman with dark-black hair, falling almost to her waist, walked by not three metres in front of him. Her graceful steps had her floating out from the throng of bodies making up the bedlam of the party. She wore a sleek, green dress, cut just above the knees. It hugged her curves as she slowed in front of Ryder. She turned slightly, so he could see her scantily covered bosom. She saw his eyes widen, and her face grew even more enticing as a wide smile formed; she truly was beautiful.

Ryder didn't blush. As primor of the Gunn family and, arguably, the most eligible bachelor in Talus, these flirtatious advances were commonplace and, most often, irritating. He turned from her and faced the bar, tapping the surface, indicating his need for a refill to his glass. As he lifted the refilled glass to his lips, a sharp slap to his back almost spilled the contents. He tilted his head and peered up at the tall man standing beside him.

"Cousin!", the man exclaimed, his speech slightly slurred by an over abundance of alcohol.

Ryder turned and half-smiled. "Gaylin, as always, you're having a good time."

Gaylin snapped his fingers above his head as he glared at the server behind the bar. Once their eyes met, Gaylin put his empty glass on the countertop. At six-foot-two inches, Ryder was tall, but it didn't compare to Gaylin's lanky frame at a full six-foot-six inches. His body never grew out of his gangly, uncoordinated build, nor did his features ever become handsome. His face was drawn out with a long, protruding chin dominating his face. His hair was jet-black, the same colour as the short, trimmed beard and moustache he wore to help camouflage his chin. Gaylin retorted, "I always have a good time, Cousin. How about you? How many young women have come by to show their wares?"

Ryder smiled from under the short crop of neatly-trimmed, brown hair. He pulled his hands in front of himself and bent his fingers down one after another, until he ran out of fingers. He blurted out a laugh before saying, "It seems I have lost count!"

Gaylin joined in the laughter. Once it subsided, the corners of his lips turned down, and his tone lowered. "Has your mother come to you yet, to see if you have a selection?"

Ryder's chest relaxed with his sigh. "Not yet, but we both know she will find me before the night is over."

Nola Gunn, Ryder's mother and Gaylin's aunt, had become vidame of the Gunn family after the death of Natalie Gunn, and that only a year after Arlo Gunn's death. The family was in odd circumstances. Nola led admirably, but anyone who knew anything about the family circles within Talus, knew, in many ways, the matriarch was more of a figurehead. There were many others behind the vidame who ran the businesses and most family affairs.

Gaylin Gunn was such a man. The Gunn family controlled the pharmaceutical industry within Talus, and Gaylin, at 38 years old, was the *Chief Executive Officer* of the business. He was also *Second in Line* to Ryder in the family hierarchy. If anything happened to Ryder, Gaylin would be the next primor, and if Vidame Nola died, Gaylin's wife would be the next vidame. With all this considered, setting aside superficial perceptions, it was actually Gaylin who was the most powerful person in the Gunn family.

It should have been Ryder, but Ryder's mind was distracted from such affairs. The last thing he wanted was to be mired in the family business and the politics coming with it. Since he had a different dream, it had been difficult enough for Ryder to accept a position as *Administrator of Family Relations.*

Ryder had been momentarily daydreaming. Gaylin cackled and snapped his fingers in front of his cousin. In a mocking tone, Gaylin said, "Still thinking of the stars and flying off into the cold, quiet of space?"

Ryder took another drink from his glass. "You know I dream of being in the Explorer's Corp. I want to be out there with the Korians who go forth and search for a new world, one we can call our new home."

Gaylin's voice changed to a sarcastic tone, and he bobbled his head as he said, "But mommy won't let you go out into space." He waggled his finger in front of Ryder's face. "It's not appropriate for the primor of the most powerful family in Talus to take such risks and not participate in family activities."

Ryder glared at Gaylin as his cousin shuffled away. *Yes, Gaylin was an asshole.* Ryder had no memory of his fall from the tree as a child. He knew he had climbed the tree many times. He knew every handhold, every foothold. He wondered if Gaylin pushed him, but he never knew, nor did anyone else. The relationship between the two cousins changed from that point. They no longer had competitions between them. As they grew into young men, Ryder developed a relaxed personality, learned of his disdain for bullshit and realized his amazement of the stars and the mysteries they held.

Alternatively, Gaylin also developed his unique personality, one focused on attaining power, and that meant, one day, leading the Gunn family. He married young; it was an arranged marriage to Urslla Zaf. The Zaf family controlled all aspects of power generation, making them one of the nine powerful families within the Talus Council that ran all things. Although Urslla was beautiful, their marriage was open, and both of them had others to fulfill their diverse needs.

Gaylin was taller than anyone in the throng of partiers. As such, yet unfortunately, Ryder could not lose sight of him. Gaylin's one arm was high in the air, the liquid in his glass sloshing about. His other hand was gyrating as it swung up and down. Eyes closed, his head snapped back and forth, completely out of sync with his arm and the music. Ryder shook his head. He had seen this act many times before, the uncoordinated movements he had come to call the *crazy dance*.

Thankfully, his view of his cousin was blocked by an older man, accompanied by a younger woman. He knew the man well. He was Jerik Oro, primor of the Oro family. The Oro family was responsible for what can be best described as water farming. They owned many ships that roamed into the expanse of space searching for water, in most cases in the form of ice. It was actually quite plentiful; most comets were made of ice, although some had impurities rendering them useless, but most were pure or, with a little refining, could be made useable.

Of course, water was critical to the people of Talus, not only to drink, but it was a significant source of oxygen. Utilizing an advanced electrolysis process, water was separated into oxygen and hydrogen. This source, along with the oxygen created by the genetically modified oxygen vines, maintained an ample supply of breathable air inside Talus.

Jerik said, "Primor Gunn, may I present my niece, Mattie Oro."

As is the custom, she held her hand out, palm down. Ryder slid his hand under hers and gave her delicate hand, under a white, lace covering, a warm embrace. His gaze caught hers. She was truly a beauty and clearly not a day older than 19.

"My niece will be coming of age in two months," Jerik offered. "The Oro family is already well aligned with the Gunn family, but a fresh union would certainly cement our relationship."

Ryder saw through his words that were actually a not-so-well disguised threat. The families of Talus were constantly making alliances. Right now, the Gunn family had strong alliances with the Oro and Vad families, making their alliance, arguably, the strongest in Talus. There were constant manoeuvres by other alliances and families in an effort to change the balance of power. Presently, the Fyr family, controlling the military, allied with the Zaf and Pym families, were the primary competition. By referencing their present relationship and implying it might need strengthening, Ryder knew Primor Oro was making a threat to their alliance. Before Ryder could respond, a dark shape came into view beside Jerik.

Ryder's mother, Vidame Nola Gunn, was wearing a black pant suit. Although it might sound bland, the jacket was interlaced with black sequins, as was the short hat, the lip of which was adorned with a silver feather. Of course, Ryder had seen his mother at many official functions, but it still caught him off guard, how stunning she looked, even now at her 63rd birthday party.

"Primor Oro, so nice to see you." The vidame looked around Jerik at the young woman. A sound came from her throat, almost like a purr. "My, my, Jerik, you have chosen young. Is this your wife, or perhaps someone you don't want your wife to meet?" Nola threw her head back, laughing at her joke.

Jerik fumbled for words as the look of innocence on his niece's face changed, first to pink with embarrassment, then red with contained rage. Jerik muttered, "No…my niece…"

Vidame Gunn flicked her hand in the air. "Jerik, I need to speak with my son. If you would…" Her hand now gave the same motion again, like she was flicking a particle of dirt off a table. The two Oro's slunk away, leaving Nola Gunn with a smug look on her face. Ryder's eyebrows were lowered, the inner edges almost hitting his nose, in a disapproving look.

His mother threw her hands in front of her, palms up. "What? She's his niece, daughter to a third sister, and no where in line to a position of importance in their family." Nola wiped her fingers down the lapel of her jacket, and in a hushed voice, offered, "That's just insulting."

"Of course, *Mother.*"

Nola Gunn's lips turned into a frown. Her son knew she despised when he patronized her with the tag, *mother.* She leaned over and gave her son a loving kiss on his cheek. "Come, let's get some air on the balcony."

Ryder didn't respond. He was looking into the crowd on the dance floor. A young woman was dancing, not with anyone in particular—rather, with everyone, it seemed. Her hand came up behind her neck, rolling her shoulder-length, red hair over her head, when she caught Ryder staring at her. She froze, her hand still in the air, aggressively returning his stare. To Ryder, it was like an electrical charge just ran through his body—a connection at some different level. He took a step forward when his mother's hand landed lightly on his shoulder.

He tilted his gaze to her as his mother whispered, "Come with me, Ryder."

When he returned his gaze to the dance floor, the redhead was gone, swallowed up by the throng.

His mother's fingers squeezed his shoulder; then, she made a path through the crowded floor to the far side of the room and the large balcony there. He followed and he knew, somewhere behind him, would be three security people. Two would be for his mother, and one was his own personal bodyguard.

Once out in the open air, with the city in the panorama behind them, three other guests quickly went inside once they saw the vidame and the primor. They were alone. Ryder leaned forward and gave his mother a huge hug. Mothers will act as mothers have acted for thousands of years, just as they will act for the next thousand. He loved her dearly. Once Ryder pulled away, he smirked and said, "That was actually pretty funny."

Nola's face changed. Her eyelids opened wide, and the tip of her tongue came out to touch her upper lip. It was a look of pure mischief. She couldn't hold the pose for long as, finally, her mouth stretched wide, letting out a cackle. "Do you think so?"

Ryder was trying to distract his mother, but his efforts were not successful. Nola whispered, "Did you meet anyone you liked?"

Leaning back against the stone railing, the vision of the redhead on the dance floor flashed across his mind. He rubbed his chin and replied, "No, mother. I told you, I will let you know when I am ready to be with another woman."

Once again, his mother put her hand softly on his shoulder. "Tamara has been gone for four years now. It's time to move on."

He slid out from under her touch. The sound of her name caused his heart to pound. Tamara was a woman he loved, the mother of their six-year-old son, Romy. She was in the military and had died on a mission, leaving he and Romy behind. He loved her deeply, and he thought back often, wondering, *why did she have to die?* She was a nobody. She was part of the Fyr family, so low down, she was of no importance and had no ambitions or goals to a position within the Gunn family. Her honesty and her lack of ambition to power was a large part of why he loved her so much. He was about to revoke his position as primor and marry her, when she died.

Ryder's eyes turned towards his mother's. His were dark as he was about to let her know, sternly, he didn't need matchmaking help, but when he saw his mother's eyes, there were tears in them. He knew what she was thinking, and he slipped his hand into hers, knowing she would tell him in any case.

"I love children," Nola softly declared. "Not only my children, but all children. I like to have them around: spoiling them, helping them and giving them my love. Just as I love you, I want you to give me more grandchildren to love." Her eyes were searching, but Ryder remained quiet. He knew there was more. "You're my remaining child. Emmaril, my daughter, died in childbirth."

Nola became silent, and Ryder gave her a minute. He thought back to his sister, whom he never met. *She died two years before he was born, yet his mother, to this day, still thinks on it often.*

Nola's words came back to her, as did the regal tone coming with her position. "My son, you're 40 now. For a primor to be unmarried at 40 is unheard of. Most family primors are married in their early 20's." Her lips stretched into a tight line as she continued. "Think on it. If something happens to me, Gaylin is next in line. Let's face it, although no one can run the business better, he has no people skills, and certainly, he's no leader!" The last few words came through clenched teeth.

Ryder saw his mother getting herself overexcited. He nodded his chin up and down and said, "I will find some one soon, Mother. I promise."

That seemed to satisfy his mother who gave him a warm smile before she walked back into the main reception. Ryder turned and put both his hands on the stone railing as he looked out into the city. In the distance, he saw two other spires as well as the curve of the city drift off in the distance. He was still in awe, especially when he viewed the city from a greater height, how the Korian builders, thousands of years ago, built the great cities within this asteroid.

The asteroid was cigar shaped, a cylinder 100 kilometres long and 16 kilometres in diameter, making the exterior circumference at the crust a little over 50 kilometres. The circumference was important because the great chambers the Korians lived in were carved out 300 metres under the crust, the floor of each being curved to match the shape of the surface. There were 20 such caverns just under the surface. Five caverns were in line around the circumference, with approximately 100 metres of rock between each. These five great caverns in line made up what the Korians called a ring, and there were four such rings down the length of Talus.

Ryder was always amazed when he thought of the 100 years it took their forefathers to carve out the caverns, but he was more amazed at the logistics. Thousands of years ago, on Kor, just as it is on Earth, all life stands on the planet and gravity holds them to it. Here, in Talus, the gravity was insignificant, so it was simulated by rotating the cigar shaped cylinder around its central axis. However, there were limits to how fast the vessel could be rotated. Ultimately, the balance required left the centripetal force, simulating gravity, to be only 70 per cent of what they knew on Kor, ironically very similar to the force of gravity on Earth.

Of course, as odd as it sounded, that meant they were all upside down in the chambers in Talus. Ryder looked down at the floor of the cavern, 28 floors below him. Three hundred metres beyond that was the cold vacuum of space. Then he looked up, knowing the center of the asteroid was several kilometres above the roof of the cavern.

The music from the party behind him faded as he thought of the world the Korians had lived in for two thousand years. They had become used to it, but for him, he wanted to find a world where there were jungles and free animals. He wanted to feel rain on his face—and snow—something he had only heard of. That's why he wanted nothing more than to be an explorer.

Ryder looked off in the distance, seeing the city curving off into the horizon. If it was morning, with the full simulated daylight, he knew he would see the far wall of the cavern. It had its own sense of beauty, the beauty the people found wonderful, but he found adequate at best. He was restless and he wanted more.

Chapter 3: The Firefight

Curran Morant, the commander of the Sholite farming ship, *Arkala*, knew he was taking a risk. The search for methane had been successful, but certainly not easy. They'd been searching for a week and were ready to turn around, when their forward scanners found a huge gas cloud. Probes were launched, and the ten-man crew whooped with joy when the message came back that there was a heavy methane composition.

The collection sails were unfurled, and as the 200-metre-long vessel passed through the cloud, the many ports on the sails collected the gas particles. As they were directed into the plenum tank, the particles were heated before passing through the electrically charged filters. Then, the pure hydrogen gas was compressed into several high-pressure storage tanks. At the same time, the carbon monoxide and carbon dioxide by-products were expelled back into space.

The collection process took time—precious time the crew knew would put their remaining air in short supply. Now, on their return trip to the Sholite fleet, Commander Morant decided the risk of running out of air was higher than that of coming across a Korian ship in Korian space. The Korians claimed a distance of 800 million kilometres in any direction from Talus as Korian owned space. Morant decided he would need to cut through a corner of that space, otherwise the crew could be at great risk of suffocating.

For the last three hours, they'd been moving along at 25 per cent speed of light, commonly referred to as *SOL*. They were almost out of Korian space when a cry came up from his communications officer. "Contact! Bearing 280, 30, 150, distance—80 million kilometres." The contact coordinates, as all contacts were reported, was a point in a three-dimensional coordinate grid with the ship at the origin. Morant rose from his chair and strode the few steps to the communication station. While putting his hand on his officer's shoulder, he reviewed the radar screen. By the coordinates and the blip on the screen, he could see the other ship was between them and Talus.

Have they seen us?" Morant asked in a calm voice.

His officer's eyes were fixed upon the screen as he said, "No. They haven't changed course—wait!" The officer's voice took on a high pitch. "They're turning to an intercept course!"

Taking a deep breath, a slight growl came from between Morant's lips before the question, "Is he close enough for identification?"

The communication officer's fingers moved to a second keyboard. After hitting several keys, a second monitor beside the radar screen came to life. "Sir, the beacon from the ship indicates it's a Korian navy vessel." The officer's head tilted up and his eyes were wide, his brow heavy with beads of sweat. "It's an Eagle-class cruiser."

Morant took the few steps to the round, glass table beside the far wall of the control room. He glanced at the communications officer and said, "Transfer."

Almost immediately, the table changed to black with a white, luminous grid superimposed on it. In yellow was a representation of their ship. In red was the pursuing Korian cruiser. "Projected trajectories, please."

Two green, dashed lines appeared from the front of each ship. They crossed at a point on the glass top. "How far to intercept?" the commander asked.

"Distance – 154 million kilometres. Time – 45 minutes."

"We're done unless we get some help," Morant muttered. He turned around, facing a woman seated at a station along the back wall of the control room. "Break radio silence. Send out a mayday, all trade and military frequencies."

Sumi Ornesco was the admiral on board the *Cordoba*, a Buffalo-class Sholite battleship presently patrolling along the plane between Talus, 5 billion kilometres on their starboard side, and the Sholite fleet, the same distance in the opposite direction. Although their quad electromagnetic drives could propel the 500-metre-long, two-thousand metric-ton spaceship to a maximum speed of 20 per cent SOL, the ship was now cruising comfortably at five per cent. Their tour, so far, had been routine—until Ensign Broderick called out, "Admiral—we have a distress call from a Sholite farming ship. They're being chased by an Eagle-class, Korian cruiser!"

There were four large 3D monitors on the front wall of the central control room. Sumi, who had been standing behind her command chair, now turned and put both hands on the top of the chair back. She leaned forward, eyes squinting, as if she could somehow see the enemy Korian ship. "Situation!" she yelled out.

Broderick had earphones on and raised a finger in the air as he listened.

Finally, he pulled one earphone off, turned in his chair and reported, "Sir! The call is from the Arkala, a hydrogen farming ship out of space station *Marrinota*. They're just inside Talus space, 100 million kilometres distant. The Korian Cruiser is 80 million kilometres behind them.

Sumi Ornesco had been in the Sholite navy for 25 years. She was a crafty veteran of the ongoing war fought between the Sholites and the Korians for thousands of years. In that time, so long ago, the advanced societies on the planets Kor and Shol, fought a cruel, merciless war. Battles were won and lost, but the war was a stalemate. The real losers were both their planets, destroyed by nuclear poisons, toxic gas and environmental carnage.

The Korians built five Talus asteroids in secret. As they tried to leave their galaxy, four were destroyed by superior Sholite spaceships. Only one Talus ship escaped, and now, the surviving Sholite fleet of 700 ships, including seven massive space stations, mirrored the path of Talus.

Ornesco was a warrior, as was her father and grandfather. She was born for battle as were many Sholites. As children, Sholites learned how to count, how to repeat their alphabet and how to hate the Korian enemy. Many had forgotten the instigation of the war. Was it an assassination? Was it a political coup—or perhaps something as simple as a difference of opinion? It hadn't mattered for a long time. For thousands of years, as friends, parents and grandparents had died in their ongoing war, it was now about revenge and getting even.

That was Sumi Ornesco's thought. She could launch a rescue mission, but it was clear it wouldn't arrive in time. However, there was a good chance they could destroy the Korian cruiser. She reached down to the microphone attached to the arm of her chair and coolly said, "Cobra teams one, two and three, prepare to launch—three minutes."

The Cordoba was the pride of the Sholite fleet, one of 20 similar battleships patrolling space. It was an impressive weapon of war, but it didn't give that appearance. It was a long cylinder, and at the front and rear third of it was a much fatter cylinder, rotating around the central core. The purpose of this was to give at least some sense of gravity to the crew. These were used only when crew members were off duty. The critical operations were in the central core, and here, the crew members wore ingenious, compensating magnetic boots. As one's foot flexed, the magnetic field would adjust so that, to the person wearing them, the feeling was similar to walking in full gravity.

Between the two fat cylinders, six smaller naval vessels were moored to the core of the battleship. Two were Eagle-class cruisers, but there were four faster Cobra-class gunships. These gunships were really nothing more than a powerful electromagnetic drive motor, 20 missiles and a small compartment for the three-man crew, all in a thin, airtight, metal casing.

A voice came through the speaker system. "Admiral, Cobra's ready to launch."

Ornesco was just sitting down in her command chair. She lifted the microphone and hissed, "Launch Cobras!"

There was a light jostle of the large warship as the clamp arms detached, followed by the side thrusters of the three Cobras firing. Once they were clear of their mother ship, their drive motors were engaged, and they were only a blur on the large front video screen in the command room of the Cordoba.

Thirty minutes later, the Korian cruiser was almost on top of the Arkala farm ship. Commander Morant knew rescue was coming from the Cordoba, but he also knew they wouldn't make it in time, so he made a decision. He lifted his communication microphone and said, "Rico, come in Rico."

There was an electrical squawk, then, "Rico here."

"Rico, we're not going to make it." Morant paused. "Blow the hydrogen."

"We can't blow the load! That's a lot of money…"

Morant cursed, "Fuck, Rico! The load is gone one way or the other, just if the pressurized hydrogen explodes, the two escape pods won't survive."

"Escape pods?"

Shouting into the microphone, Morant ordered, "Abandon ship! All hands to the escape pods. If you're not on them in three minutes, you'll be staying here with me for the party."

The four crew members in the control room didn't move; they were frozen with shock.

"Move!" Morant cried out.

After that, there were no words between them as the four people moved out the door, down the central passageway, towards the escape pods. A *thump* was heard, and Morant knew the compressed hydrogen was being expelled into space. He moved to the radar screen and saw the Korian cruiser in close proximity. Moving back to his chair, he looked down at his arm console. There were two red lights. One turned green, then five seconds later, the other did the same. The pods were ready for launch. Morant slapped his hand down on the black button beside the lights. The two escape pods were deployed. He snickered. *They have enough air for two days. They'll be safe when the Cordoba picks them up in a few hours.*

An alarm went off in the control room. Morant popped up and went to the radar screen. He saw the Korian cruiser, but there were also four small, red blips—high-speed missiles closing on the Arkala. He stared at the screen as they came closer and closer. He had some magnetic chaff countermeasures he could launch, but there were four missiles locked on the Arkala. *Why waste the energy?*

Moving back to his chair, he flopped into it. His eyes were tired more than his sixty years. There were four large monitors on the front wall of the control room. Top-middle was the front view out of the space ship. The left and right monitors showed the view out their respective sides. The lower-middle screen held the view aft of the vessel. Morant saw the blips for only a second on the lower screen. They were that fast. He was halfway through muttering, "Fuck," when the ship exploded into a thousand pieces.

Spaceships moving at 20 to 40 per cent SOL don't make sharp turns. Consequently, after verifying their kill, the Korian cruiser made a wide arc as it turned for Talus. The three Sholite cobras from the Cordoba were almost on top of them, but spaceships also don't stop easily from a high speed. Consequently, the three Sholite ships made an arc in the opposite direction, pulling them further away from the Korian cruiser, but they were quickly able to come around onto a pursuing intercept course.

At the point, where the Korian ship and the Cobras came within the closest range, the lead Cobra fired off two missiles. One was taken out by a countermeasure missile, the other by a field of magnetic chaff released by the Korian weapons officer. The Korian spaceship was racing back to Talus at a full 30 per cent SOL. With 40 per cent SOL fully engaged, the Cobras would catch them before that. It was just a matter of, would their path be clear, or would they encounter other Korian ships as they moved further into Talus space.

Maydays from the Korian cruiser were sent out to Talus. In response, five of their own Cobra-class gunships were on their way, closely followed by a Tiger-class destroyer—the *Reliant*. There were 150 crew members on board the Reliant, all the responsibility of a grizzled veteran of the war—Captain Kriton Fyr.

The destroyer had picked up the distress call from the Korian cruiser and was now pushing through space at a maximum 25 per cent SOL. The captain was standing at the navigation table, viewing the position of the Korian cruiser that was losing the race to the three pursuing Sholite Cobras.

Beside the captain was Ensign Marcus Fyr, the captain's nephew, and this was his first live mission. His mouth was open wide as he saw the situation on the navigation table, including the five Korian Cobras quickly closing the distance to the Korian frigate. The young ensign began to slowly shake his head. "The Sholites are crazy. At their speed, they won't be able to evade our Cobras."

"They don't care," the captain quietly replied. "They just want their revenge. Death is better than returning to their fleet without results."

"It's madness," Marcus muttered. His eyes opened even wider, making him look younger than his 18 years.

"Sholites have launched missiles targeting the frigate, Captain." The voice came from the radar operator. She looked intently at her radar screen. "There are five—ten—no—15 missiles launched." She popped her head up and looked at the captain. "The Sholites are breaking off in a turn."

Captain Fyr's second in command quickly moved over to the radar station. Sewel Edy turned to the navigator and barked out, "Course change to bearing 180, 50, 120—now!"

As the Korian destroyer veered to their left, a bright flash covered the central monitor at the front of the command deck. Even though they knew the inevitable outcome, young Marcus Fyr threw his arm up in front of his eyes in surprise when five of the Sholite missiles exploded the Korian cruiser.

The captain had been through this scenario many times. The cruiser and her crew were casualties of war—time to move on. The five Korian Cobras had already changed course to intercept the three Sholite Cobras now on an escape trajectory. The paths of the Sholite and Korian Cobras would cross, and that is exactly what he and his nephew saw when they watched the image on the navigation panel. There were 20 missiles released from the Korian ships at short range. In their high-speed turn, the three Sholite vessels released all the countermeasures they had: missiles, magnetic chaff and mines.

The image on the table was a blur of white lines and red circles as missiles exploded. When this cleared, they saw only one Sholite Cobra remaining. His Second knew his business when he changed course. The remaining Sholite Cobra would come within range of the destroyer's arsenal within two minutes.

The captain gave his nephew a slight tap with his elbow. "Watch this."

Sewel Edy moved over to the targeting officer. "Lock port batteries, one through ten, when the asshole comes in range."

A minute later, the targeting officer said, "Locked."

"Fire!" the Second cried.

All eyes in the control room of the destroyer were locked on the left side monitor at the front of the room. The cameras magnified the image of the Sholite Cobra on the screen. Each of the ten batteries let out a massive laser burst. The ten streaks of yellow energy sped to the target, hitting it in a staccato of destruction.

After five seconds, Captain Fyr announced, "To everyone on the deck. Well done! As usual, it's my honour to serve with you." He then turned to his nephew and said, "Follow me to my command quarters. Let's see what you learned."

There was a pneumatically controlled door bisecting the far wall. It opened automatically when the captain came near. Within, he moved around his desk, and Marcus took a chair opposite to him. The door closed, silencing the bustling noise from the command room. The captain saw his nephew, fingers intertwined in his lap, knuckles white—just not as white as his face. One eyebrow raised as the captain asked, "What's wrong Marcus? You just participated in your first battle, and it was a victorious one."

Marcus lifted his chin. His eyes were wide and innocent. "I don't get it. In fact, I don't get any of this."

"What do you mean?"

Marcus sat back and sighed. "There are many things, but the first coming to mind is the action of the Sholites. They could have turned off once they saw our countering force, but they didn't." His voice began to quiver. "They knew they were going to die, and it didn't matter."

The captain's eyebrow now lowered. He was becoming irritated. "I'm not going to say the were brave; rather, they were stupid."

A meek voice replied, "But why?"

A frown formed in the captain's thick white beard. He didn't want to yell, so he kept his teeth clenched tightly together. "Because we are at war!"

Marcus sat up straight in the chair. His voice was deeper. "Why? Why are we at war?" Before the captain could answer, he continued, "I know the war has continued for thousands of years. I know millions of people have died on both sides. We've lost family and friends, but the war continues, and we lose more family and friends. The crew on our frigate had family; the crew of the three Sholite vessels had family. Tell me, please, why did they die, Uncle?"

The captain leaned forward. He was not sure what to say. He scratched his head as his eyes looked furtively around his room, as if the answer was there—somewhere. It wasn't, just as it wasn't when his fingers scratched through the bristly beard covering his chin. He loved his nephew—almost as much as his son who died in the war five years ago. The memory was one he avoided, but now he saw his son sitting in front of him, not his nephew.

Running his finger under his nose, he sniffed away the tears that were about to fall. He returned his gaze to his nephew sitting across from him, the picture of innocence in a military uniform. The captain had come up with an answer to the question, just not a good one. In an uncomfortable tone, he whispered across the table to his nephew, "I have no idea."

Chapter 4: The Council of Nine

Ryder heard yelling from the other side of the bathroom door. He placed his wrist interlink against the sensor on the wall and the door slid open. He just finished his shower, and with a towel tied around his waist, poked his head out from the rolling steam. "Guys! Keep it down!"

His six-year-old son, Romy, stopped for a moment as a twisted look came across his normally cute face. "C'mon, Dad. We're playing, *Battle of Fort Nelson*, and I'm Nick Anderson."

Shaking his head, Ryder stepped back into the steam stating, "Fan on High. Door close."

Away from the watchful eye of his father, Romy lifted the plastic gun, yelling, *"Bang! Bang! Bang!"* He ducked behind a chair crying out, "Logan, I need help!"

From across the living room, behind the dining table, Fehyr cried out in a shaky voice, one filled with pain, "You got me, but only in the shoulder. You will have to do better than that to kill Adrian Jenk, supreme leader of the Sholite army." Fehyr lifted his own fake gun above the table and said, *"Bang, Bang! Bang, Bang!"*

Ryder's bodyguard, Linkin, was pretending to be the famous Logan Russell. He had his back pasted against the wall of the kitchen. He didn't have a gun, so his one hand held the fist of his other hand just under his chin, with the index finger pointed up. He looked over at Romy behind the chair. Romy flicked his head towards the far side of the dining table. Linkin nodded his understanding. The bodyguard jumped out from behind the wall and slid across the polished floor to a shooting position with his finger aimed at Fehyr. The older man was agile for his 65 years. He bounced to his feet and spun towards the other side of the table. Coming face to face with Romy, his wrinkled face under a thick head of white hair feigned shock, and his voice quivered. "No—please no."

Romy, his eyes narrow slits, sneered, "You don't deserve mercy, you Sholite bastard!"

Fehyr, playing the diabolical Adrian, threw his arms up in front of his face, whimpering, "No—no."

Romy had the gun trained on Fehyr's forehead, but now tilted the gun on its side. "Kill shot! *Bang!*"

Fehyr threw his head back as if a bullet really did hit him in the forehead, just before he slumped to the floor.

Ryder, now fully dressed, caught the end of the battle as he came out of his bedroom. "Romy, what's with the swearing?"

Romy lowered the gun behind his back, and his face was filled with innocence once again. "Oh, sorry, Dad."

Fehyr jumped to his feet and said to Romy, "Well played my boy! You caught me completely by surprise." He retrieved the cup of hot cocoa milk from the table and handed it to Romy. The flavored milk, a favorite among many Korians, was made with a genetically enhanced cocoa pod and sugar to suit. The pods were purchased in a freeze-dried form, then placed in the hot milk. As it rehydrated, the pod expanded and infused the milk with a massive amount of cocoa flavour. Consumed in a hot or cold format, it was available in many flavours: orange, lemon, berry, vanilla and mint, to name only a few. However, cocoa was Romy's absolute favorite.

Shaking his head, Ryder explained as he had explained many times before, "Romy, you know that's not how it happened. It was actually your great grandfather, known as Josh Harris at the time, who shot Adrian. Logan had a part in it, but Nick was not even in the room."

"I know, Dad," Romy replied. "Nick, the *Tiger of Moscow*, was outside, killing the rest of the stinking Sholites!" He lifted the cup of cocoa in celebration of his victory.

Ryder laughed. Once the Korians on Talus heard the events on Earth, almost leading to the destruction of their world, the Battle of Fort Nelson became more than famous. It was written into history, monuments were made for the combatants, and even the projectile guns, common on Earth, were made as toys and sold to the children. And much as Romy had done today, there were many different, embellished versions of the battle.

It seemed Ryder was shaking his head a lot this morning, and he did so again. He turned to Linkin and urged, "We need to leave, or we'll be late for the Vidame Council." He then switched his gaze to Fehyr. "Try to keep Romy—or Nick Anderson—or whoever he is, out of trouble."

"Yes, Sir," Fehyr replied. Fehyr was Ryder's butler. As such, he took care of all affairs regarding Ryder's household, including looking after Ryder's son. In actuality, *butler*, was a term not worthy of Fehyr's position. He had been with Ryder since Ryder was 25, so with Romy for all of his young life. He occupied a large room in Ryder's spacious apartment and was correctly thought of as a loving member of the Gunn family.

After giving his son a kiss goodbye, Ryder and Linkin left the fifth-floor apartment. They took the elevator to ground level and exited to the sidewalk with Linkin just ahead, inspecting for any possible threat.

Ryder's apartment building was in a rear neighbourhood of C21. Over the two thousand years since the builders carved out the 20 caverns within Talus, the naming convention of the chambers had been simplified. There were four rings, each consisting of five chambers. So the chamber Ryder lived in would have originally been described as Ring 2—Chamber 1. This was simplified to R2—C1, then C2,1 and finally, C21. All 20 chambers were named accordingly, from C11 to C45.

The Council of Nine was a monthly event where the vidames of the nine families in power met to discuss critical issues and make important decisions. The meeting was in C35, one ring closer towards the far end of Talus, and one chamber away, circumferentially.

Transportation within Talus was accomplished via one of two methods. About one third of Korians owned a family, electric vehicle. There were also the public trains—what people on Earth would have called a subway. The builders were ingenious and skillful. Beneath the floor of the chambers, between it and the asteroid's surface, they cut round tunnels in two layers. There were trains that travelled in the direction around the circumference of Talus in the upper layer of tunnels. There were lines travelling longer distances and others stopping at each chamber. Within each chamber was also a short haul train, making several stops within it. However, since *circumferential* is a difficult word, these trains were simply dubbed, *Ctrains*.

There was a second series of underground rail lines running perpendicular to the Ctrains and just underneath them. These were similar but called end trains, or *Etrains*, running in the direction from the front ring to the rear or end ring. And there were front trains, or *Ftrains*, running in the opposite direction.

Utilizing this system of trains, anyone could efficiently travel from one point in Talus to any other. Even residents who wanted to use their cars could use specialized lines, where the family car could be connected to the monorail of a separate series of private rail lines.

Ryder and Linkin were walking the quarter kilometer to the rail station. The brightness of the simulated daylight was consistent, notwithstanding where one walked, due to the strategically placed banks of lights. Of course, there were exceptions where areas were designed to provide shade, again simulating a real-world environment.

Ryder looked up. High above the cavern, he could see the bottom of one of ten vine bridges running between structural columns, and the combination ran the nine-kilometre-width of the chamber. Wood was a rare commodity in Talus. There were some trees growing within the many farming areas, but with the knowledge, *you can't eat wood,* these farms were primarily used to grow fruits. However, the oxygen vines offered a solution. Hanging down a good 50 metres from the bridges, the crowded vines were a mass of metre-long, light-green leaves. The oxygen vines had been native to Kor, but they'd been genetically modified. As most plants do, during their photosynthesis process, they consumed carbon dioxide and expelled oxygen, albeit oxygen vines did so at a phenomenally accelerated rate. Even during the lower, nighttime-simulated light levels, the oxygen vines expelled a vast amount of oxygen. The accelerated photosynthesis process would take its toll on the plants. The leaves both grew and died off quickly, constantly replaced by fresh growth. The brown, dying leaves were harvested, and when mixed with water and fruit rinds, created a solid, lightweight, wood-like structure used in many applications within Talus.

Most buildings were under a 100-metre height, with a limited number allowed to reach 200 metres, and then there were the Spires, stretching from the floor to ceiling of the chamber. Only five of these were allowed per chamber. These structures were all made of some form of stone, varying in its exact material, therefore colour, and also the finish. The simulated oxygen vine wood was used only for trim.

Above, there were a vast number of bridges between buildings. Some were narrow for foot traffic, and others were vast, supporting floating parkettes. Sometimes it was easy to forget they were inside a rugged piece of rock, flying through cold space at six per cent SOL.

A loud siren began to blare, and emergency lights began to blink at multiple locations. This brought back the reality that the hunk of rock they called home was really a gigantic spaceship. Yesterday, officials had announced, that in the ninth hour, an asteroid course correction would be made. Typically, these rare course corrections were made no more than once every month due primarily to disturbances from space's electromagnetic waves or gravitational affects from large bodies—especially black holes.

Today was such a day. Talus contained three electromagnetically-enhanced nuclear reactors supplying power to the asteroid, including the four electromagnetic drive, rear engines and the multitude of smaller thruster engines strategically mounted to the crust of Talus. The master computer system, when a course correction was required, computed the thrust required, what engines required firing, and the order and interval of the thrusts. The red, flashing lights indicated this was about to happen. Occasionally, there was a slight joggle of the asteroid, but most often there wasn't a noticeable effect. As recommended, Ryder and Linkin found a secure location, in this case a bench. Other than the alarm, there was quiet.

This type of event had happened many thousands of times, but still, people's fear stopped their chatter. Then, as quickly as they came on, the sirens and lights turned off, and the Korians internal world came back to life.

Ryder and Linkin boarded the Etrain. Fifteen minutes later, they stopped in C31 and subsequently boarded a Ctrain, transporting them to C35, ten minutes later. From there, it was only a five-minute walk to the Talus Government Center, another beautiful spire in the conglomeration of government buildings.

The two-story high council hall was on the first floor. Outside the main doors of the hall, Ryder asked Linkin to wait for him since there was no need for security inside the massive council room. Linkin knew the drill and headed for a side room, where he knew there would be refreshments, along with many other security personnel.

Ryder headed in the opposite direction, towards a series of nine doors on the far wall. These were private anterooms assigned to the vidames of each of the nine ruling families. Ryder entered the fourth door and found his mother, Vidame Nola, Gaylin and Ryder's great uncle, Alton Gunn, seated comfortably on couches surrounding a large table.

Gaylin, drink in hand, tilted it towards Ryder. "Cousin! I wasn't sure you'd make it."

Ryder, dropped himself into an armchair, and in a sarcastic tone, replied, "Gaylin, you know how much I enjoy these political events. I wouldn't miss it for the world."

Nola interrupted, "Ryder! You haven't been here five seconds, and already you're moaning like a child. You're the primor of the Gunn family— the next in line, and the family needs you at these events."

A waiter brought Ryder a drink; he knew what the primor liked and placed it on the table beside him. Gaylin gave Ryder a sly wink, emphasizing the dressing down his mother just gave him. Ryder was not sure what he despised more: political events, or just being in close proximity to Gaylin's obnoxious nature.

A call came over the intercom system for all delegates to enter the council hall. When it came to official events, each family had an identifying colour. The Gunn family colour was green, as evidenced by the long, flowing dress Ryder's mother wore. There was black trim at the neck and wrists of the long sleeves, the colour matching the black shoes customary when on official family business. *Flashy* was not seen as acceptable.

Vidame Nola led the way out of the room, followed by Ryder, then Gaylin, then Alton. The three men were not only members of the Gunn family, but they were also the vidame's advisors. It was customary at critical family functions, including council meetings, for the advisors to accompany their vidame. In fact, it was common knowledge the advisors, along with other senior members of the family, were really the ones doing the critical legwork and the ones making the important decisions. Since Ryder shied away from these political activities, Gaylin, who was born for them, now led them, as Alton did as primor of the Gunn family before Ryder and Gaylin had come of age. Notably absent was Pateer, Ryder's father, who had died of a lung disease four years prior.

Within the two-story, grey-walled council chamber, in a semi-circle across the front of the room, were family boxes. These were made of the pressed oxygen vine wood, stained a warm, deep-brown colour. In each family box was a table and enough chairs for the vidame and her advisors.

Across from the family boxes of the nine, were smaller boxes in rows facing the powerful families. These other boxes were aligned in raised tiers, all the way to the back of the room. Other families of import, considered secondary families, were assigned these boxes as observers, but occasionally, they brought forward issues and petitions for the Council of Nine to deliberate.

The council moderator hit his gavel on his desk and leaned over the microphone. "The council will come to order." The din of conversation subsided and he continued. "Thank you." He looked down at his prepared agenda. These were items agreed to in advance by the council to be discussed at the proceedings. "The Fyr vidame has been asked to summarize the Sholite attack occurring two days ago."

Since the Fyr family, one of the powerful nine, coordinated all military operations, their vidame leaned forward towards the microphone. "One of our Eagle-class cruisers came across a Sholite farming ship within Talus space. They know any Sholite ship in Talus space is seen as an act of aggression, so our vessel fired upon and destroyed the Sholite spaceship. Three Sholite Cobra-class ships were deployed to pursue our cruiser. Unfortunately, they destroyed it before our forces retaliated, destroying all three cobras..."

From the tier of secondary families, The Jez family vidame interrupted, "Are you saying we destroyed a farming ship and three smaller gunships, and we lost a cruiser?" The Jez family controlled policing; they were powerful, aligned with, but subservient to the Fyr family. Historically, they'd made several attempts to unseat the Fyr family on the Council of Nine.

Vidame Fyr pulled the microphone from its stand and rose to her feet. "Are you implying this was not appropriate?" There was venom in her voice.

Vidame Jez knew better than to challenge the Fyr vidame by rising to her feet. She wanted to make a point without making herself a political target. Consequently, in a more respectful tone replied, "I would like to bring to the attention of the council that a simple farming ship and three small gunships, might not be adequate compensation for the loss of a one-year-old cruiser—one of our latest—and one costing this council three thousand pentokens to build."

Sitting down in her chair, Vidame Fyr glanced at her allies on the council: Vidame Zaf controlling the power utility, and Vidame Pym controlling all interior farming. Then, she glared at the members sitting within the smaller Jez family box, impunity filling her eyes. "We'll take your concern under advisement, but understand, we're at war and war has losses. We'll continue to lead the war effort, always with the best intentions for Talus."

The following silence signalled the matter was over. Afterwards, there were several other issues discussed. Ryder couldn't help but yawn through them. On the other hand, Gaylin sat on the edge of his seat, continually whispering advice into Vidame Nola's ear. At one point, a bulletin from the Gunn family was announced as next on the agenda. Gaylin gave a last whisper in his aunt's ear just before she rose to her feet.

She cleared her throat and began, "Unfortunately, some of the materials we require, supplied by the Oro family, have recently become scarcer in local space. They charge us more, so we have no choice but to pass on the costs. This means the gravity patches we supply through our pharmaceutical company will increase in price by two tokens for a monthly batch."

There was an uproar from almost every family box. Since the simulated gravity in Talus was comparable to only 70 per cent normal Korian gravity, over the long term, there would be significant negative effects such as muscle mass loss, bone density loss, irregular heart function and eyesight degradation. To conquer this, gravity patches were developed as Talus was launched thousands of years ago. They contained medication, slow released into the upper arm. A new patch was required every week, and since a month's worth supply of patches cost 40 tokens, and every person in Talus required them, this was the proverbial goldmine that made the Gunn family the top of the Talus family hierarchy.

As Gaylin directed, Nola added with just enough feigned regret, "Again, the Gunn family apologizes, but we're just passing on the costs we receive from the Oro family." She sat down, having nothing further to add.

It didn't take long for the discontent to subside. After all, what could they do? They had to have gravity patches, or suffer what they referred to as the "gravity bends." In any case, the wealth sharing system within the families in Talus adjusted and compensated, at least in part. In a case like this, where one family had increased profits, they retained 40 per cent, and the balance was shared between the remaining families, prioritized by family position. This is why it was so important for families to increase their rank within the hierarchy.

That, ironically, brought the council to the last item on the agenda. The council moderator asked the vidame of the secondary Mal family to put forward her petition. The vidame rose and read from a document in front of her. For 20 minutes she detailed the accomplishments of her family. They were powerful, having monopolized all legal activity across Talus. This included, lawyers, notaries and legal assistants, to name only a few. They were making a formal petition, one that was put forth rarely. They proposed that they were more important to the operation of Talus than the Edy family controlling all aspects of entertainment. The Edy family were long standing members of the Council of Nine, aligned with the Krl family controlling manufacturing and the Sny family controlling all retail operations.

When the Mal family vidame finished, the petition was put to a vote. Since the Edy family vidame was not allowed to vote, that left eight votes. Each vidame thought of their family connections. *Who had married into their families? Who had been rebuffed? Who had an alternate agenda, and who wanted to tip the balance of power?* In reality, of the Council of Nine, three were the core. The Gunn, Fyr and Krl vidames voted first. They voted against the petition. Seeing this, the remaining five voting families, not wanting to create turbulence in their own alliances, did the same.

Ryder paid attention during the petition. He tried not to laugh, but it was difficult when he thought of the Edy family: actors, athletes, artists and troubadours. The lawyer family had made a strong case, one Ryder would have voted for, if he had a vote. It said something when the lawyers were seen as a lower family than the clowns and performers in the Edy family. No wonder he didn't want any part of politics and just dreamed of being an explorer.

Chapter 5: Company Business

There was a most unique, private athletic club on the 89th floor of the Gunn Spire, exclusively for use by members of the Gunn extended family. Of the eight million inhabitants in Talus, just over 30 thousand were descended from the ancient Gunn clan from Kor, or were absorbed into the family. Six hundred worked in the Gunn Spire, of which about a third used the athletic club regularly. The club had the typical fitness machines, free weights and courts for different racquet sports popular in Talus, but the unique aspect of the club was the running track.

A large, open-air veranda hung off the spire, creating an observation post on the 89th floor that was exhilarating in itself. However, even more amazing was the air bridge with one end attached to the veranda and the other end connecting to one of the oxygen vine bridges, 200 metres away. From that point, the six-metre-wide running bridge ran alongside the larger vine bridge, until the two parallel bridges connected to one of the huge, 100-metre-diameter stone columns supporting the vine bridge, one kilometre away. There was a rest stop one-half kilometre along the bridge and a full-service restaurant on the balcony surrounding the end support column.

Ryder was leaning against the bannister of the wide, supported deck beside the restaurant and pulled his wrist up under his gaze. All Korians in Talus had a monitoring system integrated into their anatomy when they turned 15 years old. A 10 mm-wide band of metal curled around his wrist as it did on each citizen. Each Korian had a large selection of artistically designed bands to choose from. These bands had two small ports in them for the purpose of injecting medications or taking samples of blood.

Just above the band, on the inside of the wrist, was a 100 mm area where nano electronic circuits were integrated. The result was a group of three small, light sensing buttons used to flip the active function through a multitude of options including a phone and an array of bio health sensors monitoring blood pressure, pulse, body temperature, blood sugar levels and copper content. Ryder pressed the *change screen* button several times until his blood pressure and pulse were illuminated in green through an opaque layer of skin. Here again, *green* had been his choice from a vast array of colours available to the 15-year-olds when the bionic devices were installed.

He ran his fingers through his short brown hair. Since he'd run at a good pace for the entire distance from the athletic club, beads of sweat covered not only his brow, but his entire head. A shiver ran through him as the breeze hit the perspiration. He thought, *this was another amazing feat created by the builders*. At the front end of each chamber was a bank of huge fans. At the rear of each chamber was the same number of ducts leading to the fans in the next chamber. Of course, the ducts at the back wall of the end chamber had to recirculate to the front chamber—a distance of 100 kilometres. This was accomplished in the central core of the asteroid where the return ducting passed through it. Along the way, the air quality was checked and the air scrubbed. Huge tanks of nitrogen, hydrogen and oxygen also ran down the central core of the asteroid, and the air passing back to the chambers was supplemented from them as required.

At ground level, the movement of air was only slightly noticeable, but here, near the ceiling of the chamber, a strong breeze could be felt. Ryder had never been on a planet, but he was taught wind was evident on many worlds, just as rain and snow fell from their skies. His hope was that, one day, he and all Korians could feel such climatic events. Strangely, Ryder dreamed often, and almost always he found himself on some unknown, fantastical world, where he would live out the feelings of wind, rain and snow. The dreams seemed realistic, increasing his need to have other Korians share in his need to have such a fantasy come true. It was one of the reasons his mind always went to his desire to explore space.

Turning his wrist again, in a loud voice he said, "Time." The wrist interlink also had a voice sensor tuned to his voice.

The response came back, "11:15."

"Oh, shit," Ryder mumbled. The company board meeting was starting in 45 minutes. He would have to hurry to make it there on time.

As he started his jog, he passed a young woman running in the opposite direction who gave him a cute smile and a wave. Ryder had no idea who she was, but he politely smiled back. These subtle advances were something no longer happening to him very often. When he turned 20 and ascended to the rank of *eligible bachelor* of a powerful family, he received a plethora of such advances. Many were not as subtle; women waited outside his apartment. Some even followed him when he was shopping. After a time, the women weren't as persistent, with the thought, *maybe Ryder was gay*. Some men had evolved the same idea, and there was a period when it seemed it was their turn to follow him with cute smiles and winks.

The time on his wrist indicated, 11:35. He just came out of the shower, then quickly changed into his work attire. Ryder liked bright colours, but he knew he needed to tone it down for the annual board meeting of *Gunn Pharmaceutical*. His slacks were grey, matching his waist-length jacket. There was a short, 2-centimetre, vertical collar on the jacket, and just under it a wide, single lapel that one could button across the chest. Here, Ryder left the lapel hanging open, revealing the bright-red, round-neck shirt he wore underneath. The ankle-high black boots completed his outfit.

As family primor, he received many, "hello's," and salutations as he made his way to the meeting. He arrived in the large board room with the last two members just behind him. Thankfully, he wasn't last, so he wouldn't receive the customary, sly insults from his cousin, Gaylin. As Ryder sat down with the last two members, there were now 12 board members seated around the large, simulated oxygen vine table.

Seeing all members were present, Gaylin, sitting at the head of the table, pressed a button on the console in front of him. Blinds lowered in front of the large picture windows filling the wall behind him. At the same time, the interior lights increased, maintaining the illumination in the room.

Pulling in his chair, Gaylin nodded to the woman on his left. She looked at the group of seven men and four women, stating, "You have the annual report in front of you. The agenda for today is on page one."

Raising his finger in the air, Gaylin interrupted. "I have one item before we start the official meeting."

Ryder, sitting at the opposite end of the long table from Gaylin, rolled his eyes. As primor, he had to be present for the meeting that, in his opinion, was too long as it was, but was now being hijacked by an impromptu interruption by his overcontrolling cousin.

Gaylin reached to his side, and a small cardboard box was now pulled directly in front of himself. "I received this package yesterday at my office down the hall." He pulled open the cover of the box and pressed his hand inside. He pulled out one piece of bright-green cloth, then a second similar piece in pink. As he pulled apart the shiny fabric, there was a collective gasp from the other members of the council. Held carefully between the tips of his fingers, as if they might somehow get soiled, was a pink thong. After the sigh, the room was silent, and Gaylin's whisper was loud enough for them to hear his abashing words. "Do I look like the kind of person to wear these?"

The people around the table didn't know if Gaylin really expected an answer or perhaps a nod of their heads. None were that brave; they just sat still with their eyes averted from the offensive piece of clothing—all except for Ryder who blurted out, "I don't know. Would you?" His light-blue eyes were full of mischief.

Ignoring the comment, Gaylin turned his glare to his right, towards a man who seemed to slink even lower in his chair, likely wishing he could altogether disappear. Sliding the box across the table to him, Gaylin asked, "Who is the package addressed to?"

The man's hands were shaking as he rotated the box and pulled it under his gaze. Tilting his head towards the head of the table, he said, "Gaylin Gunn?"

Gaylin's frown grew longer. "You idiot! Are you asking me or telling me?"

From behind his spectacles, the man cleared his throat and repeated. "Gaylin Gunn, Sir."

"Gaylin Gun, what?"

The man took another quick glance at the box. "Gaylin Gunn 283." His face suddenly froze, then turned deep-red. "My apologies, Sir."

Gaylin intertwined his fingers on the table. "I see, you see the problem—your problem. This is the fifth package this year I've received that is destined for Gaylin Gunn 283. I will remind you again, for the last time, I'm Gaylin Gunn 149." His gaze was so intense, as if two holes were being bored into his *Manager of Shipping and Receiving.*

Korians didn't use middle names, and since society was divided into families, 3,288 registered families to be exact, obviously, there would be some duplication of names. Long ago, Korian officials decided to use a three-digit numbering system to differentiate these people. They weren't sequential since, in these cases, the numbers would, at a glance, look similar. Rather, a random three-digit number was used as a unique identifier for all Korians.

Gaylin wasn't really overly concerned about receiving a package meant for the Gaylin Gunn who worked on the tenth floor, in Chemical Engineering. He wasn't even really unhappy the man was having sexy underwear delivered to his work address, likely to keep the contents associated with his perversions hidden from his wife. He just wanted to use the moment as a vehicle to set the tone for the meeting, one he knew would soon reveal some unsatisfactory results.

There was a crack breaking the awkward silence as Gaylin snapped his fingers. Satisfied with the reaction as three board members jumped, he turned to the woman on his left. "Please continue, Carmen."

Carmen opened the report to the agenda and read out, "Results from the Council of Nine Meeting—Gaylin."

"Thank you." Gaylin explained the Council of Nine events from two days earlier. The main focus of the summary was to explain the two-token increase to a monthly supply of patches, resulting in a potential five per cent increase in profits. Since there were just under eight million people in Talus, that would create additional annual revenue of 160 million tokens, or 51 thousand pentokens, considering, in their base five monetary system, there were 3,125 tokens in a pentoken.

The next order of business was a presentation of the results of a clinical trial to reduce the chemical content within the gravity patches by five per cent. Gaylin had set the trial in motion six months earlier, in the hope of an expected increase in profits by watering down the chemical composition in the patches.

The Bli family, controlling all medical applications across Talus, was closely aligned with the Gunn family. As such, their primor was on the Gunn board, and today, he brought with him their Chief Medical Officer. The medical officer rose to his feet and asked the meeting members to turn their report to page eight. He explained the results of the study that, in summary, failed to meet the requirements. Five per cent less medicine in the patches would not allow the effectiveness to last for a month.

There was a loud *crack* as Gaylin's palm slapped down on the table. His eyes were once again smoldering under the mop of jet-black hair. "That's unfortunate. Run the trial again at three per cent."

The medical officer furtively looked around the room at the other board members before he stuttered, "But—but the results are quite predictive. It shows success at three per cent is highly—improbable."

Gaylin slapped his hand on the table again as he sneered, "I said—run the fucking trial again at three per cent!" He turned to Carmen. "Next!"

There were six more items on the agenda, and each of these were discussed in detail. Understandably, they were all monetary in nature—everything from asset values to tax levels to depreciation carrying costs. These mundane topics were giving Ryder great difficulty in keeping his eyes open. But of course, he did listen; he was a great listener, and he was responsible. Although others might think him unconcerned, in fact, he forced himself to absorb every fine detail. He didn't trust his cousin one bit, and although he'd passed his responsibility of running the business to Gaylin, with support from his mother he could reclaim it, although he was loath to do so.

The final agenda item was a summary of the family's profits. Gaylin was once again unhappy. Although the ten thousand pentoken annual profit was higher than the prior year, it was below expectations. The exact impact of the lower profit margins was not readily understood and would need further analysis. This was because, as all Korians knew, in the Talus wealth sharing system, family profits were divided amongst the families. This meant additional profits, from increases such as the two per cent being applied to the gravity patches, would not only go to the Gunn family. In fact, the Gunn family would receive 40 per cent of their family's profits. The other eight families on the council would receive two per cent each. The 70 secondary families would receive one per cent each, with the remaining smaller families in Talus claiming the remainder. Obviously, in such a wealth sharing system, it was important to improve the status of one's family, especially in light of each family's stipends and pensions being paid from the family funds available.

After blaming several members of the board for the company's poor performance and berating them accordingly, Gaylin closed out the agenda. As was customary, Carmen questioned each around the table, asking if there were new items to be discussed. They all knew better than to add to the day's carnage—all except Ryder. When the board's attention came to him, he nonchalantly said, "I have one issue, but it's relative to family business more so than company business. I will need to speak to the vidame personally before I share it here."

No one thought any more of it; they all just wanted out of the room. It seemed to be just a comment in passing. Once Gaylin announced adjournment of the meeting, the members of the board could not leave the room fast enough. As his cousin rose from his chair, Gaylin urged, "Ryder, please stay for a moment."

Gaylin strode over to the far wall where a well-stocked bar provided refreshment. He poured two glasses of light-blue fruit punch—a drink he knew his cousin favoured. He sloshed a measure of alcohol into his own glass before moving back towards Ryder, placing one glass beside his cousin, then lowering into the seat beside him.

Gaylin took a deep drink from the glass, then turned his gaze towards Ryder. "What's this family business you need to speak to the vidame about?"

"I told you, it's family business. My mother needs to hear of it first."

"I'm in charge of all aspects of company business. As such, you should trust me."

Ryder's nose wrinkled and creases formed on his brow. "I told you, it's *family* business."

Gaylin tilted the glass over his mouth, emptying the contents. He then lowered it onto the tabletop—hard—creating a sharp *clang*. His eyes narrowed as he chirped, "In Talus, there's no family business that isn't company business!"

Ryder enjoyed goading his cousin, but there came a time when following, what he thought was correct protocol, just wasn't worth the future aggravation Gaylin would cost him. He was already at the point where he considered the length of time he had been in the meeting and thought, *that was two hours of my life I'll never get back*. Rather than prolonging the pain, he smiled and said, "It's actually good news. I have a meeting with officials of the Zaf family in two days. They're considering leaving the Fyr alliance to join ours."

Gaylin's eyebrows shot into the air. "That would be amazing! If they joined us, then our alliance would include four of the families within the Council of Nine. The Fyr alliance would only have *two* families; clearly, we could monopolize council decisions!"

Placing his hands palm down on the table, Ryder replied, "Relax, Cousin. It's early in the negotiation process. I need to hear my mother's opinion on the matter before I speak with them."

"Of course! Of course!" Gaylin uttered. He leaned closer to Ryder. "Do you need help? Maybe I should go to the meeting with you."

Ryder chuckled. "No, I don't do much to help this family, but *I am* the *Director of Family Liaisons*. I can handle this as I have done with all other changes affecting our family."

Gaylin nodded. "Very well." He rose to his feet and moved back to his chair at the head of the table before watching his cousin leave the room. Once the door closed, Gaylin tilted his wrist and pressed a virtual button on his interlink. A deep voice answered, and Gaylin brought the bionic device closer to his lips. "Byron, come to the board room."

A few moments later, a tall man with a full head of curly, black hair, entered the room. He wasn't quite as tall as Gaylin, but his muscular physique filled out his black suit more proportionately. Surprisingly, for a large man, his steps were soft and he moved quietly across the stone floor to the chair beside Gaylin.

Byron Gunn was Chief Security Officer of the Gunn family's security and intelligence service, reporting directly to Gaylin. He led a team of 50 specialists who supplemented the services the police typically provided. This meant, in many cases, the Gunn security personnel stretched the rule of law to make sure the family's interests were maintained. Byron was the perfect man to lead such a group. He was a man of action and few words. "How can I help you?" he asked.

"Tell me what you know of a meeting between Ryder Gunn and Zaf family officials."

Byron had a square face. Chiselled was the best word to describe it, and it really did look like it was hewn from a rough piece of stone, with his heavily pockmarked cheeks adding to his unemotional appearance. "It was in my written report a week ago. The meeting is set in two days at the Park of Heroes in C11."

"I read that report. Is there an update?"

Once knowledge of the meeting came to Byron, listening devices were arranged in several Zaf offices and even some of the official's homes. "It's all a scam—subterfuge, intended purely as a distraction. In reality, they have a move to the Krl alliance all but signed."

One eyebrow rose on Gaylin's face. "All but signed?"

"That's correct, Sir."

Sighing, Gaylin continued, "Then, we'll have to make sure that signing never happens. Is that understood?"

Byron was 50 years old and a veteran of the Talus police service before joining personal service to the Gunn family. Old habits didn't leave him easily. Consequently, he sat in the chair with his back perfectly straight, and throughout their short conversation, his eyes had been locked on a point on the far wall. His thin lips were in a long line, perfectly square, not allowing a hint of emotion on his stoic face. But now, as he heard the open-ended direction, his dark eyes lit up, and one corner of his mouth rose in the slightest of smiles. He whispered, "Oh, yes, Sir."

Chapter 6: I'lish Mann

Ryfoss Space Station was one of seven massive ships flying through space at the core of the 700-ship Sholite fleet. Each cylindrical space station was almost identical, with each having a diameter of three kilometres and a length of six. To manage at least a semblance of gravity, the entire cylinder rotated, with increased simulated gravity at the outer edges of the cylinder, incrementally reducing for the inhabitants residing closer to the central axis.

Of course, it made sense Sholite living quarters only filled the outer kilometer of the space station. Here, the marginal gravity along with magnetic shoes, created a bearable environment to live in. The inner two kilometres were used for technical applications, including manufacturing facilities, the electromagnetic power plant and the drive engines.

I'lish Mann, standing with her fingers clasped behind her back, watched as a sleek space trawler came into view through the thick, triple-pane, panoramic observation window. She was looking along the right edge of a web-like steel structure hanging off the back of the station. This structure had the same diameter as the station, but its length was only 200 metres.

The trawler, *Nemesis*, appeared to be rotating in a loop as it came closer to it. However, this was just an illusion, since in fact, it was the space station rotating. The Nemesis adjusted its course as thrusters fired. Slowly, the spaceship started to loop as well, speeding up until their rotation matched that of the station. Oddly, now the illusion was that the ship was no longer rotating, but looking in the distance it appeared, incorrectly, as if the stars in the background were rotating.

The web-like metalwork was a parking structure, and the Nemesis was one of I'lish's fleet of six trawlers she owned and operated. Now that the rotations were matched, the Nemesis carefully glided into an empty cell. Magnetic catches locked on, indicating the docking was successful.

I'lish spied a group of lounge chairs in the corner of the observation room, lowering herself into one of them. She crossed one long leg over the other, knowing it would take half an hour for her second in command, Tanner, to deboard and meet her.

At 42 years old, she was an imposing figure in her black slacks and knee-high boots, complemented by a dark-green, loose fitting shirt, hanging down to the top of her thighs; the shirt was tied at the waist with a black cord, the sign of the Space Mining Union. Her face was narrow with high cheek bones highlighting her dark eyes. Her complexion was mulatto, but appeared lighter because of the long length of black hair, tied in a braided ponytail, the tip of which was just past her waist.

She was the granddaughter of Lashkar Mann and Nancy Tellman. Lashkar Mann was almost as famous as Duggan, Arlo and Natalie Gunn. He was part of the Earther group duped by the Sholites in an effort to destroy Talus 3, 64 years earlier. Nancy, an intelligent, Sholite computer programmer, had a romantic relationship with Lashkar during that time. Realizing she had strong feelings for Lashkar, she saved him from the battle of Fort Nelson. Comically, she drugged him, resulting in a deep sleep, leaving him completely oblivious of the deadly battle. When he awoke, it was to find the fighting over, the Sholite leaders dead and Nancy a captive of the Korians. As was customary in the ongoing war, a few weeks later, there was a prisoner exchange, resulting in Nancy's return to the Sholite fleet.

Lashkar, heartbroken but enthralled by the higher-level alien technology he was introduced to, decided to leave Earth and finish his life with the advanced Korian society in Talus—at least, that was the plan, and as often happens in life, plans tend to become susceptible to change. Nancy really did love Lashkar, and secret messages were sent to him. Lashkar realized his love for the Sholite woman had never left him. With the help of Natalie Gunn, an arrangement was made, and Lashkar was allowed to leave Talus to live out his life with Nancy Tellman within the Sholite fleet. So that's exactly what they did; they lived happily and had a daughter together, who in turn had her own daughter. They named her I'lish.

Life was not easy for her as a young girl, with mixed blood many Sholites disparaged her for. In addition, her grandmother had failed with the Sholites on Earth. I'lish endured insults and a few physical beatings, but these just made her stronger. As she grew older, and typically taller than her peers, she now more often reversed the intended beatings.

She also didn't adapt well to a classroom education. But her mind was sharp, so she read book upon book, absorbing a vast amount of information. As a result, she honed her mind, and along with her growing strength of character and dark, mysterious countenance, she was ready to challenge the vastness of space.

Ironically, she looked like an outlaw—a little wild and nonconforming. It didn't completely shock some when she took up such an occupation. There was a healthy black market between the Sholites and Korians from time on end. The people who conducted these activities were called smugglers and, at times, pirates. However, in reality, these people were needed on both sides of the war. This is how technology and innovations were shared, maintaining a balance between the two races.

I'lish thrived in this environment. She loved the thrill of a good chase, taking risks and enjoying the exultation when a close call was averted. It wasn't long before she commanded a smuggler ship, earned a vast amount of money and was able to purchase her own trawler. This was a turning point in I'lish's life. She could have continued to smuggle and live a life of deception, or now, having the funds, she could live a legitimate lifestyle.

Consequently, she purchased her own space farming trawler, and in the following years, she showed herself just as adept in the legitimate search for necessary materials held within the comets and meteors speeding through local space. She had a nose for it, having a knack for finding ice comets, not only to provide water for the fleet, but often they contained ammonia salts and hydrogen deposits, all sold for top token.

Now, she owned six mining ships and was the head of the Space Mining Union with 30 thousand members. That said, with many responsibilities and never enough time, it was not surprising she had an involuntary look of disdain on her face as she impatiently waited. Such was the woman, I'lish Mann.

It was just as she glanced down to check the time on her wrist interlink, when Tanner walked through the door into the observation room. She slapped her palm down on the arm of the chair and chirped, "Finally!"

Tanner hastened his pace across the room, sitting in the chair beside her. His eyes searched the room. Seeing it empty, he reached into his pocket, pulling out a folded piece of paper. I'lish already had her hand out as he handed it to her. Her eyes darted back and forth as she quickly read the report. Satisfied, her gaze came up to Tanner as she said in a commanding tone, "Flame."

Her second in command pulled a small silver box from an inside pocket. He dragged his finger down the side and a small flame flashed from the top. I'lish held the corner of the paper over it until it caught. Once the flame expanded to the point it could not be stopped, she dropped the paper onto the metal tabletop beside her. Hoping the fire alarm wouldn't be set off, she quickened the pace of her words. "I'm hearing rumour of several meteors seen on long range sensors, heading through sector 32 towards sector 31. Take the *Nemesis* and the *Challenger* out to see what you can find. Just remember, in six days you need to meet with our associate from Talus at the same location as the last meeting."

Tanner rose, his black-bearded face looked stern, carrying a long scar along his jaw from a past violent encounter, one of many he'd lived through. He nodded and began to turn away, but she caught his wrist with her long fingers. As he turned back, she rose and wrapped her arms around the burly man. She whispered, "Thank you for everything you do for me."

With her chin sitting on his shoulder, she couldn't see the smile on his face. This was why people followed her. She led with a stern hand, spoke with a direct, truthful voice, and cared deeply for the people she led. I'lish pulled back with one hand still on his shoulder. "On your way now. Give my regards to the crew."

I'lish followed Tanner from the room, but as he continued along the curved hallway, she turned and made her way to the next docking station. Here, two Sholite military guards stood on either side of the docking door. They knew I'lish on sight; no other identification was required as she nodded to them before boarding the shuttle.

There were four other ministers on board the shuttle when she took her seat. She gave a polite smile to them as she heard the shuttle door close and seal. She engaged her seat belt, knowing in a moment the shuttle would disconnect from the station. It would slow its rotation, and gravity would be lost.

A few minutes later, the shuttle had stopped its looped path and was sailing towards the Central Council ship. It might sound odd that a meeting of the Sholite President's Council was held on a smaller ship, but when considering all the facts, it made sense; a smaller ship was a smaller target and the Central Council ship was very mobile—in fact, it was the fastest ship in the fleet. If any type of attack came, it was designed to evade and escape anything the Korians had to offer. It was also beneficial that a top-of-the-line, Sholite Buffalo-class battleship was parked one hundred kilometres off its starboard side.

Looking out the small, round window, I'lish tilted her head, searching for the battleship she knew was there, even though it was too far to see with the naked eye. She looked directly out the thick, glass pane. She saw empty space, but she knew five billion kilometres away was the border between Sholite and Korian space, where five more Sholite battleships, numerous space destroyers and frigates, patrolled. The trip from the Sholite fleet to the border could be accomplished in 25 hours; another 25 hours and they could be at Talus.

I'lish's attention was drawn away from the daydream as the shuttle slowed and then docked with a *clunk*. There was a pneumatic *woosh* as the door opened, and the pressure equalized. *Thank our ancestors for magnetic boots,* she thought as she unclipped the seatbelt.

In the center of the Council spaceship was a round room, and not surprisingly, in the center of it was a large, round table. There were 12 ministers on the president's council, their election to it the result of a democratic vote. Any Sholite name could be put forth as a potential minister if they had a petition of names indicating the support of followers. The candidates with sufficient followers were put forward into an election, and a general vote selected the successful 12 Sholites to the council.

Each term was three years, and I'lish had been on the council for two terms. This wasn't surprising considering the vast following of her union membership, but there were many more additional votes than just those. She was popular with the people, seen as a woman of action, one that would do what had to be done for success, all the while not taking a back seat to anyone.

She took her place, and the meeting was brought to order by the Sholite president. President Balorian was 85 years old, a veteran of the war from his younger days, and an experienced politician, having held the office of president for the past 15 years. His body was frail, his back stooped and his fingers shook, but his mind was still sharp and his voice could still command a room. He read out the agenda and brought forth the first topic for reading.

The next 90 minutes was less than captivating, with mundane topics of economics and supplies, and a few irritating requests to review complaints. I'lish suffered through the boredom by watching the ministers. She was a good observer of people and a better judge of character. Most often, she watched Ministers Brighton and Merrick. Brighton was also an experienced representative on the council, who looked older than his 50 years. He had a reputation for closing issues, heightened by his reputation for often illegally coming to those results, at times, with opponents mysteriously disappearing. He typically wore black, and between this aura and his scrupulous reputation, he was known as *Black Brighton*.

Merrick, or correctly, Admiral Zane Merrick, was the leader of the Sholite military. Although his reputation was also darkly stained, it was from a different source. He just hated Korians—vehemently. In battles he held no mercy, and he promoted the same sentiment amongst his captains and commanders. It was rumoured he enjoyed torturing Korians, and in secret, had done so numerous times.

During the meeting, I'lish watched both of them. They glanced at each other, made slight signals, and at times, their faces also told I'lish the messages they conveyed to each other. Merrick's love of the war was obvious, but she also saw Brighton was an advocate. When a peaceful solution to an issue was entertained, he would roll his eyes. When a recommendation of military action was nominated, a cruel grin would cross his face.

"I'lish Mann."

I'lish, having been distracted, now turned back to the president.

"I'lish, have you any news of Talus?"

She smirked. Smuggling, pirating and spying were illegal, except when it was beneficial to the government. She was a reputable owner of a trawler business, but they knew she had contacts and knew how to get things done—discreetly. She didn't mind playing the game, so she began her report. "I have one item of interest. There's some discord within the Talus Council of Nine. As you know, there are three alliances keeping the balance of power."

"This is not news, Minister Mann," Admiral Merrick scoffed.

I'lish thought Merrick was an ass and paid no attention to him. Historically, at these meetings, when his brazen words didn't illicit a response, that was when his level of frustration heightened. Consequently, she didn't even give him a glance as she continued. "My sources in Talus tell me the Zaf family, presently aligned with the Fyr family, is contemplating a move to the Krl led alliance."

"What impact would this have on us?" the president asked.

Shrugging nonchalantly, I'lish replied, "Right now, the nine families are divided equally into three alliances. If the Zaf family moved to the Krl alliance, accounting for four families, that would leave the Fyr alliance with only two families. This would significantly reduce the influence of the Fyr family."

Rubbing his chin, the president was considering this, when Admiral Merrick blurted out, "If this happens, we must attack Talus! With their military weakened, we could change the stalemate we have had for centuries."

President Balorian slapped his boney hand down on the table with a surprising amount of strength. Merrick's head snapped towards the sound, catching the glare of the older Sholite leader. Balorian had lived a hard, younger life in the military. In that past time, his eyes were cold, steel blue, but now, in his old age and reported waning health, they were most often a softer, lighter hue. It surprised I'lish, at least for the moment, to once again see the dark glare he gave the admiral. "War, fighting and killing! That's all you think about."

"More than that," Black Brighton interjected. "It's about revenge." Brighton, as the head of the Sholite intelligence services, was a staunch proponent of the war, having lost his wife and son many years before.

President Balorian slumped in his chair and rolled his eyes. "You too? Does everyone just want to continue this war and the killing of your loved ones?"

I'lish was once again intently people watching as spirited opinions came from around the table. Brighton and Merrick were on their feet, imploring their position as a warring state. Others were calmly supporting the president's more peaceful stance. There were also a few who stayed silent. Over the past year, several times, President Balorian had put forth his support for peace, and each time, the council meeting became a proliferation of differing opinions—anything but a council of unified direction. However, this time, I'lish noticed only four ministers were pressing their position of hate and revenge. She grinned. The president was making headway.

The President rose to his feet and slapped the table. There was no response, so he did so again. It wasn't until the third hit that all the ministers were sitting, showing an acceptable level of decorum. He coughed, then cleared his throat. There was a sickness inside him, one his physician said had no cure. An exact timeline was not known, other than it was short. One fact he did know was a peace treaty or even a truce, would not come readily through this council. He had to find another way. He brought the meeting to a close and released the ministers.

As they were leaving, he requested, "I'lish, please stay for a moment."

I'lish turned and returned to a seat beside Balorian. When the council chamber doors closed, the president mumbled, "Fucking idiots," as he pressed his shaky fingers through his thinning, white hair.

Pausing, I'lish replied in a noncommittal tone, "You handled them very well."

"Not as well as I would like," the older man replied with a disgruntled tone. He locked eyes with I'lish as they searched her. "You seem neutral on the idea of this ongoing war. I am not. I think it has been clear for some time now, I would like to pursue peace with the Korians." He leaned closer to the woman and his voice became more whimsical. "We send explorer ships out every week to search for a home, so hopefully, one day, we can leave the confines of these ships. The Korians do the same. I wish we could use the ships of war to accelerate our search. Right now, our efforts are insufficient and pathetic." He put his hand on top of I'lish's and whispered, "Most of the others respect you. Which way do you lean on the matter of war?"

She placed her free hand on top of his and, in a subdued voice, asked, "How much time do you have left?"

Balorian was not surprised at her astute observation. He shrugged. "I'm not sure, but not long enough to convince some of the obstinate members of this council." He tilted his gaze, knowing this was a critical moment. "My hope is for peace before I die. I suspect, to do this, I will need to use other methods outside the council. Although, it won't be popular amongst some, I do have some underutilized powers I can invoke. Can I count on you to support me?"

I'lish pulled her hands out from his. She needed a moment to think. *Was she committing treason? Did she even care if she was?* In her life, doing the right thing always outweighed what ink put to paper. She remembered an aspect of her life she had compartmentalized in a corner of her mind. For only a moment, she peeked in, and her decision became simple. Her lips spread into a wide smile, brightening her face. "Of course, you can count on me. My wish is for peace between the Sholites and Korians."

Admiral Merrick and Black Brighton scurried into an anteroom when they left the council chamber. Merrick's face was still red as he slapped the wall. "Can you believe the old man! Every time we meet, he seems closer to offering a peace treaty to the fucking Korians."

Black Brighton lowered into a chair. His smile was filled with evil. "We don't have much longer to wait. In three months, it won't matter."

"I'm not sure we should wait. I could have a squad take out the president."

"Complete anarchy would be the result," Brighton growled. "Besides, my alternate plan in Talus is still in play. Rather than killing the president, we need to keep him alive. My sources tell me he's deathly ill; he has six months to live at the outside, and we need him and his indecisive ways to remain with us for only three months." His voice had a deathly chill. "That's when my plan will be sprung."

Merrick sat in the chair across from Brighton. He glanced around the room before he whispered, "Are you referring to the six agents you have in Talus?"

Brighton leaned forward and whispered back, "Very few people know of this plan. Five years ago, we began a detailed infiltration. We selected six Korians who had positions with access to critical installations or critical officials in Talus, who also had specific medical conditions. We lured these six people to a medical professional, a person who was really a Sholite operative, for treatment of their conditions. However, while doing so, they were drugged and brainwashed with our latest techniques. This included a kill order to be initiated, simultaneously, in three months."

"So, unknowing, they're sleeper agents," Merrick interjected.

Black Brighton's eyebrows lowered with irritation. After all, it was *his* story, describing the plan *he* set in motion. "Yes, they're sleeper agents. Each has a deadly mission embedded in their subconscious, but with a twist. Their missions are irrevocable, except with a stop code phrase—a phrase known to only a very few Sholites."

"Therein lies the flaw in your plan," Admiral Merrick offered. "President Balorian is one of those few people who knows of the six sleeper agents, and he also knows the stop code phrase. If he decides to, he could reveal these to the Korians."

Throwing his head back and laughing, Brighton boasted, "You underestimate me, friend." He lifted a hand and a twisted finger curled, urging Merrick closer. Once Merrick's face was close, Brighton whispered, "You're aware all Korians have a first name, a family name and a three-digit sequence number when clarification is required."

Merrick gave a slow nod.

Through a sly grin, Brighton continued. "I made an adjustment to one of the six names. It's not unusual for Korians to have the same last name. It would be horrible if, when I gave the president the list of six names, one of them, accidentally, had the wrong three-digit number."

Eyes wide, Merrick mumbled, "You didn't…"

"Oh, I did."

"Who knows?"

In his excitement, Black Brighton snorted, then in slowly paced words, replied, "Only me—and now you."

Chapter 7: Take Shelter

Waiting outside his apartment building, Ryder looked up towards the roof of cavern C21. What he saw was a constant, each and every day. There was either daylight, or the subdued lighting applied to simulate nighttime. As he waited on the carved, stone sidewalk, he remembered the stories his grandmother, Natalie Gunn, told him. On her home world, Earth, she described the clouds floating across the skies. Often, they were white and fluffy, but at times, they would hold turbulent power, bringing high winds and even torrential rain. He dreamed of seeing and feeling such events, one day, on a planet the Korian people could call their home.

It was well into the tenth hour. Many people were walking along the sidewalks and a few vehicles passed by him. In the distance, he spied a red and yellow, three-wheeled vehicle—really not much bigger than a cart—coming towards him. Ryder raised his hand in the air, causing the vehicle to slow and then stop directly in front of him.

The taxi driver, a cute female, smiled and offered, "You need a ride, Sir?"

"Thank you," Ryder replied as he stooped while entering the rear compartment of the vehicle, just before Linkin, his bodyguard, slid in beside him. Since smaller taxis in Talus were limited to 40 kilometres per hour, many, such as this one, were open air with only a tarp over the top. "Please take me to the Gunn Memorial Wall," Ryder directed.

Instantly, an electrical hum began as the vehicle accelerated towards the specified destination, six kilometres away. The Gunn Memorial Wall was a location where the Gunn family dead were remembered and honoured. There was no room for cemeteries in Talus, so the customary way to take care of the remains of the dead, was to expel them into space during a formal funeral. Ryder's grandmother had told him it reminded her of the way sailors on Earth were buried at sea. Yet there needed to be a place where family members and friends of the deceased could go to remember their loved ones. That was where Ryder was headed now to meet his mother for a ritual he participated in once every three months.

The taxi drove towards the back wall of the massive cavern. The configuration of the streets in Talus was straightforward, with all streets travelling in a direction parallel to the centre axis of the asteroid. However, since the Korians numerical system was based on the number five, a circle had 500 degrees, not 360 as the people of Earth would be familiar with. The names of the streets were identified by their position, in degrees, around the circumference of the rings with the Talus Government Center in C35 as the origin. Since the chamber Ryder was travelling in was C21, its width was between 50 and 150 degrees, and all streets in this zone, fell within these bounds. As such, the taxi was travelling towards the back of chamber C21 on 140th Street.

Since the crossroads were shorter, they were all referred to as lanes, and they took on a similar naming convention, defined by their location along the length of the asteroid. Since they were in the second ring, all lanes in C21 had names between the 28th and 48th Lane.

Ryder leaned forward and peered upwards under the front lip of the black tarp. No matter how many times he saw it, the 300-metre-high, rough-cut, stone wall at the back of the chamber was an imposing vision. The primary colour of the stone was a reddish-brown, but it was filled with streaks of coloured minerals; the green, purple and orange lines made the wall both beautiful and fascinating.

When it seemed the taxi driver was about to drive into the rock face, she made a sharp left turn onto 48th Lane running directly alongside the vertical face. They drove for two kilometres, passing many buildings on their left, most of them being small factories. But at their destination, there was a large four-story shopping mall filling a one-kilometer length along the far side of the laneway.

The taxi driver leaned back towards Ryder and handed him a small scanner. "One token please." Ryder lifted his wrist interlink and swiped it under the scanner. There was a *beep*, indicating the successful transfer of one token from his bank account to the taxi company.

Ryder thanked the driver before exiting the vehicle, followed by Linkin. With the shopping complex behind him on the far side of the lane, Ryder was face to face with the stone wall looming in front of him, not 30 metres away. At the base of the rock wall, between it and the lane, was a wide area paved with a mix of stone containing a red, crystalline formulation. Linkin remained close to the laneway as Ryder walked across the sparkling, paved surface, through several long, raised flower beds.

From behind him, he heard his mother's voice, "Ryder!"

He turned to see Vidame Nola Gunn exiting the family car, followed by her two bodyguards. One stayed by the roadway while the other walked just behind her towards Ryder. His mother never seemed to have a bad day—at least as one could tell from her appearance. Today, she was wearing a tight-fitting black and green, ankle-length dress. The colours alternated in horizontal rings down the length of the material. Her wide smile as she approached Ryder only made her look that much more elegant, albeit with a casual overtone, something he thought only his mother could pull off.

They hugged and Ryder gave her a kiss on her cheek. "You look great," he complemented while taking her hand and leading her towards the wall. As they came closer to it, the reddish-brown colour at the base of the rock took on a golden hue. Since they had been here many times, they knew it was not from mineral inclusions. Rather, it was from a multitude of gold plates, each one-half metre square, running the length of the wall.

Now, Vidame Nola walked faster, leading Ryder to the location she knew very well. Here, on the other side of a curved, raised flowerbed filled with green and yellow flowers, was a location on the wall reserved for the Gunn family leaders. In the middle, top position was a gold plaque with the inscribed name, *Vidame Natalie Gunn*. Underneath it was the dates of her birth and death. On its left was a similar plaque with the name *Primor Rowan Gunn*. However, in addition to the dates was the inscription, *Known as Josh Harris, hero of the Battle of Fort Nelson*. There was a similar plaque on the other side of Natalie's for Arlo Gunn. His inscription read, *Known as Logan Russell, hero of the Battle of Fort Nelson*.

Underneath Arlo's plaque was another for Vidame Nola's deceased husband, Pateer Gunn. Ryder stood back as his mother put her hand on this plaque for a moment. She smiled remembering the life they had together, but quickly, her hand moved to the plaque to the left of her husband's. The name inscribed on it was, *Emmaril Gunn*. The inscription below had her date of birth, and beside it were the words, *Died in Childbirth*.

Ryder moved closer and put a reassuring hand on his mother's shoulder. A beam of light from one of the many light fixtures hanging off the front wall of the shopping mall across the street, caught the ring on her mother's finger. The family ring was three thousand years old, but it looked like it was brand new. The dark-blue, almost black ring, with light-blue tendrils through it, was maintained on a regular schedule. Blemishes or chips were repaired, leaving Ryder wondering, *how much of the original family ring was left*. Nevertheless, it was the symbol of their family and needed to look the part, as it did today.

After several minutes, Nola turned and her son saw the tears in her eyes. In a solemn tone, she confided, "It's difficult losing a child at any time, but Emmaril left me instantly. I never even heard her cry." A sob began in her throat, but she managed to hold it back.

There were no words that could change what happened to his sister, so Ryder remained quiet while giving her a comforting hug. After a few moments, his mother pulled away, her eyes wide. "Don't get me wrong, my son. I love you more than anything, but boys and girls are not the same. I don't mean to say a bond between a mother and daughter is stronger than that which I have with you, but it is different." Her wide eyes searched his for understanding, and when he smiled, her body relaxed. "I miss her so much."

They turned, hand in hand again, and walked back to the Gunn family car. Nola asked Ryder if they could drop him somewhere, and he accepted. Once inside the vehicle, Ryder directed the driver to drop him at the nearest train station.

His mother asked, "Where are you off to today?"

Ryder reminded her, "Remember, I told you about a meeting I'm having with an official of the Zaf family. They are leaning towards leaving the Fyr family alliance and joining ours."

"Where are you meeting?" his mother inquired.

"Heroes Park in C11."

"Isn't that a little too public?"

"I consider it like hiding in plain sight," Ryder suggested with a coy smile.

The family car turned a corner and then stopped. They were at the train station, so Linkin pressed the side door open before stepping out on the sidewalk.

As Ryder followed, the vidame leaned her head forward, her gaze on Linkin. "Now, you look after my boy," she implored as only a mother could do.

While Ryder rolled his eyes, Linkin gave a curt, "Yes, Ma'am."

Their railcar ride was a direct shot under 110th street, across the length of C21, then through the four kilometres of rock separating C21 and C11. A little over half way across C11, they exited the Ftrain and moved up to ground level. Here, there were taller ten-story office buildings on three sides, but in front of them was an open area covered in green, artificial grass. There were large flower pots and flowering trees bringing the park to life, along with a wide, crushed-stone pathway snaking through it. The two men didn't make it more than 50 metres, when they heard a squeaky voice from their left. "Dad!"

Ryder turned to the familiar voice to see his son, Romy, running towards him followed by the huffs and puffs of Fehyr, who was struggling to keep up. Ryder leaned down and Romy jumped into his arms. Heroes Park was one of Romy's favorite places, and it didn't take Romy long to reveal why.

"Dad, can we go see Great Grandpa?"

Earlier in the morning, Ryder had made arrangements to meet Fehyr and Romy here, and he gave himself enough time to spend a few minutes with his son before the meeting. "Of course!" Ryder replied. There was a side path on their left, and Romy clamped onto his father's hand, dragging him, sometimes walking forwards and sometimes backwards, towards it. Ryder stumbled on, followed by Linkin and Fehyr. After a minute, they arrived at a 20-metre-wide, paved circle surrounded by gold statues. Gold was fairly common in the meteors mined by the space farming families, so it made sense to make these monuments from it.

Romy shook free from Ryder and sped off towards a statue on the far side of the circle. There, two men were immortalized in a running position. Side by side, they both carried assault rifles, and the artist had masterfully captured the satisfied look of victory on their faces. The statue was four metres tall, and when Ryder strode to Romy, it was to find his son looking straight up, his jaw slack with awe.

The visage of Rowan Gunn was on the left with his brother, Arlo, on the right. Ryder thought the statue was a great likeness, but deep down, he didn't like how it glorified the war. However, as he turned, he saw all the statues around the circle were of war heroes. That's when the swatch of colour caught his eye.

He grunted, "Look at that," as he pointed to a specific statue. There, across the front of a military admiral's statue, a man who died more than 600 years ago, was a huge letter, *A*, painted in pink.

As they walked towards it, Romy asked, "What's that all about?"

His father chose his words carefully as he explained, "Most people in Talus don't eat meat. Maybe 30 per cent, us included, still do. It's still an accepted way of life, but there are radicals who despise us for doing so. That admiral ate meat so the radicals protest by writing a big *A* across him."

"What does the *A* stand for?"

"Animals matter."

Romy scratched his head. "I still don't get it. I love animals, especially bacon; it's my favorite!"

The three adults couldn't help but laugh. Ryder pressed a virtual button on his wrist interlink and checked the time. His meeting was in five minutes. He encouraged Romy, "Why don't you go to the playground for a little while. Fehyr will go with you." Before Ryder finished the sentence, Romy was off like a shot towards the swings with Fehyr struggling along behind him.

Another 100 metres further into the park was a group of picnic tables. That was where he had made arrangements to meet the two Zaf family officials. He whispered to Linkin, "Give me a bit of room," as he headed for the location.

Linkin allowed the distance between them to grow to 50 metres as Ryder saw the two older men waiting at one of the painted, oxygen vine tables. At 52 years old, the younger of the two men was Primor Cohen Zaf, while the other man was a senior advisor. Ryder, sat down across from them, and said, "Greetings."

The Zaf primor furtively looked about before he spoke. "Salutations Primor Gunn. This is Miron, my senior advisor. We have had some correspondence already on the topic, but we would like to pursue further the—" Primor Zaf's eyes darted about again as his voice lowered to a whisper "—the possibility of the Zaf family leaving the Fyr alliance to join the Gunn alliance."

"It's something that would benefit both our families," the Gunn primor forecasted.

Primor Zaf grumbled, "Certainly, with a definite, clear majority on the Council of Nine, the Gunn family's benefit is obvious. Not so much for the Zaf family."

Ryder lowered an eyebrow. He didn't like negotiating, but he knew this would be part of the arrangement. "What are you proposing?"

Intertwining his fingers on the table, the Zaf primor suggested, "We want to be second seat on the Gunn alliance."

A wry smile crossed Ryder's face. He knew this was just the start. The Bli family was their closest partner in their alliance. Since they controlled medical operations, their close relationship to the Gunn family's pharmaceutical prowess was logical and necessary. "The Zaf family can be third seat."

The Zaf primor chuckled. After a moment of contemplation, he purred, "We'll take third seat, on one condition."

"Which is?"

"You'll marry a Zaf family member. We have several beautiful women for you to choose from."

Ryder tapped his fingers on the table top. He knew an outright "no" would stop all further discussion. "I will consider your list of women. I'm not saying I will marry one. After all, that will make her the next vidame of the Gunn family, so my mother would also need to review such a list."

Primor Zaf's eyebrows lowered. He wasn't confident Vidame Nola would approve. Historically, she had implied the Zaf family was weak.

Ryder was amused to find these negotiations always revolved around women and money, and seeing Primor Zaf hesitate, he countered with a monetary offer. "Third seat and four per cent of the Gunn family profits over two years."

Primor Zaf's eyes lit up. "Third seat, and seven per cent over three years."

"Third seat and five percent over three years."

A half-smile of satisfaction came over Primor Zaf's face. "It's reasonable. I'll take that offer to my mother, Vidame Zaf."

"I hope to hear from you soon..."

No sooner had the last word left Ryder's lips, when a blaring siren was heard. It wasn't the same alarm from a week ago for the asteroid course correction. This was a different—*whoop—whoop—whoop!*

Ryder recognized the signal as the air raid siren. In all likelihood, just as it had been for over four hundred years over which time a Sholite attack had never come directly at the asteroid, this was only a drill. Still, it was one to be taken seriously. As he rose to his feet and left the table, he shouted into his wrist interlink, "Linkin—get Romy!"

"Already on my way," came the reply.

Off in the distance, Ryder could see Linkin undertaking a brisk walk towards the playground. He followed at the same, quick pace. All Korians had been trained on such drills. From that came the knowledge not to panic. Don't run. Don't trample. Just be quick and efficient.

Once Ryder caught up to his son, Linkin and Fehyr, they headed directly to the closest support spire, 50 metres outside the park. There was a steady flow of people towards it, just as it would be at every spire in the asteroid. Inside the spires were turbo elevators taking large groups of people at unbelievable speeds to the many air raid shelters in the inner core of the asteroid, just above the spires. It only took two minutes for the group to scurry into one of these elevators. Their stomachs were seemingly forced to their feet, only to find, a minute later, their stomachs tried to push into their chest. The huge elevator was filled with 50 people—50 silent people except for Romy, who blurted, "That was awesome!"

The elevator doors opened on four sides, revealing square tunnels cut into the rock above the chamber. Ryder led his group to the closest, and soon they found themselves in a large air raid shelter. There was row upon row of benches, but most were already occupied. The push of people forced them further in, towards the end. A flash of red caught Ryder's eye, and he did a double take. There, sitting on the bench in front of him, was the same redheaded woman who had caused him to catch his breath at his mother's birthday party. It was the young woman who, in only a moment, had so intrigued him.

All the seats were filled, and Ryder was coming to the realization they would be standing for a while, when a voice carried to him. "Your son looks tired. Please let him sit here." The voice came from the woman who was sitting beside the redhead. She rose to her feet as Ryder gave her a quick thank you.

There were bars hanging down from the roof of the shelter and Ryder held one. He didn't notice, 30 metres away, the woman who had given up her seat, squeeze by a large man in a dark suit—nor the man slipping a 50-token chip into her hand. The man lifted his wrist interlink to his lips. "So far, it's going as planned," he whispered.

Sitting in the neighbouring air raid shelter, Primor Zaf listened to the words. "Very good," he whispered. The primor knew it was unlikely Ryder would accept an arranged marriage—at least knowingly. Consequently, his back up plan was in play.

Romy, sitting beside the redhead, poked her leg. When she looked down at him, he said, "How did you like that elevator ride? Wasn't it exciting?"

She smiled, and it caught Ryder off guard. She was not traditionally beautiful, but there was something about her that made her extremely appealing. He interrupted his son and said, "Romy, leave the people alone."

The redhead looked up at Ryder, and her smile widened. "It's okay." She turned her gaze back to Romy. "It was a blast. Do you like rides?"

"Oh, yeah!" Romy blurted. "I love the fair and the rides there, especially the *Rocket* roller coaster."

She gave a soft laugh and offered, "That was one of my favorites when I was your age." Her blue eyes turned back to Ryder where she caught him staring. "Have I met you somewhere before? You look familiar?"

"I believe I saw you at Vidame Gunn's birthday party. I was about to ask you to dance when you disappeared."

"My loss," she purred.

Their eyes were locked, much as they were at the birthday party, when a squeaky voice broke the trance. "Say, do you like bacon?"

The redhead frowned and gazed down at Romy. "Say what?"

Romy had a quizzical look on his face. "Well, my Dad likes bacon, and from the way you two are looking at each other, it would be swell if you liked bacon as well."

A slight blush came over her face as she glanced back and forth from Romy to his father. "Well, I love bacon, but I'm sure your mom does as well."

An involuntary frown crossed Ryder's face as he interrupted with a whisper. "His mother is no longer with us."

As she glanced at Ryder, her large eyes became even bigger. "I'm sorry. You look like you're raising a great son."

"And you look like you're great with kids," he offered.

"Well, I have no kids, other than the few I teach piano to."

Romy began to squirm, and in a loud voice, exclaimed, "I always wanted to learn how to play the piano!"

"Shhh!" Ryder lifted a finger to his lips. The redhead started to laugh and Ryder explained, "He has wanted to learn piano for a while. Do you have time in your schedule?"

Romy tugged on her coat and blurted, "Oh, do ya? Please!"

She lifted her hand and tussled Romy's hair. "I can probably fit you in." She reached into the pocket of her jacket and pulled out a business card. She handed it to Ryder and said, "My name is Shareen—Shareen Zaf."

"I'm Ryder Gunn."

"I know," she said in a low voice.

"You're okay with that?"

She shrugged coyly. "Well, you do like bacon. Maybe you're not as bad as your reputation."

Through a chuckle, Ryder muttered, "My reputation? Now what would they be saying?"

Her eyes smiled at him. "It depends who *they* would be, but *they* could be wrong. After all, you don't have horns—not even a tail."

Ryder rolled his eyes. "Romy thinks you are cute."

Romy's chin flew up and down at a tremendous pace. Shareen saw this and turned her gaze back up to Ryder. "And you?"

His voice moved to a deeper tone, and his words were slow-paced. "So far—so good."

"Good," she decided. "I'm sure we can work out the time for piano lessons—maybe around a coffee?" Her blue eyes were hopeful.

Across the room, the man in the dark suit lifted his wrist interlink to his lips and whispered, "This is going better than expected. Very heavy flirting…"

In the next chamber, the Zaf family primor had a smug smile on his face. This was going even better than their plan could have forecasted. He knew Ryder would never agree to an arranged marriage, but neither Ryder nor Shareen knew this *supposedly accidental* meeting was devised well in advance. The primor thought, *one way or the other, we're going to get what the Zaf family wants.*

Chapter 8: Indiscretion

Gaylin Gunn sat in a low, cloth armchair against the wall of his apartment in chamber C33. Chamber C33 was populated primarily by members of the Fex and Rok families. Both were farming families with the Fex family focusing their fleet of ships on recovery of nitrogen, most commonly in the form of ammonia in the vast coldness of space. The Rok family, aligned with the Fex, were similar only they sent their ships out in search of hydrogen clouds. Both groups, as you would expect from farmers, were laid back, resulting in one of the quietest neighbourhoods in Talus.

It was a perfect location for the covert apartment Gaylin kept to feed his vices. The curtains of the bedroom were cracked open, allowing a thin streak of light to play across his face. Beside him, on a side table, was the incense stick, popular among the elite. It provided the mildly hallucinogenic effect presently fogging his mind. In his hand was a short glass filled halfway with ice and a deep-amber liquor. A quarter-empty bottle and a bucket of ice sat on the table next to him, ready to provide the next refill.

Gaylin took a slow drink of liquor from the glass.

On the far wall, across from Gaylin and beside the window, was a narrow floor to ceiling mirror. Sitting in his underwear, he looked at himself in the dim light. He cocked his head to the side as he considered his long face partially hidden by his black, trimmed beard. He was not overly handsome, but surely not ugly. He was tall and lean, but a little soft, he thought, as his fingers squeezed the little roll of fat across his stomach. It was a good thing he had what was more important than classic beauty or a rippled abdomen; he had power—power over people because they feared him. At his whim, as he had done at times, with a single word he could ruin a person and their family, or give them ultimate opportunities.

That thought brought his mind to the girl. He glanced at the bed with the sheets bundled to one side, next to where their urgent lovemaking had occurred only 30 minutes before. A frown formed. He knew himself as a wonderful leader, and as such, he was a wonderful communicator. Within that, he considered himself also a great listener, except when people just began to whine and complain, which seemed to happen much too often. But right now, he couldn't remember the name of the girl. Was she Mira or Mina? He rubbed his chin and tried to remember—Marla—Marna? Finally, he put the troublesome mental block down to the drug coming from the incense stick.

Gaylin took a slow drink of liquor from the glass.

He had an excellent assistant who often surprised him. She was a woman who seemed to deal with his vices admirably and without judgement. Accepting or understanding them was not something Gaylin was concerned with—as long as she did his bidding. That she did, and he paid her well for it. On the first day of every work week, when Gaylin entered his outer office, Tala, his assistant, sat ready with her pad and pen. As he walked by, he would utter just one word. It was either, "Blonde, redhead or black." The odd time, he would just say, "Exotic." From that, Tala would find an open morning— it always had to be the morning—when she would arrange for a woman to spend time with him. The requirements were simple. She had to be stunningly beautiful with not even a slight blemish on her skin. Of course, the women had to be clean and were sent to a doctor prior to the *event* to verify this.

Gaylin took a slow drink of liquor from his glass.

He glanced at the bed once again. The girl this morning was excellent. She was of medium height with long legs. She had a great smile that never left her face, no matter what Gaylin did to her—and he did a lot. He used her in every way possible. But he knew it wasn't the exorbitant amount of money he paid her keeping the smile there. Rather, it was her hope she would be asked back and become a regular, allowing the money pot to become a waterfall of tokens. Even though he told every girl, "they were wonderful, and he would certainly call them back," he never did. He told them, "their discreet silence might draw them here for a second romp," but it never did. Gaylin wrinkled his nose and muttered, "Fucking sluts." Then he thought, *maybe her name was Milo.*

Byron, his head of security, was the only other person who knew about his weekly morning of indiscretion. Right now, he was waiting in the lobby. Each time, he was assigned to pay the girl and arrange her a taxi. Byron was one of only a few people who understood him.

Gaylin's eyes rotated back to the mirror as the hallucinogenic drug interlaced deeper into his brain. His gaze was again squarely on his form he saw in the mirror through the incense-laden haze. He enjoyed his position as one of the most powerful men in Talus. He enjoyed being a leader; in his mind he was good at it.

Complete in many ways, he still held one thought that often bothered him—a thought that often came up during these drug-induced periods of self reflection. This predicament was the knowledge he was not doing anything *good*. As a leader in business and in the community, there should be something he could say he did that was *good*, yet when he evaluated his life, he couldn't come up with even one individual instance. Sure, he gave the girl today—whatever her name was—an impressive tip, *but doing good must be more than that,* he thought.

Gaylin took a slow drink of liquor from his glass.

The topic ate at him in such a manner that he even researched the word *good,* discovering there were many definitions. The one he found most appropriate indicated *good* was the advancement of prosperity or well being. Immediately, he realized he did many good things, but right after that, he realized that was because he was the recipient of that prosperity and well-being. That wasn't the interpretation bothering him. He tried harder. Several times, he called a random employee into his office to give them a large bonus. Every time, he almost did, but ultimately after some hesitation, he didn't. The company gave money to charities, but of course, he saw this as free advertising. When he tried to make personal donations, he could never follow through with it.

He didn't know why it bothered him so much. At 38, he still had the majority of his life left to live. He was successful and held the power that fueled him, but still, he felt incomplete with the knowledge he was not a good person. He wouldn't go as far as to admit he was a bad person. His mind would let him go as far as admitting he needed to perform some good endeavors to complete his life. *He had time, but—fuck—at some point, he better get on with it.* Ironically, he knew this to be true because, why else, at 11:00 on a weekday morning, would he be sitting in his underwear in a dark room, in such a drug and alcohol induced, melodious state?

The melodious state was about to become complicated as there was a *buzz* from the metallic ring associated with his wrist interlink. He tilted his wrist and rolled his eyes when he saw the source of the incoming signal. He pressed the virtual button and lifted his wrist close to his lips. "Hello, My Love."

There was a momentary pause before his wife, Urslla, inquired, "Where are you, Darling? I called the office, and Tala told me you were out on business."

"I just finished a business meeting, and you caught me just on the way back to the office," Gaylin lied.

"I hope the meeting was useful."

"As always."

"The reason I called was to remind you we're having dinner with Vidame Gunn this evening," Urslla said.

Gaylin chuckled. "Actually, I did forget all about it. What would I do without you?"

"Mmm," she purred. "I'll see you tonight. Make sure you're not too tired."

Gaylin's jaw slid open as his mind tried to catch up with an appropriate response. His wife saved him the effort as she disconnected the call. He downed the remainder of the liquor in his glass, pressed the virtual button, then lifted his wrist interlink to his lips. "Byron, get the car ready. I'm going to have a quick shower, then meet you in the lobby in 20 minutes."

It was only a five-minute drive in Gaylin's private car, across C21, from his home to that of his aunt. Both their homes were close to the Gunn Spire which he could see to their right, out the tinted window of the car. The roads in this high-end part of Talus were painted black, flanked by deep-red coloured sidewalks. Byron was driving, and as usual, he said little to nothing. Gaylin and Urslla had not spoken much since the call in the late morning. Gaylin thought he had escaped an inquiry, but as they were coming up the driveway of Vidame Gunn's home, Urslla chirped, "So who was it this morning? Was she pretty?"

It's not that Gaylin lied to his wife about his extra-curricular affairs, he just didn't offer information willingly. This time, since she asked, he put an unusual look on his face—one he hoped showed a lack of interest in the topic, and he replied, "She was attractive in her own way."

Gaylin and Urslla had an open marriage. It was arranged between the two of them when they married. Although Gaylin thrived in the freedom it gave him, Urslla also undertook enough of her own discrete affairs. However, it didn't stop the occasional jealous needling. "Have you fathered any children?"

He grumbled, "Nope—no children." He understood the meaning of his wife's question. They had a daughter, but no sons, and sons were needed by the second in line of any family. If death should befall Ryder, then Gaylin would be primor. Urslla would be the next vidame, and if they had a son, he would be in line to be primor in the next generation.

The electric hum of the vehicle stopped as they pulled in front of the double doors of the large house. Urslla peered at the yet unopened doors before she whispered, "This family is comical. Ryder is the primor with no wife and you are second in line with no son." She rolled her eyes to ensure the comment punished her husband as deeply as possible.

Tapping Byron on the shoulder, Gaylin directed, "Let the butler know we'll be along in a moment."

Byron departed the black vehicle and stepped up to the front door, just opened by the vidame's servant. Now alone inside the vehicle, Gaylin admonished his wife. "Be careful what you say and when you say it. Byron is the one person I trust the most, but every man has a price."

Urslla was absolutely beautiful. Gaylin would have no less. As she slunk back in the seat and crossed one thin leg over the other, she had a devilish look on her face. It elevated her beauty, giving him pause. Her voice was melodic as she suggested, "I'm not the problem. Ryder is the problem. Are you ever going to do something about him?"

Through clenched teeth, Gaylin indicated, "You don't need to worry about Ryder. I'm not saying that as a casual, flippant comment for you to discard." His eyes bored into hers. "Stay out of my business!" he hissed. "I have an expert following Ryder. If need be, when the time comes, I just need to snap my fingers and he'll be removed—just like that." As the words left his lips, for emphasis, he snapped his fingers right under her nose.

A chill went up her spine as she heard the cut-throat menace in her husband's tone. She was frozen, not sure how to respond. Gaylin was maniacal. From one instant to the next, his face brightened and suddenly carried a wide smile as he urged in a now playful voice, "Let's go eat. I'm starving!"

Nola Gunn's home was a three story, stone structure. Its size befit someone of her standing, as did the accompaniments. Inside the grand front vestibule, the walls were covered by many paintings depicting the history of the Korian people. Most of these were thousands of years old, painstakingly preserved.

Once the front door closed behind the visitors, Byron slid down a side passage he knew led to the living quarters for the butler. There, he would wait as he had done the few previous times he had visited.

The butler greeted Gaylin and his wife before scurrying off to announce their arrival to the vidame. A few minutes later, Aunt Nola entered the vestibule from the wide main corridor running the length of the house. Her face framed a polite smile for the two of them. Her feelings towards her nephew were confused, at best, ever since the time Ryder fell from the tree behind this same house, then occupied by her mother. Ryder was as sure footed as anyone, so when he fell, there was a suspicion Gaylin pushed him. There was no evidence, just as there was no solid evidence Gaylin really conducted the dastardly deeds many told her he concocted as an adult. He was her nephew, and he begot the benefit of her doubt, as fragile as that may be.

As they entered a side parlor, benefiting from different shades of blue on the walls and furniture, the butler brought wine. Their banter was light and courteous as it was during dinner. Gaylin expected this. It was not common for he and his wife to be invited to the vidame's household without other guests. Typically, Ryder would be invited, or some other important members of the Gunn extended family. It was obvious, since there were only the three of them at dinner, the vidame had a sensitive topic to broach.

He assumed a difficult discussion would result after the fine lamb dinner. Of course, *lambs* didn't exist in Talus, but the lambs known to Earthers were the closest resemblance to the herd animals raised on the vast farms in C22 and C42. These lamb-type animals were slightly larger and had long, fast growing horns. The builders stocked them from Kor thousands of years before because the species were multipurposed. Their horns could be used to manufacture tools and other items of value. Their hair also grew quickly, and when shorn, was a critical supply of wool. They also provided a fine milk and lean meat—such as the wonderfully cooked cuts they just finished eating.

With the meal finished, Nola led them back into the parlor, where all three of them sat in round, wingback chairs. The butler brought a tray with a decanter of potent liquor often served after such a fine meal. It was a viscous fluid the butler poured into three tiny glasses. Once they all had a drink in front of them, the vidame nodded her chin, bringing the coloured liquor to her lips.

Gaylin did the same and tipped only a small amount of the thick liquor down his throat. That was the point. Supposedly, as the legend had it, the liquor has medicinal qualities for the throat. He felt the slight burn of the liquid, then tilted his face up towards his aunt. It seemed, with some difficulty, she smiled and said, "Well..."

Oh, fuck, Gaylin thought. *Here it comes.*

Vidame Gunn held the smile, peered at Gaylin, then Urslla, then back at Gaylin. The subtle nuances were over. "When will I see a nephew from the two of you?"

Crossing one leg femininely over the other, Gaylin replied, "Hopefully soon. We practice constantly." He waggled his eyebrows to indicate his humorous interpretation of the question.

Nola waggled her finger back at her nephew. She laughed politely for only a moment, before a stern countenance pushed it aside. "How often?"

Urslla, as she was apt to do, won the alcoholic consumption contest for the night. She blurted out a laugh, but offered no more. She would leave it to her husband to handle his aunt.

Gaylin knew better than to think the vidame was kidding. "It varies, but at least a couple of times a week. Sometimes more."

"Then, what do you think the problem is?"

Gaylin shrugged. "You know as well as I do what the problem is. The ongoing life we lead in space takes many tolls. One of these, quite unforeseen by the builders, is the negative effect low gravity has on the Korian male's sperm count. That's why, when your mother, Vidame Natalie Gunn, came to Talus, there were a little over eight million inhabitants. Now, 64 years later, our population sits at the same number."

Nola flicked her hand, shooing away the explanation. "Are you taking your medications?"

"Of course!"

"Then I'm not sure exactly what *your* problem is," Nola chirped. "There is the option of having a sperm donor who has a higher sperm count."

"Really!" Urslla blurted. Her eyes were wide, indicating she was not at all against the idea.

"To be a primor, the son would have to be *my* son. I don't know why I have to explain this," Gaylin scoffed as he ran his fingers through his hair.

The vidame rapped her fingers off the arm of the chair. "That's only if people knew. Of course, if necessary, it would be done in secret."

"Would I get to choose?" Urslla asked expectantly.

The vidame smiled coyly at her step-niece. "Well, to a point, yes."

"An advance sneak peek?" Urslla asked with a carnal gaze.

"Perhaps…"

"Hey! I'm still in the room!" Gaylin shouted.

"My apologies," Nola offered in a less-than sympathetic tone. "We were just kidding. But understand, we have some serious issues in the structure of this family. They need to be fixed."

Seeing the opportunity to jab back at his aunt, Gaylin clarified, "You mean Ryder."

It was odd to Nola how families fought. But not only that, they fought with veiled methods such as seen in the banter now. When she saw it, she tried to correct it as she would do now. She leaned forward in her chair; her words were meant to leave a mark. "Ryder is a problem, but at least his sperm is not. He has a son, but no wife. A wife can be found in a day, and one day, if need be, that will be the case." Her eyes bored into Gaylin. "Your problem cannot be fixed in a day. I'm not unsympathetic, so I'll give you a year to give Urslla a boy. If not, I'll take matters into my own hands. Is that understood?"

Gaylin's face was deep-red. Briefly, he thought it would take only three strides of his long legs, and he could have his fingers around her neck. He could kill her and be done with it. Byron was here, and if anyone knew how to clean up such a mess, he would. However, Gaylin was a survivor. He knew the cameras saw him come in. If he ever did more than fantasize about his aunt's death, it would not be so impulsive. All he could do was catch his breath and reply in as steady a voice as he could manage, "Of course, Vidame. As you wish."

Chapter 9: Broken Mirror

Integrated into Ryder's wrist interlink was a narrow slit. Doctor Dana Bli placed the thin strip of white plastic into it. After a few seconds, she withdrew it and introduced it into a similar slit in the medical kit open on the desk. It didn't take long for a green light on the apparatus to brighten, indicating the blood analysis was complete.

Earlier, the doctor had inserted a similar strip, previously introduced into Ryder's urine stream, and those results were already on the small monitor integrated into the briefcase-type medical kit. With both sets of results now available, the doctor was scrolling through them with a long finger rhythmically tapping her chin. Occasionally, a "hmm" or an "aha" would quietly press through her lips. Finally, as the two of them sat in his study, she turned to Ryder, stating, "The results are acceptable. Your sodium levels are high, but that's easy to rectify."

"How so?" Ryder asked.

Dana Bli was young—29 years old, with short, platinum-blonde hair. She grimaced at Ryder before answering in a berating tone. "Stop eating so much salt!" Simultaneous with the last word, for emphasis, she slapped the two sides of the medical kit closed.

The Bli family, aligned with the Gunn family, controlled all medical practitioners in Talus. Simply explained, there were three levels of doctors. There were specialists who handled the more involved cases and also the surgeries tending to go with those. There were also the general practitioners who looked after basic conditions, and were also the first line of evaluation, who might refer Korians to the specialists. Dana Bli was within the third category of doctors, and in fact, these lower-level doctors were only slightly more qualified than nurses. These were the doctors who made house-calls to all Korians every three months to evaluate their blood and urine, allowing them to adjust the chemical composition of their gravity patches.

Doctor Bli also carried a small carrying case which she was searching through. Mumbling, "there they are," she pulled out two small boxes. Her large brown eyes, under unusually dark eyebrows that were a mismatch to her light-coloured hair, turned towards Ryder as she pushed the two boxes of patches across to him. "There's no need to change the formulation."

Ryder smiled and rose up from behind his amber-coloured, oxygen vine table. It was a meticulously maintained antique from the Gunn family, passed down from primor to primor. The panelling, halfway up each wall, was also made of the often used, pressed oxygen vine material, stained with a colour to match the desk.

As Ryder led the doctor from his study, the change was startling. Where the study was dominated by simulated wood targeting a theme from centuries ago, the rest of the apartment was modern, mainly white and black with touches of grey. Ryder saw the doctor out, then turned, the odd silence giving him some cause for concern. After all, such silence with a six-year-old in the home was indeed unusual.

Since Ryder had asked Fehyr to keep the boy quiet during his medical appointment, he assumed the two were in Fehyr's room. When Ryder knocked on his door, he heard his son's squeaky voice blurt out, "We're busy!"

After hearing further subdued mumbles, these were followed by Fehyr offering, "Come in, Ryder."

When he did so, he saw Fehyr and Romy sitting on a couch not far from the video monitor. His son was on the edge of the cushion watching an episode of *Captain Courageous*. It was a cartoon where Captain Courageous was the captain of a Wolf-class frigate, the bravest person in the Korian navy, and apparently, impervious to the multiple lasers and missiles having hit him over five years of episodes.

Ryder was interrupted by a *beep* from his wrist interlink. He pressed one virtual button, frowning as he didn't recognize the incoming caller, but he pressed a second button to connect it anyway. As he left Fehyr's room and closed the door, he said, "Hello, Ryder Gunn here."

Even though the man's speech was slow, the tone sounded like it came from a younger person. "Sorry to bother you, Mister Gunn. I'm Detective Taylor Jez of the Talus police. We have an ongoing investigation we need your help with."

As soon as Ryder heard it was a police call, he began to pace across his living room towards the far windows. "Are you sure?" He questioned. "I have no idea how I could possibly help you."

There was a brief pause before the detective continued, "Do you know a man by the name of Wilam Fex?"

Ryder froze. "Well—yes. Many years ago, we were good friends in college. We still see each other, but I think the last time was six months ago." Briefly, his mind went back to their college days when they were inseparable, but for the most part, in the years following, they had lost touch. "I still don't understand how I can help you."

"Mister Gunn, I'm sorry to tell you, Wilam is dead. There is something here at his apartment I need to show you, if you could make your way here."

A good half-minute of silence passed.

"Mister Gunn?"

Ryder's thoughts came back to the call. Considering he had the rest of his morning free, he replied, "It's not far to the train station. I'll be on my way in a few minutes."

"No need for the train, Mister Gunn. I have a car waiting outside your apartment."

By now, Ryder was at his window; he pulled back the curtain to see the red police car just off the edge of the sidewalk. He smirked and replied coyly, "Of course, Detective. Your forethought is appreciated."

After disconnecting the call and collecting Linkin from his room, the two men were on their way down to the first floor. The police driver opened the door for the two men, who entered into the large passenger compartment, then lowered into two of the inward-facing, bucket seats.

There was a private train line five kilometres away which the policeman drove the vehicle towards. Wilam Fex's apartment was in C45, a good 65 kilometres away, so connecting the police car to the private rail line was the fastest route that would take them approximately one hour. The car weaved from street to lane, back and forth, until a ramp appeared on their left. It spiraled downwards for 30 metres to a point below the level of the public trains. Here, the car was corralled towards the entry to a private rail line. Talus's primary transportation computer kept control of all vehicles along the private lines. The vehicles were kept 100 metres apart, allowing incoming vehicles to enter when a gap became available. However, police vehicles had priority, so in these cases, oncoming vehicles were slowed, making a gap for them.

As they were ready to load onto the monorail, the driver called out, "Watch your feet. Chairs are going to rotate in three—two—one..."

Both Linkin and Ryder leaned back in their bucket seats as all the sideways mounted seats rotated on their pedestals so the occupants were facing forwards. In this way, as they accelerated, their backs and necks were supported properly. In a similar manner, just before they slowed at their destination, the seats would rotate 180 degrees for the same purpose in deceleration.

Once they were shuttled onto the main monorail, two rail attachments lowered from the police car and latched onto the electrified monorail. The car lurched forward as the city computer took over control of the vehicle, soon bringing it up to its maximum 80 kilometre per hour speed.

Ryder had given Linkin a brief explanation of the reason for their trip. After that, Linkin saw Ryder silent and deep in thought. Ryder remembered his friend, Wilam, and their early school years in a much different educational system from that known on Earth. In Talus, elementary school ended when children were 16. From that point, college began in five-year increments and was considered an ongoing life process. Therefore, people in Talus were recognized with five, ten, fifteen and twenty-year degrees. Only the first five years were compulsory, full-time attendance. After that, the education could be, and often was, part time studies given equivalency towards a full year of courses.

Ryder had completed his 5-year degree with Wilam. Wilam continued in full time courses while Ryder continued with both part time and on-line courses. At 40 years old with a ten-year degree under him, Ryder had slowed the pace of his educational activities.

The police car veered left in a banked turn on the underground monorail. Ten minutes later, their car was slowed and sent along a side rail towards a flat top area. The policeman took over control of the vehicle, now firmly supported on its rubber wheels. They proceeded up a spiral ramp and out into the simulated daylight in chamber C45. Three turns later, the red police car came to a stop in front of a 20-story apartment building.

Ryder and Linkin exited the vehicle, where a police officer at the door came to them. Once Ryder's identity was confirmed, he was escorted into the building, leaving Linkin to wait inside the front lobby. The elevator stopped at the 15th floor, and the officer led Ryder to one of the apartments as they passed several other officers and forensic personnel, milling about in the hallway.

When Ryder came closer, a tall, young man in a long, black coat raised his hand. He met Ryder just outside an open apartment door, introducing himself as Detective Taylor Jez. "I'm sorry for the loss of your friend, Mister Gunn," the detective said in a scratchy voice.

Pointing at the apartment door, Ryder whispered, "Is he in there?"

The detective had a face that seemed to be in a perpetual frown, something that can happen to someone who never smiles. "No, Wilam Fex was found deceased outside a bar in C24. When the bar owner was closing up, he saw the body beside a garbage dumpster." Detective Jez elaborated in a softer voice, "It was a quick death—professional."

"I'm not sure how I can help you, and even more confusing to me is, how can I help you here at his apartment?"

Nodding his understanding, the detective suggested, "Follow me into the apartment, and I'll show you." Without waiting for a response, Taylor Jez strode through the open doorway.

Inside the apartment, Ryder saw the contents had been turned upside down. Chairs were flipped, cushions were torn, cupboards were turned over and paintings had been ripped off the walls. His eyes narrowed as he turned his judgmental gaze to the detective. "Why did you do this?"

Detective Jez pulled a pair of thin, plastic gloves from his pocket and pulled them on. He returned Ryder's cold stare. "We didn't do this. We found Wilam's apartment in this condition. It appears, from his death and now this, someone was looking for something."

All Ryder could manage was a slight nod as the confusion clouding his mind grew.

"Follow me and don't touch anything," Detective Jez directed. He then walked down a side hallway and into a large bedroom, it's state of dishevelment matching that of the living room. He passed into a large bathroom and turned to Ryder, "Watch your step. There's broken glass."

Ryder's speculatively inspected the bathroom. There was a storage cupboard that had been emptied onto the floor. Bottles of all sorts were strewn on the floor, and the large mirror had been pulled off the wall, the sharp, broken pieces from it, being the source of the shards across the tiled floor. "I still don't know why I'm here," Ryder grumbled.

The detective raised a finger in the air. "Of course," he replied. He leaned down and retrieved the bent frame of the mirror leaning against the wall. He pulled it up and twisted it around so the two men were looking at the felt backing. There was a tear along the back, and the detective pushed his finger into it. "When I found this there was only a small tear, but through it I saw a streak of red. I tore it further, and I found something—perhaps the thing the people who killed your friend were looking for."

Taylor Jez flicked his finger and a wide strip of torn felt fell open. Ryder's eyeballs almost exploded when he read the message on the backing of the mirror, hidden under the felt. In red marker it read, *Tell Ryder Gunn to visit the Talus Dogs.*

"What does that mean!" Ryder blurted.

The detective managed a slight grin, the closest he could come to a smile. "I was hoping you could tell me. What can you tell me of the *Talus Dogs?*"

Shrugging, Ryder explained, "I know what everyone else in Talus knows.

Talus Dogs are the most elite group of fighters within our military." Ryder summarized it well. The Talus Dogs was a nickname for an elite group of first line, shock troops within the Korian navy. They were considered the best of the best, sent on the military missions having little hope of success and even less hope of survival.

"Do you have any association with them, or do you know if Wilam did?"

Ryder shook his head. "I don't, and Wilam was a reputable scientist, following in the footsteps of his father. I have no idea why he would have any relationship with the Talus Dogs."

Sighing, Detective Jez muttered, "I guess we'll have to go visit the Talus Dogs."

"We?"

Ryder didn't know it was possible to chuckle without smiling, but the detective managed it, after which he chirped. "It's not my name on the back of the mirror. It reads, *Tell Ryder Gunn to visit the Talus Dogs.* That's you," he noted as he pointed directly at Ryder.

"Okay—okay. When..."

Detective Jez interrupted. "I'll be tied up here the rest of the day. I'll call you in the morning, and we'll take an excursion to the military docks."

Ryder took his leave, collecting Linkin in the lobby before they made their way back to the Gunn Spire. Ryder didn't have many scheduled meetings with the ten people on his staff, but he liked to have impromptu meetings, and he wanted to have one this afternoon. He gathered his staff and sat on a random desk as he typically did. The people working for him knew the process, and they knew this was always an opportunity to update Ryder on progress and issues. For Ryder, it was an opportunity for him to encourage his workers. Although he hadn't thought about it much, Ryder had excellent leadership skills. He was a good listener and had the ability to envision projects well ahead of completion. He wasn't the best problem solver, but he knew that, so he surrounded himself with those who had strength in that capability. He wasn't aware how well his management skills had progressed, but that wasn't a surprise. Those who self-profess themselves as great leaders often aren't, and those who are great leaders, don't have to. Others do it for them, and those who really knew Ryder well, did so.

Ryder left work early since he had a date—the first he had planned in longer than he could remember. Young Romy had had three piano lessons with Shareen Zaf. She and Ryder had continued their playful banter until, finally, he asked her on a date. Tonight was the big night.

Avoiding the family colours, Ryder dressed in a light-blue, long-sleeved shirt, covered with a dark-blue waist-length, casual coat; his slacks matched the colour of the jacket. As he was doing a final inspection in his full-length mirror, Romy whipped around the corner, placing his fists on his hips. He scrunched up his face and tilted his head, judging his father's appearance. Seeing his son's reflection, Ryder turned and asked, "What do you think?"

Romy lowered his eyebrows, causing his face to scrunch even more. He scolded, "I think me and Miss Shareen get along really well." The boy crossed his arms. "I think it's yours to screw up, so don't, Dad," his son advised in an accusing tone.

Shareen Zaf lived close to Ryder's apartment, in the adjoining chamber, C25. She resided in an elegant, but not overly large, second floor apartment. In the same building, she rented a room on the first floor for her piano lessons. This was where she asked Ryder to meet her at the arranged time at the top of the 18th hour.

He didn't hear music playing on the other side of the door, so he slowly opened it to find Shareen and another man having a conversation, with each holding a cup of hot, flavoured milk. Ryder entered and cleared his throat. "I'm not interrupting, am I?"

Shareen turned her face, and it was overtaken by a wide smile at the sight of him. She waved him over while replying, "Not at all."

Ryder took appraisal of the man as he walked closer. He looked a little younger than Ryder, with a similar height and build. He had light-brown hair to a length covering his ears, with the slightest hint of grey at the temples. Ryder didn't know why, but he leaned in and gave Shareen a kiss on her cheek, then smiled at the stranger.

Through a slight blush, Shareen said, "Ryder, this is Soren Pym. He's come here inquiring about piano lessons."

"Greetings. I'm Ryder Gunn. It's nice to meet you." It wasn't customary in Talus for strangers to shake hands, so they didn't. "You look familiar. Have we met before?"

Soren Pym hesitated for a second before he replied, "No, I would certainly have remembered if I did."

Chuckling, Ryder commented, "That could be taken two ways, Soren." The comment had a prodding intent, but since there was no reaction, he added, "Forgive me, but aren't you a bit old to begin piano lessons?"

With a wave of his hand, Soren corrected Ryder's assumption. "The piano lessons would just be a refresher. I took lessons as a child, but lost touch with the art over time."

Shareen interrupted while handing Soren a business card. "We've discussed my pricing and the open spots in my timetable. Let me know if you'd like to proceed."

Taking the card, Soren placed the empty cup on the table. "It's been nice meeting both of you." His gaze on Shareen seemed a little too long until his eyes fell on Ryder and stayed there for even longer. Finally, he whispered, "Have a great day," then he made his exit from the room.

Shareen led Ryder to a chair overlooking the manicured garden, and told Ryder to wait until she quickly dressed in her apartment. Once she left, Ryder glanced at the time on his wrist interlink and mumbled, "We're going to be late."

However, Shareen made a hasty change. When Ryder heard the door to the piano room open behind him, he turned his face. For a moment, his breath was taken away by what he saw. Shareen was wearing a pale-yellow dress, cut mid-thigh. The floral pattern on the backless dress added both dark and light blue petals. Over her shoulders was draped a silk, dark-blue shawl, completing the vision.

As Ryder walked towards her, his voice came back to him. "You look fantastic." He couldn't help but glance up and down, now noticing the elegant sandals. She had nice feet and toes, the nails of which were painted light blue.

She gave a nervous chuckle and spun on the toes of one foot before coming face to face with him again. "So you approve?"

He gave her a quizzical look, one acknowledging her silly question in the face of the obvious. Taking her hand, he led her out into the foyer where she was introduced to Linkin. She wasn't surprised, going on a date with a man of importance, that a security guard would be present. However, when the three of them traveled on the public train back to the Gunn family space docks, and Ryder told Linkin he would need to wait for them at that point, she was surprised.

Shareen understood when Ryder took her to one of the smaller docking bays where a small two-seat racer was held in docking clamps. "Where are we going?" she asked.

As he took her hand and led her across the narrow gangway to the hatch of the space vehicle, he divulged, "There is a great nightclub in the Casino ship."

As she scooted across the small cabin of the racer and lowered into the seat, with excitement in her voice, she replied, "Really? I haven't been there in many years. Do you gamble?"

Ryder took the seat beside her. While he secured his seat belt and began to flick various switches on the dash, he muttered, "No, I don't gamble, but I like watching people and it's a great place to do that."

Shareen didn't respond as Ryder put on a headset and continued to engage switches in a start-up sequence. The glass surround hatch cover closed, and Ryder communicated with the Talus station tower. There was a *woosh* as the two large bay doors beneath them swung open. A few minutes later, with Talus station in control of the space racer, they were given clearance to launch. The station's computer set the racer's drive unit to match the rotation and speed of the asteroid as the docking clamps released the vehicle. Thrusters were fired until the racer was clear of the bay doors, and the Talus tower operator told Ryder he was clear to take manual control.

He acknowledged the tower's direction and placed one hand on a ball atop the dash. As he slid his hand forward, the racer sped away from the asteroid. With his other hand, he set small dials on the space vessels computer, entering coordinates of the Casino ship before pressing a flashing green button to engage the auto pilot.

There were many Korian ships in four armada's in close proximity to Talus. In total there were 582 ships including farming trawlers, hydroponic farming ships, Explorer Corp. ships, and of course, the vast Korian navy. Ryder veered the racer out of Talus's rotation as the speed increased, from the six per cent SOL speed of Talus, to the ten per cent required from the drive unit in the racer. The racer could go as fast as 40 per cent SOL, but since the specific armada they were travelling to was five thousand kilometres away, it only took ten minutes to arrive at the Casino ship.

This armada held 120 ships of every size and configuration. Most obvious was the military quadrant, where four Korian battleships were predominant within the vast number of smaller vessels. Also prominent was the five-kilometre long, recently commissioned oxygen vine farming ship. In case of a mishap in Talus, the Korians had redundancy in their systems, such as this vast oxygen farming ship, just as there were livestock farming ships and even residential ships.

As Ryder slowed the racer, he turned and pointed at a huge metal framework. Attached to it, and rotating in sync with the framework, were five large, but sleek space vessels. The red paint on them, identified them as ships of the Explorer's Corp. These stripped-down vessels were sent out regularly in every direction from Talus. They could travel up to 35 per cent SOL, and as a result, would travel up to six months in advance of the asteroid in their search for a world the Korian's could call home.

The Sholites had similar, red-painted explorer ships, none of which were weaponized. Both races had an agreement that Explorer ships were strictly off limits as military targets. Both worlds knew the discovery of a new world was paramount to both civilizations, trumping the need for war.

Ryder thought better than to open the date with his obsession for the Explorers Corp. Instead, he just calmly said, "Look at that."

They were given clearance to dock at the sizeable Casino ship, and they did so. After deboarding, they followed a wide hallway towards the din of voices and music. There was a massive internal archway, and beyond it they found themselves in the midst of ringing bells and spinning wheels, adding to the voices and music. They took some time to walk along the colourful carpets between the vast array of machines and tables. For a time, they stopped at a table where a couple were on a lucky streak. They seemed to win with each roll of the dice, and each time, while screaming, they both would throw their hands in the air. This happened several times until one roll was not as cooperative. As the Casino attendant pulled the massive stack of chips away from the couple, their jubilation was destroyed, and both hung their heads in dismay.

"That's why I don't gamble," Ryder offered.

Shareen nodded her head in agreement as Ryder led them through the throng of people. Shareen grasped his hand so as not to lose him. He intertwined his fingers into hers and didn't release her, even when their path was clear.

The large gaming room was three stories high. As Ryder searched out the balconies on the second level, he found the night club where he'd made reservations. Leading her up the stairs, he announced their arrival, whereby the maître d's eyes widened with the attendance of, what he considered, a celebrity. Immediately, they were whisked to a preferred corner table, overlooking the gaming floor.

Once they were seated, Shareen said, "This is wonderful. Thank you for bringing me here."

Ryder had mixed feelings. He felt silly and downright giddy, but at the same time, he felt like he wanted to tell Shareen about his entire life—the good—the bad—absolutely everything. He confessed, "I haven't been on a date in a long time. I wanted to do something special."

She whispered back, "It has been a while for me as well." Their gaze locked, interrupted by a sharply dressed waiter arriving at their table. They both ordered their drinks and a trio of appetizers to share. Once the food arrived, and the appetizing aroma hit their senses, they both realized how famished they were. They both dug into the finger food, making short work of the heaping plates of vegetable and meat slices, finished in several tasty ways.

Finishing the last wedge of battered, fried vegetable, Ryder wiped his fingers on a napkin before changing the subject. "Romy really likes you."

Letting the blue shawl fall back on the chair, revealing her pale, white skin, Shareen replied, "He's a great kid, and he's learning to play the piano with a lot of excitement. I enjoy teaching him."

"That Soren fellow was a little odd, I thought."

"I don't teach many adults." She took a drink from her glass, then added, "He did ask some odd questions that seemed to do with more than piano."

"Odd indeed." Questions came to his mind, but there would be time for that later. Right now, Ryder was with a woman he was attracted to, and he redirected his questions there. "You live in a nice apartment building. I didn't know piano teachers did so well."

Under her head of thick, light-red hair, she laughed, and her face lit up. "I should've told you. I teach piano in my spare time, mainly on evenings and non-workdays." As she elaborated, Ryder was fixated on her lips, coated with a thin layer of pink colouring. "I have a regular day job as the assistant director of the Rossnol Nuclear Plant in C25."

"Wow. You mean like second in command of the station?"

After she sipped from the edge of her glass, she nodded her head up and down. Once she put her glass on the table, her voice took on a more serious tone. "I am a Zaf, so the powerplant work is natural for me." She cleared her throat and tilted her soft gaze up to Ryder. "However, I'm not an *important* Zaf. In fact, I'm near the bottom of the family tree. I'm not in the group of beautiful, young Zaf women who are being shopped around to primors of important families. And you are the primor of the Gunn family—*thee* Ryder Gunn."

Ryder didn't realize he had a scrunched up look on his face much like the one Romy carried when he scolded him earlier in the afternoon. "I don't think anyone has ever called me—*thee* Ryder Gunn."

"Well, I did," she whispered.

"Say it again."

"What?"

"I liked it. Say it again."

"You're kidding?"

"Please?"

The corner's of Shareen's lips turned down; her lower lip began to tremble.

Ryder tilted his head and smiled wide. "Yes—I'm kidding!" He reached out and placed his hand on top of hers. "In case you haven't noticed, I'm 40 and still unmarried. There have been many suitors, including the primor of the Zaf family, but I hope you can see, *I* will make my own choice for a wife when *I* am ready, which is when *I* have found the right woman."

"I see…"

She had not removed her hand and he squeezed it. "I hope you do because I like you very much. I think a large part of that is because, just as I don't have ulterior or hidden motives, I don't think you are here with me in the hope of being the next vidame of the Gunn family."

Shareen had just taken a drink from her glass and it almost spilled out of her mouth as she blurted, "Hell no."

They both laughed loudly. The stage had been set for a relationship in the making. With the formalities out of the way—*really out of the way*—the two of them spent the next few hours talking about anything and everything. They seemed to shift closer and closer together until the two chairs were side by side, overlooking the gaming floor. Eventually, Ryder wrapped his hand across her far shoulder—and she leaned into him.

At one point, he had an irresistible urge; he leaned over and kissed the side of her head. She tilted her gaze up and through the wonderful smile, she had an *is that the best you can do* look. The answer came when he leaned down for a second time, his lips brushing hers for a moment. He pulled back, just a breath, and she whispered, "This could get complicated, Mister Primor."

He took a deep breath as her sweet breath spun his mind. He whispered back, "It can be this simple…" His words trailed off as his lips pressed to hers for a second time. It was a soft kiss, lingering, one they knew was a hopeful beginning for both of them.

If anyone from the gaming floor would have looked up at the balcony of the nightclub a few minutes later, they would have seen the two of them, cuddled close, with foolish, cheeky grins on their faces, seeming adolescent for their actual age. It was after midnight when Shareen heard a familiar song playing from the dance floor behind them. She asked if he liked dancing, whereby he rose and led her there. The music carried a slow rhythm, and he easily brought her into his embrace. Her warm breath was on his neck as they swayed to the music. They both revelled in each other, happier than they had been in as long as each of them could remember.

Human nature, for Korians and Earthers alike, can give a person a new found exuberance. This phenomenon seemed to manifest itself in Ryder as the music changed. As one song ended, the crashing, fast-paced rhythm of a second began. The electrical twang of stringed instruments and loud drums inspired Ryder. He yelled out, "C'mon!" With his eyes closed, his head tilted back, swaying back and forth.

Shareen felt his hands slip away from her. They flew in the air, one after the other and neither they, nor the sway and tilt of his head, matched the rhythm of the music. Her eyes opened wide as she saw his legs twist at awkward angles, again not matching the music or the movement of his other body parts. Others on the dance floor began to stare at Ryder's interesting style of dancing. As Shareen stood frozen, something was bothering her. She had seen this dance before. Then she almost jumped as she remembered. This was the same dance Gaylin Gunn had exhibited on the night of Nola Gunn's birthday. *It was the crazy dance, and it ran in the family!*

More people began to stare at Ryder's gyrations. Shareen wasn't sure what to do, but finally, she just gave a simple shrug. Then, as she flailed her arms and kicked her legs, there were two people doing the crazy dance on the dance floor. If she would have had her eyes open, rather than her mouth yelling out, "woot! woot!" she would have seen there were more people on the dance floor joining them in the suddenly popular crazy dance. First, only a few patrons, then more, gave their own rendition. Everyone in the nightclub was soon following Ryder down a new and unknown direction. Yes—even though it was possible Ryder wasn't the best dancer in Talus, he seemed to have a knack for leading people—no matter what the endeavour.

Chapter 10: Kidnapped

I'lish's eyelids jolted open. The sound had been slight, but she'd learned, with years of experience as a successful smuggler, to sleep lightly. Lying on her bed and without turning her head, she rolled her eyes towards the door leading to her living area. That's where she heard the creak, and as she peered through the darkness of her bedroom, she heard it again. Someone was there.

The bedroom was pitch black, in contrast to the living room receiving a frail amount of light through the curtains on the far side of that room. Seeing no one in sight, she silently rolled her long legs out from under the silk sheets. Just before she rose to her feet, she grasped the short knife from her night stand—a knife having served her well over the years.

She gave a quick glance behind her at the naked form of Paislee, her long-time girlfriend, lying serenely in the bed beside where she should have still been. Over the years, I'lish had experimented in relationships with men and women. Both had their advantages, but ultimately, she found she preferred women. It had nothing at all to do with her not understanding her sexuality, or being confused. She just found women were less complicated and more mature than men. As such, she had enjoyed the five-year relationship she had with Paislee. The only regret was with I'lish being a predominate force in political circles, and Paislee being the head of a large shipyard, it had been necessary to keep their sexual, loving relationship private, away from the prying eyes of the media.

The brief line of thought left her as she heard another creak from her living quarters; her grip on the hilt of the sharp knife tightened in response. Quietly, with slow fluid motions of her legs, she sidestepped towards the door, finally leaning her shoulder against the door jamb. She was just about to slither through the opening when, from behind her, a strong hand grasped her knife hand while a second hand clamped over her mouth. Before I'lish could respond, the hand over her mouth pulled her back against the intruder's chest.

The person's lips were close to I'lish's ear as the intruder, in an urgent tone, whispered, "Stand down. It's me, Krista."

I'lish's body relaxed immediately when she heard Krista's voice. Krista was the captain of President Balorian's personal guard. The large woman's fingers slid up along I'lish's forearm as she coaxed her into the living room.

Krista glanced down at I'lish in the short silk nightgown barely hiding I'lish's sensuous curves. It was a distinct contrast to the black, hooded cloak Krista wore over the bronze-coloured uniform of the presidential guard.

As I'lish's eyes adjusted to the still slight, but increased level of light, she asked, "What's going on Krista?"

Flicking her chin towards the bedroom, Krista whispered. "Get dressed, but don't wake her. The president needs you."

"Now? It's the middle of the night."

"Yes—now," Krista retorted through clenched teeth, indicating her growing level of irritation.

I'lish moved back into the bedroom, quickly dressing as irritation also came over her. She'd been alert enough to hear the noise from her living room, but not enough to check the bedroom surroundings. She thought, *I must be getting old having been caught out so easily.*

Now dressed in brown slacks and a white long-sleeved shirt, she strode back out into the living area to find Krista along with three other members of the presidential guard, all dressed in their uniforms and matching hooded cloaks. Krista threw I'lish a similar black cloak and ordered, "Put it on. It's unlikely we'll run into anyone, but best to keep our movements secret on this night."

Krista cracked open the main door to I'lish's apartment and snuck a peek down both directions of the wide hallway. Seeing no one in sight, she led them out. There was a wide scarf attached to the hooded cloak. Krista wrapped it around her face, pulling it around her head for the loose end to fall over the opposite shoulder. The other three guards were already wrapped in the same secretive manner, and I'lish realized she was required to do the same.

I'lish's apartment was in Vingelen space station, one of the seven massive cylindrical stations in the Sholite fleet. Her apartment was in the third row of residential apartments from the outer edge of the rotating station, and they were walking along the visibly curved floor of the hallway towards the Main Corridor. The Main Corridor, or the *Main*, was a primary thoroughfare, twenty metres wide, running down the length of the station. Part of it was for pedestrian traffic, but most was for light vehicles and two reserved, cordoned-off lanes for rail traffic.

A nondescript, covered, light vehicle was waiting for them when they arrived at the Main. They entered, and the driver immediately brought the electric motor to life. Krista was set in her ways, and as such, I'lish knew better than to ask her question again. She had already asked her once,

"What's going on?" so there was no reason to repeat it. Krista or the president would enlighten her once they arrived at their destination.

I'lish was surprised when the vehicle stopped ten minutes later. She had assumed, if they were going to see the president, they would travel to the end of the station where the main docking yard was located. Instead, I'lish was led down a narrow side hallway, then another until they reached a door with a sign above it. The sign read, *Emergency Shelter.*

Krista, ever suspicious, glanced in one direction—then the other— before she pressed open the door, allowing her four companions through. Once the door closed behind them, I'lish saw two more presidential guards with air rifles held at the ready in front of them. Surprisingly, behind them was an air lock. The group strode down the air lock tunnel and through the adjoining door to the waiting space vessel. It was a small shuttle that began the decoupling sequence as soon as the passengers were aboard.

By now, I'lish's patience had wavered. "Where are we going, Krista?"

Krista removed the scarf from around her face, a signal to her other guards to do the same. "President Balorian is waiting on a nearby ship. I'm delivering you there, where I'm sure he'll explain his need for you in the middle of the night," she explained.

As quickly as the small shuttle accelerated, soon after, it began to slow, until with a metallic *clunk*, their docking door latched to one from another ship.

Once I'lish entered the second spaceship, she realized this ship was much larger. In fact, it looked like a military, Wolf-class frigate that had been retrofit for civilian purposes. All military markings had been removed but apparently not the armament pods, as she passed several of these along the way towards the front of the ship.

They continued down a central corridor to a door on their left. Krista opened it and walked through. She stood straight, saluted, then announced, "I'lish Mann, as you requested, Sir!"

I'lish walked through the door to see the president cough into his hand. In a low voice, the president indicated, "You can wait outside, Krista. Let me know when we arrive at the rendezvous."

The door was closed by Krista, leaving I'lish alone with President Balorian. She quickly lowered into a well-padded chair, across a small table from him. The president looked hollow and grey. With genuine concern in her voice, she asked, "How are you feeling, Sir?"

The words brought a crack of a smile to the president's face. "Now don't you start calling me *Sir*, especially in private." He lifted a finger, waggling it at the younger woman.

She grumbled an "as you wish" while her eyes showed worry for him being in such obvious ill health and awake in the middle of the night. "Is this acceptable for you to be out here?"

Balorian took the question with a different meaning than that intended by I'lish. "This ship is well armed, but if that alone does not comfort you, look out the window."

Rotating her gaze, she squinted as she saw a small ship on their starboard side. However, as she recognized the shape to be that of a Sholite Buffalo-class battleship, she realized the small size was because the large ship was 100 kilometres away. "Is that the *Revenge?*"

Nodding, the president elaborated, "Admiral Jovic is in charge of the vessel." There was another wry smile. "He is a good friend of mine, and I trust him without any reservations."

On the left side of the table was a large pitcher of water. She refilled the president's glass before filling one she had retrieved for herself. "What are we doing out here in the middle of the night, Mister President?"

"We are going to a meeting."

"Odd time and place for a meeting."

Balorian shrugged nonchalantly. "Not if you're going to a peace meeting with the Korians."

It took most of the 30 minutes it took for the Sholite spaceship to arrive at the rendezvous point, for I'lish's heartbeat to return to normal. *Peace with the Korian's,* she thought. The president was trying hard to accomplish this before he died. She didn't think this would ever be possible, but as their ship stopped, and she looked forward out the side window, she saw three frigate size Korian ships, and a shuttle covering the distance towards them.

The possibility became even more real when a small group of Korians were escorted into the room they occupied. I'lish and the president rose to their feet, as a somewhat regal looking Korian man announced, "President Balorian and—" The man paused for a moment as he considered I'lish.

"I'lish Mann," she offered, finishing the Korian's sentence.

With a slight nod, the Korian said, "Of course. May I introduce, Vidame Timo Jez, of the great Jez family—" He then directed a finger towards the man beside the vidame. "—and the vidame's son, Primor Dante Jez. I am Fergus Jez, the family's chief attorney." He bowed his head, indicating the

Jez family introductions were complete.

The president welcomed the visitors, opening an arm towards the far side of the room, where two couches and several arm chairs surrounded a large, round table. Once they were seated, the president tipped his head to a man on the far side of the room. Instantly, he brought over a tray of glasses, and three bottles of drinks, including water, fruit liquor and wine. After those accepting drinks were served, the president smiled and said, "Shall we begin?"

P'lish, sitting on the president's left, was impressed by President Balorian. He no longer looked sick or frail. Somehow, he had raised the strength for the critical meeting, an effort P'lish knew would likely be harmful to him in the time he had left.

Vidame Jez, replied to the president, "Of course. First of all, thank you for accepting our invitation to discuss a possible truce in the war between the Sholites and the Korians."

P'lish now knew it was the Jez family who had broached the idea to the Sholite president. That was important. That told her the Jez wanted something more than just a truce. Korian and Sholite nature had proved this out too many times over the centuries. It only took a few seconds of thought to realize what the Jez family's motives were. It had been surprising when she heard it was the Jez family arriving for the secret meeting. After all, the Jez family was not on the Talus Council of Nine. They were, arguably, the most powerful secondary family, and in the eyes of some, wielded more influence and favour than some of the families on the Council.

The Jez family controlled policing in Talus. In a manner, this was detrimental as many thought it unwise to have two armed forces represented on the Council of Nine. This meant it was either the Fyr family controlling the military or the Jez policing family, who would have leverage. It explained to P'lish why the Jez were here seeking peace. It gave the Jez family an opportunity. She thought, *after all, how powerful is the military when the state is at peace?*

"I think your spies have told you I am amiable to a peace between our peoples," the president coyly stated.

Primor Dante Jez leaned forward on the couch. "President—spies? We have no…"

"Stop!" the president interrupted in a firm voice. He glared at the primor, then turned his gaze to the vidame. "I think, if we expect this discussion to lead to a successful result, we best both be honest with each other."

Vidame Jez smiled, and I'lish thought she saw more than a glimmer of respect in the vidame's eyes. "You're more than right," the vidame responded. "There's a long history between Sholites and Korians, and we could be here for a long time spinning our tales of woe. Instead, let's talk of the future."

In their history, long ago, there was a time before projectile guns and air guns, where their ancestors used swords as weapons. As the president understood it, when there was a duel, there was a period of what could best be described as *light forays* to test out the enemy. Such was the case here, with both sides putting forth such trolling incursions. It was time to move past that now. "I know you speak for the Jez family, but what allows you to speak for the Korian people?" the president prodded.

"I understand your concern since we are a secondary family. However, of the Council of Nine, there are three families who know we are here, and they also know the subject matter," Vidame Jez replied. "That means they'll be easy to convince. I'm confident two more families will side with us if it came to a vote regarding a truce."

I'lish didn't come to her position as a Sholite leader by not having a good knowledge of their own laws, but also those of the Korians. If any of the Council of Nine came to a peace meeting without the full authority of the council, they would be breaking the law. But no one would expect a powerful secondary family, utilizing a loophole whereby they did not have this restriction, would attend such a meeting.

"Who are the three families who know of this meeting?" Balorian pressed the question.

After an awkward pause, Vidame Jez listed the families supporting the meeting. "The Tor, Pym and Vad families know I am here."

The list was not a surprise. The three families who led the alliances— Gunn, Fyr and Krl—were absent from it. The three families mentioned all had a chance to be the lead family in their alliances if there was a significant disruption to the council. It became obvious to I'lish that the Pym family could have the most to gain. They could take over the alliance led by a weakened Fyr family, or possibly, a secret alliance between the Jez and Pym families was foreseeable.

The president had the same thoughts, but still, he asked, "Why the secret meeting then?" The president's gaze was circumspect. "We could have done this through normal political channels."

The vidame let out a light chuckle. She was over 60 years old, but her black hair was still devoid of grey, just as her face was lacking the wrinkles one would expect. "Mister President, I wanted to see face to face if the rumour of your desire for peace was sincere. I think it is," Vidame Jez concluded.

"Then, will you propose the truce to the Council of Nine?"

Vidame Jez lightly ran a stray finger across her chin before responding. "The most powerful families: the Gunn, Fyr and Krl, would be unlikely to threaten their position as the most powerful families. As I stated, there are three families easily swayed to our side, but to convince the other two families, we'll need a more substantial show of support from the Sholites to indicate your sincerity."

"What do you propose?" President Balorian asked.

In a soft voice, the vidame responded. "What can you give us to indicate your sincerity?"

I'lish saw the president was at a crossroads. His brow was furrowed and his eyes looked troubled. After a few moments, he took a deep breath and made an offer. "There are six sleeper agents in Talus. These are Korians who we've overtly turned towards secret, destructive missions in Talus. They have no idea they are sleeper agents, but in a little less than three months, without a specific word phrase to stop them, they will complete their deadly, assigned missions."

I'lish's jaw was slack as she heard the shocking news. The look on her face was almost as surprising as that on the vidame and her son. The vidame implored, "You'll need to give us the names and the word phrase."

President Balorian shrugged, and the look on his face showed his irritation. "Of course, I will give you the names. That's why I brought it up!"

The discussion had turned more than interesting. I'lish listened to the back-and-forth negotiation, but then gave pause. She hadn't said a word yet, and she didn't think the president expected her to. It left her wondering why she had been invited. However, as the discussion continued, she felt a weight beginning to press on her. It began at the platinum necklace she wore around her neck, seeming to spread an ominous dread through her being.

Vidame Jez said, "We'll need more to convince the majority within the Council of Nine you're sincere in creating a truce with us."

"More?" There was now a distinct frown on the president's face.

"You could personally present the names of the sleeper agents at the Council of Nine along with your views on a truce," the vidame suggested.

I'lish closely watched the president's face. She had known him for quite some time, and she now understood he had played the Jez family. The vidame was walking directly into his trap. She also knew there was a reason she had been invited; from that, the weight of her necklace seemed to become even heavier.

"I would bring the news myself, but my health will not allow that," President Balorian chirped. "However, I could send my vice-president."

I'lish watched as the vidame and her son looked curiously at each other. She wondered which one held the most confusion. Finally, the primor commented, "Sir, you are correct in that we have spies within the Sholite fleet, but it doesn't take a great deal of effort from them to know the Sholites do not have a vice-president."

Raising his finger in the air, the president corrected, "Today, that is true. But as president, I have special powers and tomorrow, I will announce I'lish Mann as my vice president. She will come to Talus to speak to the Council of Nine and negotiate the truce."

A silent scream thundered through I'lish's head—*No, I can't go to Talus!* Yet, as she looked at the vidame, whose judgemental gaze inspected I'lish with a new found appreciation, the vidame coolly replied, "Agreed."

Chapter 11: The Contract

Byron Gunn had been specific. He had told Gaylin, exactly at the top of the 13th hour, to leave his office in the Gunn Spire. He was to tell his assistant that he needed a break and would be taking a long walk in the park, three blocks away. However, Byron's words were clear. When Gaylin left the tall building, rather than moving towards the tail of the chamber where the park was located, he was to go in the opposite direction. A little over one kilometer away, along 58th Street, he would come across a ten-story building under renovation.

That's where Gaylin was now. He walked down the small alley on the far side of the boarded-up building to the blue door marked, *Do Not Enter.* As Byron had assured him, the door was unlocked, and Gaylin entered before making his way down the flight of stairs. As Gaylin swivelled his head from side to side in the basement level's dimness created by the sparsely placed emergency lights, he heard a short, shrill whistle. As he walked towards the source of the sound, under a faint light hanging from a stone column, Gaylin saw Byron leaning back against a decrepit vehicle, covered in dents and different colors of paint where body repairs had been previously completed. The vehicle resembled a well-used artist's palette.

Byron pushed himself off the front of the vehicle, resulting in a groaning squeak from its suspension. With his lips barely parting, Byron gave a matter of fact, "Good afternoon, Boss."

"You don't think you're taking me to this meeting in that, do you?"

It looked like it pained Byron when, only for an instant, a slight smile came over his face. Once the indiscretion passed, Byron explained, "You asked me to set up a meeting where we will be participating in an illegal activity—an extremely illegal activity. In your suit and the family car, no matter where we go in Talus, you will be easily recognized. As your Chief of Family Security, I can't let that happen."

Gaylin pushed down on the front fender of the vehicle, forcing another groan from it as he mumbled, "I hope this gets us to wherever we're going."

As Byron led Gaylin to the back of the strange, colourful vehicle, he clarified, "Sir, I work for you, but in the activity we're undertaking today, I'm the expert, so I need to lead. That means, even though you might not understand why you need to do so, you need to follow my instructions without waiver." Byron didn't wait for a response as he pulled the latch on the rear liftgate, allowing it to pop open.

As Gaylin saw the two carrying cases now revealed, he asked, "What's this?"

Maintaining a soft voice, Byron replied, "We both need to change our clothes. The outfits in the cases will transform our appearance." The security chief pulled the clothes out of the cases. For Gaylin there was a bright-green shirt with a white collar, white pants and green ankle high boots. From the second case Byron laid out a dark-blue shirt with light blue long-sleeves and collar, light brown pants and white boots, for himself.

Gaylin's lips were pinched tight, holding back the long line of curses waiting to burst out. The colourful car and the just as colourful clothes didn't make it difficult for Gaylin to guess their destination. His eyes were narrow slits, turning to Byron as he managed to say, "Don't tell me we're going to…"

Again, only for a moment, there was a hint of a smile from Byron. "Yes, Boss. We're going to Joyville."

Simply put, Joyville was a community of predominantly gay Korians, numbering approximately ten thousand, living in C22, four chambers away from the Gunn Spire. Joyville, as a gay community, had been there for many generations and was seen as unusual by straight Korians. This was because, with a matriarchal society where marriage between families either improved or degraded your family's position, same sex marriages didn't fit. For example, a family primor could marry a man; that was perfectly legal, but the partner couldn't be a vidame because that position was exclusive to the female sex. In the same way, if parents within a family wanted to marry into a powerful family, their daughter would need to marry a high-ranking male, preferably the primor. Consequently, there was an excruciating overabundance of social pressure dissuading same sex marriages.

Notwithstanding these pressures, Korian society was quite liberal, having laws allowing same sex relationships and marriages. Such relationships were intermingled across Talus, but for many gay men and women, Joyville was their escape from convention.

Many partners in gay relationships kept their family names, and this was accepted. But long ago, an alternative was created. A new family came to light—the Joy family. This family was structurally organized in the same manner as any family, with a vidame and a primor. However, even though simple thought would arrive at the conclusion either position could be filled by a man or a woman, in gay society, the fact remains only women could bear children. With a little more thought, it becomes obvious only women could hold the position of vidame. And since these positions in the Joy family were available only to people of the same sex, the primor must also be a woman.

These were the thoughts going through Gaylin's mind as Byron drove the old, colourful clunker to the private rail line where, once attached, they continued to Joyville. Byron broke Gaylin's sulking silence. "Sir, there's something I need to update you on."

Gaylin, who had been inspecting his bright-green shirt, lifted his gaze to his security chief—a sure sign he should continue.

"Your cousin, Ryder, had a date last night."

Normally, for anyone else, this wouldn't be of interest, but this was the first date Ryder had in years. Tamara Bli had been with Ryder for three years before she died while on duty on a Korian battleship. She was a doctor, trying to save lives, yet she lost hers in the ongoing war. After her death, Ryder stayed in his apartment for a good month. He grieved for a long time but finally came back to work and attended social functions as a family primor should. However, family efforts to steer Ryder towards a wife, or even a date, were vehemently shunned. Consequently, this date, an oddity to Ryder's pattern, was indeed of interest. "Was it a business date?" Gaylin asked.

"No. He took the woman to the Casino ship, arriving at the 19th hour. They had dinner, danced and appeared to be getting along very well, until they left at the second hour the following morning."

Tilting his head to the side, Gaylin asked, "Did they have sex?"

"No," came the curt reply.

Gaylin had a twisted view on sex, based mainly on his weekly encounters with women for hire at his secret apartment. Typically, Gaylin would greet the woman, and within minutes, they would be on the bed having sex. On a good day, he might even remember the girl's name when she left. Since Gaylin didn't care at all about these women, his failed logic told him, if two people have sex immediately, surely there can't be feelings between the two. The thoughts caused Gaylin to grumble, "He must like her."

"It seems so," Byron agreed. "Ryder called this morning and asked me to put a security agent on her, but to keep a discrete distance. Since he's dating her, he's worried about her safety."

In the past, Gaylin had berated Byron several times about the man Byron had following Ryder. They had changed the agent several times, and even now, Gaylin was surprised the information came from Ryder, before the agent reported it. Life would be so much simpler if Linkin Gunn could be subverted. Byron insisted several attempts had been made, using financial enticements and inuendo's involving family members having accidents, yet the security agent remained totally faithful to Ryder. A sudden insecurity came to him. *Is Byron as faithful to me, or is he just faithful to the paycheck I provide him?* "What's her name?" he asked.

"Her name is Shareen Zaf—34 years old. She's the assistant director at the Rossnol Nuclear Plant and also teaches piano as a sideline. She has been teaching Romy, and it seems that's how Ryder met her. She is far down the political ladder within the Zaf family." As usual, Byron gave a concise report with as few words as required.

"Make sure you put a loyal person on her, and make sure the reports come only to *you*. If Ryder asks the agent for an update, he is to be told that would have to come through you," Gaylin demanded with a long finger pointed at his subordinate.

Twenty minutes later, after arriving at ground level, if Gaylin thought their colourful attire was misplaced, he now realized this not to be the case. The buildings on both the left and right sides of the thoroughfare were painted a myriad of bright colours. The shops on either side were intermingled with many casual, outdoor restaurants, and all were bustling with men and women wearing clothes just as colourful as theirs. Gaylin now understood why he would not be recognized here and why Byron selected this location for their covert meeting.

The two men walked past a man singing on a makeshift stage, with a band behind him. Quite a few couples were holding hands, or some had their arm around their partner. Seeing this, Byron glanced inquisitively at Gaylin for long enough to hear him murmur, "not a fucking chance," through the scowl he wore.

The security chief led Gaylin a block up the street to a most unusual building. Certainly, the deep-red colour was quite different, but it was the narrow width, not more than five metres wide, causing Gaylin to scratch his head. The sign above the door indicated it was a tourist lodging offering excellent nightly rates.

Just inside the front entry was a wide counter with an older man standing on the other side of it. He had white hair in a long pony tail and a pretty silver ring through his left nostril. Gaylin assumed the man was gay, but his demeanour was not as he grumbled, "Can I help you?"

"I'm looking for a room with a bath," Byron said.

The old man rubbed his stubbly chin, looking first at Gaylin, then back to Byron. "I only have a room with a shower."

The code phrases were exact. Byron relaxed his finger on the trigger of the small air gun in his pant's pocket. He provided the final code phrase. "Then perhaps just a fruit drink."

Flicking his chin towards the narrow hallway along the side wall of the narrow building, the old man said, "Take the last door at the end of the hallway. He's waiting for you there."

Holding out his hand, Byron added, "You have mail here for me."

The old man leaned down, reaching under the counter, retrieving the large envelope Byron had mailed to this address two days earlier. Without another word, Byron snatched the envelope from the man's wrinkled fingers and led Gaylin down the hallway barely wide enough for them to fit through. They exited out the last door and found themselves in a tiny courtyard at the back of the building. Two round tables filled the area, and at one of them sat a man, one leg crossed casually over the other.

He was also wearing colourful clothing, but as they came close and sat in two chairs opposite to him, they saw a long scar along his jaw bone under dark eyes exuding violence. Oddly, his hair was short-cropped and tinted white-blonde, making his appearance quite unusual.

"I'm Byron Gunn," the security chief whispered. "This is Gaylin Gunn."

The mysterious man was 50 years old. When he talked, one side of his mouth tilted up and the other down, as it did now. "I'm Matteo. Nice to meet you."

Gaylin hoped his eyes did not appear to open as wide as he felt they did. *Matteo—thee Matteo—the Matteo who didn't have, nor need, a last name.* The man history knew as Matteo was a historical legend—a myth to most. He was the assassin who, supposedly, had been killed numerous times, but his continued contracts survived such rumours. Not many Korians had met *thee Matteo* and lived.

Byron was not a man to waste time. He slipped the envelope across to Matteo and stated, "I understand your standard contractual fee is 150 quadtokens."

There was a barely discernable nod of the killer's chin. Tearing open the lip of the envelope, he pulled out the large picture. After examining the face on the photo, oddly, only one eyebrow elevated, giving his white eyebrows an angle to match his lips. "This isn't a standard target, so the price will not be standard."

"How much?" Gaylin interrupted.

Shrugging, Matteo replied, "Two hundred quadtokens."

A quiet, involuntary, "fuck," came from Gaylin's lips.

A chuckle slithered across the table. "In many things, a larger appetite requires a proportionately increased budget."

As he pointed his finger at Matteo, Gaylin sneered, "Agreed, but I don't want the target killed. I want a serious injury—something permanent as a reminder Gaylin Gunn is the power of the Gunn family."

Matteo replied in a quiet voice, "I think I can do that—for an additional 50 quadtokens."

Gaylin rolled his eyes before leaning forward across the table. "I have a last requirement."

"The pattern of requests would indicate the price will likely increase again."

Money was not an issue to Gaylin; he had an abundance of it, along with a feeling much like an itch he needed to scratch, but couldn't reach it. "I want the injury to the target to occur in public where I can see it. I need to see the damage done."

Matteo slid his tongue across his thin lips before he answered. He realized Gaylin was not unlike himself. Matteo received a feeling of gratification when he killed someone. Gaylin had a similar, grotesque need to actually see the carnage. Matteo could relate to that. "I can make it happen."

"Will it cost me another 50 quadtokens?" Gaylin asked.

For the first time, when Matteo's mouth angled as he was about to speak, it opened wider into an evil, twisted smile. "No, my friend. I will give this to you as a present, from one killer to another."

Chapter 12: Dreaming

Ryder had been here before. The high, sheer rock cliff on his left was familiar to him. But what reminded him even more than that ominous sight, was the roar he heard coming from the sky. He had to find cover.

He found himself in the middle of what appeared to be a lush, tropical rainforest. The trees around him were tall, devoid of branches except at the tip, where bright-green, wide, slitted leaves were in abundance. The wind grew, causing the tall trees to sway, and even at ground level, the breeze caused the waist-high ferns to dance to and fro.

Hearing the splash of waves, Ryder walked towards the sound. Pushing aside two wide-leafed plants, he stuck his head between them and saw a large lake. Eighty metres out from the shoreline, riding on the choppy waves, was a ship best described as a barge; yet billowing out from two tall masts, were two wide sails: one green and the other yellow. There were men running back and forth across the deck. He didn't know why, but he felt the eyes of someone watching him from the ship, causing him to draw his head back from between the two plants.

He had a sense it wouldn't bode well for him if he was discovered, but he also knew he needed to move on quickly as the roar from the sky was ever louder, just as the pace of the wind was increasing. There was a thin path around the shoreline he now followed. He ran, pushing aside leaves and branches, many with sharp needles on them. As he thrust aside another wide leaf, he spied a lean-to just ahead of him. One of the four corner supports had fallen on its side, but the roof, made of sturdy branches covered in several layers of wide leaves, was still in tact.

Ryder just made it to the protection of the roof before the skies opened, dropping a deluge of rain over this land. He couldn't see through the wall of thick rain. He didn't know why he was here, even though there was a familiarity with the heavy rain, the lake and the sheer cliff wall. Ryder also knew the rain would only last a few minutes, and sure enough, it did end quickly. When he came out of the lean-to, the land was changing. The sharp needles were opening into bright flowers. Flowers opened on many of the plants, searching for the bright sun now sending tendrils of light through the canopy of overhead branches.

Deciding to continue on the narrow shoreline path, Ryder inspected all that was around him. He had seen birds in the zoos in Talus, but here he heard their chirps filling the trees. He stopped for a moment as he saw a bright-green lizard climbing a tree. The slithering creature also heard the birds, sending him off in search of breakfast.

With such distractions, it wasn't a surprise when Ryder walked past a wide tree trunk and found himself on the edge of a clearing along the shoreline. He saw the same ship he saw earlier, but now it was moored at a wide dock—old enough that more than a few boards were black with rot. He dropped to a squat, searching for the men from the boat. None were on the deck, and as he panned the clearing, he heard voices in the far distance, coming from the trees on the far side of the clearing.

Ryder wasn't sure how he came to be here, or even why, but he also knew in any unknown environment, one of the first things to secure was food. With soft footfalls, he crept towards the dock. Still seeing no one on the deck of the strange barge and no movement from the voices on the other side of the forest, he continued towards the ship, making sure to miss the blackened areas of the dock planks that looked ready to fall apart. When he found himself at the railing, he slid himself over and lowered to a squat. It appeared, so far, he hadn't made himself known.

There was a long cabin on the rear portion of the deck with three doors in the front wall. Through one that was open, Ryder could see stairs going below deck. Silently, he ran towards the door, flattening himself against the wall beside it. After a minute, hearing nothing indicating he was noticed, he slid around the corner.

Ryder's eyes opened wide. In front of him, filling the stairway, was a giant of a man. He wore pants reaching just past his knees and no shirt, revealing a barrel chest covered in black, curly hair. His head was adorned with long, black hair to match, as well as a long, thick beard, making it impossible to see where the beard ended and the chest hair began. Ryder was frozen. The large man gave him a coy grin and said a few words in a language Ryder didn't understand—he didn't have to. He knew from the man's tone the message was, Ryder was caught. The man reached out with a huge hand, his fingers long enough to almost touch at the back of Ryder's neck.

Ryder awoke with a loud gasp as his chest instinctively rose off the bed. His eyes shot open as he bolted upright. Heavy breaths continued as he wiped his hands down his face, then his fingers gingerly inspected around his neck. "Another dream," he muttered as he gazed around his bedroom. Since he was a little boy, he'd had these vivid dreams. Some were in completely unknown locations, but many would repeat—not the events— just the location. He found it odd his dreams were not like those of others he knew. For many people, dreams were nonsensical. Events would occur that simply were not possible in reality. Yet, his dreams never had these elements with such unrealistic happenings. His dreams were more than realistic, as the feel of the big man's fingers on his neck had been.

Ryder fell back onto his pillow. His thoughts changed to that of a beautiful redhead in a flowered dress—Shareen. It was the most wonderful night he had in a long time. He hadn't wanted it to end, and it almost didn't when he dropped her off at her apartment. When the family car stopped there, she had a questioning look on her face. He knew, if he walked her up the stairs, he likely wouldn't return until well into the daylight hour. Wisely, since it was their first date, he gave her a warm kiss and said goodnight.

He glanced at his wrist interlink; it was now 8:25 in the morning. He arrived home late the previous night, could not fall asleep right away, resulting in only four hours of dream-filled slumber. He had just put his wrist back down when he heard an audible, *beep—beep*.

He rolled his eyes as he pulled his wrist back up. He answered the incoming call, "Hello."

A voice answered with slow words. "Mister Gunn, this is Detective Taylor Jez. I'm following up on our visit together yesterday."

"And?" Ryder replied, more than a little perplexed.

Ryder heard a deep exhale before the detective continued. "Sir, we agreed we would go and visit the Talus Dogs naval base today."

Ryder held his fist to his forehead and scrunched his eyes together. "My apologies. I forgot all about that. When can I meet you there? And don't tell me you have a car waiting outside my apartment."

There was a light snicker from the detective before he continued. "Very well. I won't send you a car. Can you please meet me at the gate to the Fyr Naval Base in C41 at 13:00?"

"I'll be there, Detective," Ryder replied before he disconnected the call. He ran the fingers of one hand back through his hair, once again reminiscing about the night prior with Shareen. He wanted to call her right now, but he didn't want to appear overly eager, or—the gods forbid—needy.

With only his pajama pants on, Ryder left the confines of his bedroom, shuffling into the living quarters. As soon as he did, he could smell the bacon cooking. Fehyr was an excellent cook, and when Ryder turned the corner into the kitchen, he saw Romy, anxiously waiting with his chin sitting on his layered hands on top of the counter.

Romy didn't move. Only his eyes shifted. "Morning, Dad. Did the smell of cooked bacon wake you up?"

Ryder walked around the table and mussed the hair on top of his son's head. "Yes, that was it! Who can resist bacon?" His eyes turned to Fehyr as the older man turned and was ready to move the bacon from the frying pan to the three plates laid out across the counter. "What's on your schedule?" Ryder asked.

Fehyr finished sorting the bacon, then he put a few slices of fresh fruit on each plate, finally placing two slices of toast out for each of them. "I will take Romy to school, then I have to go to the market for a few things. On the way back, I will be visiting my sister. But, no worries—I'll be back in time to pick up the little rascal."

With a mouthful of bacon, Romy gave out a garbled, "Heyyy!"

The three of them finished their breakfast with very few words. Ryder felt guilty because his mind kept going back to Shareen. He frowned in annoyance as he thrust the last piece of toast into his mouth. He rose to his feet and said to Fehyr, "I'll be at work for a couple of hours, then I have another meeting with that detective."

Fehyr raised an eyebrow. "You mean the detective investigating the Wilam Fex murder?"

"For some reason, the detective thinks I can help him. I have no idea why."

Fehyr was a good man and too good to provide Ryder, a man he loved like a son, with a patronizing response. Instead, he answered with what he really was thinking. "It sounds interesting. Let me know what comes of it."

Ryder gave his son a kiss on his cheek and mussed his hair one more time before he went back through his bedroom and into a hot shower. As he soaped his body, he thought about his upcoming trip to the Talus Dogs naval yard. He had never been to the secretive site and was looking forward to it. The Talus Dogs were not totally off limits, especially to residents with rank, but they did have a reputation for not being the friendliest of Korians. Ryder decided it would be best to dress in something not so colourful—perhaps with a military theme.

As such, after his shower, he pulled out a dark-brown suit. There were faint, black pin stripes through the pants and jacket, and along with the four brass buttons on each side of the collar, this was about as military as Ryder had. As he inspected his appearance in front of the full-length mirror, he thought the black shirt, underneath the suit, matched exceptionally well.

It was just before 13:00 hours, after spending three hours at the Gunn Spire, when Ryder stepped off the railcar in C41. Most of the sector was taken up by the electromagnetic drive engines in the rear of the chamber and the factories providing parts, materials and accessories for them.

This Fyr Naval base was unique from the other military bases in Talus. It was smaller, exclusively housing the Talus Dogs division and their seven covert space vessels. The Talus Dogs used Eagle-class cruisers. With a maximum speed of 35 per cent SOL, they were the best combination of speed and maneuverability—with creature comforts being far down the list of requirements. Ryder was excited. He had never seen one of the Talus Dog ships. Supposedly they were painted black over their entire surface and had cutting edge, experimental weapons the rest of the military didn't have access to.

Ryder was waiting just outside the steel gates of the address he was given. The building behind the sturdy gates was six stories high, but he knew most of the vast naval complex would be below ground level in the crust of the asteroid. He turned over his forearm and checked his wrist interlink. Detective Taylor Jez was late.

Finally, he saw a red blip in the distance down 58th Street. It became bigger until the blip turned into a police car, finally stopping by the curb where Ryder was waiting. The detective jumped out, and the vehicle sped away. "Sorry I'm late, Mister Gunn. It's difficult to get access to this facility, and I only just now received approval for our visit."

Shaking his head, Ryder replied, "I'm still not sure why I'm here or how you think I might help in your investigation."

The corner of the detective's lip lifted in his best effort at a smile. "I'm not quite sure myself. I just have a hunch this will lead us somewhere important."

"So you don't have other leads?"

Detective Jez pulled his police badge from its pinned location on his shirt and re-pinned it to the lapel of his thigh-length, black, leather jacket. As he fiddled it into its final position, he said, "Now that you mention it, there is something interesting I came across, I need to ask you about."

Ryder twisted his head from one side to the other while holding his hands palms up and slightly out from his body, as if he needed to indicate this was a fine time for the detective to ask the question.

"Mister Gunn, did you know Wilam Fex's father—Calvin Fex?"

Ryder scratched his head as the question jogged a vague memory. "I met

Wilam's father a few times when we were in college together, but not since then."

"So you don't know he was murdered four years ago?" The detective watched Ryder's eyes carefully for any sign of distress.

"What?"

"And you don't know he was murdered while in the employ of Gunn Pharmaceutical?"

Ryder took a deep breath and almost choked. "I'm not aware of any of this." His eyes were wide with shock, and his throat tightened. He wrung his hands together, hoping to alleviate the tingling condition he felt in his fingers when he felt this type of stress. The rubbing action brought back his calm as he continued, "When I knew Wilam in college, his father worked for the Fex family as a lead scientist. I remember Wilam telling me his father was working on a more efficient process to obtain nitrogen from ammonia."

"That's odd…"

Ryder threw up his hands. "What's odd?"

"You remember exactly what project Wilam's father was working on 20 years ago, but you know nothing of his change in employment to the Gunn family, nor of his death," the detective explained.

Ryder's eyes narrowed. The detective was quite right. Ryder was the primor of the family, and he should have known of a worker's murder. *This had Gaylin's hand all over it.* He looked directly in the detective's dark eyes. "I will say this for the last time. I know nothing of Calvin Fex's death."

Detective Taylor Jez shrugged. "Then we better stop wasting time out here." He brushed past Ryder and pressed the button on the post by the metal gate. A moment later, a woman's voice came from a speaker. "How can I help you?"

Detective Jez lifted his face and looked into the camera. "I'm Detective Taylor Jez from the Talus police, with Primor Ryder Gunn. We have an appointment with Captain Langdon Fyr."

The electrical voice came back with, "one minute please."

It took more than a minute—in fact, three minutes for the voice to return. "Captain Langdon is busy today. He won't be seeing anyone."

Reaching into his inside jacket pocket, the detective pulled out a folded paper. Pulling sharply down, there was a snap as it flattened out in front of the camera. "This is an order from Primor Mercer Fyr. It indicates the captain will have time to see us at our convenience—and it is convenient now."

An electrical buzz came from the latch at the center of the gate, and it slowly swung open. The detective, followed by Ryder, walked through, covering the 20 metres to the front double door of the building. By the time they pulled it open, a young woman was waiting just inside. Her shoulder-length, blonde hair was striking under the black beret angled off center from the top of her head. The colour matched the rest of her military fatigues, devoid of any markings, military or otherwise. She gave them a smart salute and said "My name is Ensign Adley. I'll be your escort during your visit today."

Casually, the detective pointed to himself and then the primor. "I'm Detective Taylor. This is Ryder Gunn."

The ensign broke her stoic demeanour when she heard Ryder's name. Her lips began to curl into a smile when the detective cut it off. "Please, Lead the way to Captain Langdon."

The ensign held her hand up. "Sorry, Sir, but I'll need your firearm. They aren't allowed on the hanger floor."

Taylor Jez unbuttoned his jacket and removed his sidearm from its inside holster. The gun was a standard 150 mm telescoping air pistol, typical of those worn by the Talus police force. Unlike the military, the police used weapons utilizing recent technological advancements whereby compressed air was used in place of bullets. The weapon's specialized battery pack compressed a small pocket of air, then forced it down the barrel of the gun—the longer the barrel, the higher the compression factor. This explained the reason for the telescoping barrel since, at it's 150 mm length, it's lethal limit was twenty metres. When the barrel was extended to it's maximum 450 mm, its compression factor was increased, and the lethal range was expanded to 100 metres. Of course, long barrel air rifles were also available, and they could kill someone at 300 metres.

In space, where the vacuum provides no air, these weapons would be useless. Even if a firefight was engaged on a spaceship, it was not unusual for the ship to lose its environment during a battle. As such, the military still preferred projectile weapons since their jurisdiction was outside the asteroid's confines.

Once the handgun was given to the ensign, who in turn, passed it through a window opening to another soldier, Ensign Adley, instructed, "Very well, if you'll follow me please. The captain is on the maintenance deck. It's been a busy few days for us," the young ensign elaborated.

Ryder knew exactly what she was referring to. The Council of Nine and their senior advisors received critical news before the general population did. Ryder had been informed, three days ago, three Talus Dog cruisers had been sent out to the rim of Talus space. The official word was the mission was one of revenge against the Sholite battleship, Cordoba, the ship having launched the Cobra's that destroyed the Korian cruiser two weeks ago. Unofficially, the mission was to test a new weapon the Korians had developed. It was a mirroring device and it had apparently worked to perfection. When the Cordoba's sensors saw the three attacking cruisers, each was able to mirror two additional images of their ship. So in reality, the Cordoba saw nine ships when there were really only three.

The Cordoba launched one frigate and two gunships in response. These ships, along with the missiles from the Cordoba, only had a one in three chance of attacking a real vessel. Consequently, an hour later, only two Talus Dog ships were returning to Talus after destroying the two gunships and crippling both the Sholite frigate and the battleship. In fact, one Korian missile had completely destroyed the command deck of the Sholite frigate.

The Korian military would see this as a successful test with the destroyed Sholite ships as an added bonus. But, many others, and perhaps even a higher percentage of Korians, would see this as a continuing, futile loss of lives on both sides of the war.

Ryder felt his stomach lurch up into his chest. The elevator they had entered was speeding downwards to the maintenance deck. Finally, the feeling of partial weightlessness stopped, and the elevator doors opened onto a vast hanger. As they stepped out, they saw the complex, cut into the edge of the asteroid's crust, was a good half kilometre long. Ryder glanced upwards and judged the ceiling of the cavern was at least 150 metres from the metal grating they stood on.

Thirty metres distant from them was the ominous, black shape of an 80-metre-long, Talus Dog cruiser held firmly in place by docking clamps. As they walked towards it, Ryder glanced down through the floor grating, and below it, saw huge metal plates. He knew, for the purpose of either docking or launching a ship, the metal grates would retract into the crust, and the metal plates would, with the assistance of powerful hydraulic motors, swing open.

Now that they were closer, they saw the cruiser was damaged. They could see buckled hull plates, large charred areas and a gapping hole in the prow. The ship was built in modules and some of those had been removed, either for replacement or repair. Consequently, on the metal grating sat three laser cannon modules and what appeared to be one of the drive motors.

There were men in red coveralls working on the modules. As Ryder and

Taylor walked past a laser cannon module, from the other side of the next one, they heard a loud voice bellow, "Put your backs into it, you asses! How long does it take to remove six bolts on a cover plate?"

As they passed the next module, they saw a tall man in black coveralls, the front buttons open down to his waist, revealing a wide chest. The man was bald with a thick, black moustache, the edges of which hung down lower than his chin. From under it he yelled, "C'mon people! This ship needs to be back in operation by the end of the week—not next month!"

Ensign Adley, once she arrived at the captain's side, sharply saluted, then announced, "Sir, I have visitors requiring your attention."

The captain snapped his head towards the ensign, then peered by her at the detective and Ryder. His jaw lowered and his eyes narrowed. "Visitors— you have to be fucking nuts. Can't you see I'm busy?"

Rather than arguing with the captain, Detective Jez pushed the letter from Primor Fyr into the man's large hand. The captain's head shifted from side to side, just as he read, line by line. A look of disgust came over the captain's face as he thrust the paper back at the detective. "You have five minutes," he growled.

The detective took out an old-school pad and a pen, to take notes. "Captain, we had a murder in the city two nights ago in C45. Do you know of a man named Wilam Fex?"

Placing his fists against his waist, the captain spread his feet in an aggressive stance. "Fex—a nitrogen farmer? No, why would I?"

The detective wrote on his pad while he asked, "How about Calvin Fex?"

The captain's head tilted forward, closer to the detective. "Maybe you didn't understand. I don't have time for *any* nitrogen farmers."

"Got it," the detective mumbled.

The captain angled his face towards Ryder. "Why are you here?" At the same time, the captain reached into his pocket and retrieved a *smack*. Smack's were small drug-laced candies some in Talus enjoyed. They would give the person a slightly mellow state, and if enough were taken, a sense of euphoria.

Ryder thought, *you need to take a lot more of those* as he answered, "I'm with him. We're a team, and there's no *I* in *team*."

The captain shook his head and mumbled, "Smart-assed fucker…"

The detective continued the line of questions. "Sir, have any of your Dogs been on furlough the last few days?"

"Probably."

"I'll need a list of those names, Sir"

The captain popped another *smack*. "That's classified."

The detective tilted his dark eyes up at the captain. "How about you? Where were you two nights ago?"

The captain sneered, "Your five minutes are up." He turned his glare to Ensign Adley. "Get these two—*cividiots*—off my deck." Without another word towards the two men, the captain stomped towards the dismantled laser cannon, bellowing further obscenities in the direction of the workers there.

The ensign led the detective back towards the elevator while Ryder lagged behind, his eyes drawn to and mesmerised by the sleek lines of the frigate. As he passed the damaged drive module, he heard a sharp whistle. Turning towards the direction of the sound, he saw a frail man on a maintenance cart roll himself out from under the drive. He had short white hair, was at least 60 years old, and half his coveralls were coated in black oil and soot.

From his prone position with a large wrench in his hand, the man looked up at Ryder through eyes showing more intelligence than his general appearance did. "Hey, Mister. It wasn't difficult to overhear your conversation with the captain."

Through a smirk, Ryder replied in a sarcastic tone, "I never would have thought that."

"Yeah, yeah," the man replied as he itched his cheek, not realizing he put another streak of black oil there to mingle with the dried-on layer. "I'm trying to help you son, so listen up."

Squatting down, Ryder whispered, "What do you have?"

The old man's words came up to Ryder in a squeaky tone. "I think you might have the wrong *Talus Dogs*. The men who work here are killers, but they get their fill out there." He pointed to the ship. "They wouldn't be killing anyone in Talus."

Ryder nodded his understanding. "But you said I had the *wrong* Talus Dogs. What did you mean by that?"

The old man's eyes lit up, and through a smirk and a wink, he whispered back. "You need to go to aisle 21, the Galactic Fair. You might find what you're looking for there."

Chapter 13: The Galactic Fair

Two weeks had passed since Ryder's date with Shareen on the casino ship. It was the best two weeks Ryder could remember—back as far as his time with Tamara. A day didn't go by when they didn't at least talk, and on most days, they saw each other for at least a short time. It didn't seem to matter what they were doing, as long as they were together. That's when they both appeared to be happiest.

With Ryder trying to maximize his time with Shareen but still spending ample time with Romy, and of course, he had duties with work and his family, it wasn't a surprise he forgot all about the Talus Dogs. He was only reminded of it when Shareen suggested a different kind of date—an evening at the Galactic Fair.

The Galactic Fair was a large, two square kilometre amusement park in chamber C32. There were thrilling rides, many of which had the patrons screaming in fear. Other rides were designed for smaller children, who also screamed, but with exhilaration and joy. One-third of the 24 aisles were populated by such rides; the remainder were filled with small eating venues and gaming tents, and of course, loud music of all types.

Ryder hadn't been to the fair for a year. That was the last time he took Romy. Now, as Shareen suggested a night there, Ryder remembered about the confusing advice from the old mechanic at the Talus Dogs shipyard. He'd said, "You need to go to aisle 21, the Galactic Fair. You might find what you're looking for there." The grizzled, old man was referring to the unusual message written on the back of a mirror in Wilam Fex's apartment. It was the message that brought Ryder and Detective Taylor Jez to the Talus Dogs shipyard in the first place.

Ryder left the Gunn Spire at 18:00 hours and took the public Ctrain to C25. As the doors to the railcars opened at the Rossnol Station, he popped his head out through the opening. Shareen, two cars down, saw him and scooted over. They sat down and Shareen put her hand on his jaw, pulling his lips to hers. "Hello, Handsome," she said through a smile.

There were quite a few patrons in their railcar, and the kiss caused Ryder to blush—not that he minded her warm lips. He rolled his arm around her shoulder and replied, "Hello, Sexy."

The ride to the Galactic Fair would take 40 minutes. During that time, Ryder confessed he had an ulterior motive in visiting the Galactic Fair. He explained the entire story of Wilam Fex, the murder, the mirror and the subsequent visit to the Talus Dogs.

"You never told Detective Jez about the clue from the old man at the shipyard?" Shareen asked.

"No. At the time, it seemed like the words of an eccentric old man. I didn't want to bother him with it. But now that we're going to the fair, I might as well check it out."

They switched trains in C22. Their trip, so far, was along the arcing circumference of the asteroid. Their final leg was taking them towards the back of Talus. When they exited the Etrain at the Galactic Fair Station, fast-paced music was already playing through speakers mounted throughout the underground station. Once they arrived at ground level, they found themselves in the middle of the fair, where it cost them a token each to proceed onto the grounds.

They didn't have any firm plans for dinner, but the aroma of a plethora of different foods, both savoury and sweet, assaulted their senses. Immediately, Shareen pulled on Ryder's arm, dragging him towards a food stand exuding an especially sweet smell. "We have to have space balls!" she urged. A space ball was a dessert delicacy of extremely light dough filled with a sweet, spice mixture of grated, dried fruit. The ball was fried in hot oil until golden brown, then coated with a sticky syrup.

"We're starting with dessert?" Ryder scoffed.

Shareen let out an evil chuckle. "I didn't set up the geographical location of the food stands. I can't help it if someone decided to put a dessert stand right beside the entrance to the fair. So tonight, we're starting here and heading that way." She stretched her arm out down the direction of the long aisle. "I'm thinking whatever order the remaining stands are in, will determine the order of food we eat."

Ryder had a silly grin on his face. "I see."

"Good." Shareen stated as she lifted two fingers in the air. She said to the proprietor of the space ball stand, "Two space balls—*each*."

They made two more stops at food vendors. One was for a meat sandwich and a cold drink. The other was for ice floats. That's when Shareen, more so than Ryder, realized it was a mistake to start their tour of the fair with food. The next aisle was filled with rides—and Ryder liked rides. He enjoyed the feel of pulling high g's. It reminded him of space flight, of which, he had much more experience than Shareen, so he handled the rides better than she did. It was after the fourth daring ride, with Shareen looking a little green, that she determined her participation for the evening was over.

Ryder didn't mind. He just enjoyed being with her. They strolled down one aisle after another. They found enjoyment in watching the people at the fair. All types were drawn, and Ryder and Shareen took turns, slyly pointing at someone, trying to guess what family they were from and what occupation they held. They held hands the whole time. It made it easier for Ryder, occasionally, to drag Shareen down one of the narrow aisles between tents, usually filled with boxes of supplies. He would find a space between them and drag her into it, where he would give her passionate kisses. His hands would wander under her shirt, causing her to let out delicate moans. When they were both almost at the point where their clothes would truly become an encumbrance, Ryder would grin and drag her back out into the main aisle.

Ryder would chuckle as Shareen, wide eyed with flushed skin, would be putting her disheveled hair back in place. Eventually, each time, a grin would form on her face. "You're terrible."

"Yes, I am," he confided. "But it's your fault."

"How so," she blurted.

With a sarcastic grin, he pointed an accusing finger at her nose. "You were the one who dragged me here. We could have been at your apartment where I could truly be ravaging you right now."

The flush began to return to her face. Her voice was almost a purr. "Good things come to those who wait."

They turned the corner into aisle 21, the aisle where the old man told them to find the Talus Dogs. This aisle was filled with gaming tents from one end to the other. As they strolled up the aisle, hand in hand, Ryder muttered, "Have you wondered why they have tents?"

Raising an eyebrow, Shareen said, "What are you going on about?"

"Look, every stand is under a tent. Why? In Talus, there's no wind or rain, so what purpose do the tents serve?"

Shareen's eyes now narrowed in a speculative gaze. "You've got some strange thoughts bouncing around in that head of yours, Mister Gunn."

There was mixed music playing in this aisle as almost every gaming stand was playing their preference. As they moved up the aisle, one song would fade, only for another to replace it. That's when they both heard a strange moaning in the distance.

"What's that?" Shareen asked.

104

Ryder shook his head as they continued towards it. It grew louder as they came closer, until finally, they heard the words coming through a speaker, "Doggie, doggie." They moved closer and the words were louder. They were said in a moaning drawl feigning sympathy. "Doggie, doggie. Where's my doggie?"

On their left was a less than appealing gaming stand. The table at the front was covered with a stained cloth, matching the tent overtop that was also stained, although Ryder wondered, *what could possibly stain it from above like that.* Behind the table was a middle-aged man wearing a baggy shirt with the sleeves cut off. He held a microphone in front of his saggy face, made to look even longer by the brown beard hanging only from under his lower lip. He had warm, sagging, brown, puppy dog eyes, matching his pathetic look, best described as one drawing sympathy. "Doggie, doggie. Where's my doggie?" the man exuded into the microphone.

Ryder and Shareen were shuffling past, staring, then they stopped in their tracks. Hanging from two thick chains above the man was a rusty sign. Painted on it, in crudely painted letters were the words, *Talus Dogs.* With their jaws dropped, as they both turned to each other, they looked quite silly. Walking to the mellow fellow holding the microphone, behind him, Ryder saw there were three bins filled with cute, stuffed dogs of every type, in three different sizes: small, medium and large. It almost made sense why the stand was named - *Talus Dogs.*

There were four small baskets on the table, and in each was a small ball. Three metres away, were four small, round tables. On each of them was a pyramid of six tins, three in the bottom row, two in the middle with the last on top. The man pointed at the basket and said, "Show the lady how good you are. One token for a shot."

Ryder knew this game. It was almost impossible to win since the bottom of each tin was weighed down. It was easy enough to knock them all over, but almost impossible to knock them all off the table. And that was the requirement to win. "I'll pass," Ryder told the man.

The vendor turned to Shareen. "Why not show him how good you are?"

She shrugged. "I might have, if you asked me first."

The man rolled his puppy dog eyes, before returning them to Ryder. "I'll give you two shots for one token." Ryder hesitated. "Don't let her walk home empty handed," the man added.

Ryder stiffened up as his pride came to the forefront. "That's a deal I'll take," he replied as he lifted a token piece from his pocket and placed it on the table. The pressure was on. His girl was watching with a stuffed animal lying in the balance. He picked up the first ball, aimed and whipped it at the six tins. There was a loud clattering, but two tins were on their side, still on the table.

"So close," the vendor said in a voice with even more sympathy exuding from it. "Maybe not so hard and more arc," the man advised with a saggy-eyed wink.

As the vendor set up the tins for a second throw, Ryder had an irritated look on his face, made worse by Shareen clapping her hands and cajoling, "You can do it!"

The pressure was intense. The vendor was right. A softer throw, with more arc would hit more tins. It was about finesse, not speed. With increased confidence, Ryder slung the ball at the tins in what looked like a perfect shot. When contact was made, five tins flew off the table. The last was knocked on its side, spinning towards the edge of the table. Unfortunately, when the spinning stopped, the tin was teetering on the edge of the table, but still on it. Ryder turned towards Shareen and blurted, "So damn close!"

From behind him, Ryder heard a clatter as the vendor slapped the last tin off the table before he, in his melancholy voice, said, "A winner."

Ryder turned in surprise. "But, it…"

The man interrupted as he said for a second time, "A winner every time!" Oddly, the man didn't reach into any of the three bins of stuffed dogs; rather, he reached behind them, and from a shelf, pulled down a large-sized, light-brown, stuffed dog.

With a frown, Shareen asked, "Don't I get to pick?"

Ryder was still confused about winning with one tin still on the table, as the man walked to the edge of the table. He looked at Shareen and adamantly said, "No." Then, after his puppy dog eyes glanced back and forth down the aisle, he leaned over and whispered to Ryder. "Mister Gunn, there's a message from Wilam in the dog. He told me to give this to you if you came."

Ryder was perplexed. *How could Wilam have possibly known this man?* His eyes became wider. *How does he know I'm Ryder Gunn?*

The vendor pushed the stuffed dog at Ryder, who had no choice but to accept it. Ryder turned the dog one way and another, until he pushed his searching finger into the dog's mouth.

A slow chuckle came from the saggy-eyed man. "No, that's not the right hole."

Through clenched teeth, Ryder replied, "You're kidding."

"Nope. Good luck. Now move on before someone sees us," the man whispered before he walked away from the table.

As Ryder and Shareen shuffled away from the Talus Dogs, more confused with every step, from behind them all they heard was, "Doggie, doggie. Where's my doggie?"

Ryder and Shareen were walking down the stairs towards the underground railcar. The three hours they spent at the fair were, to say the least, interesting. Ryder flipped the stuffed dog upside down, and with one eye closed, peered down at the animal.

Shareen slapped his hand and warned, "Don't do that here. Someone might be watching."

She was right, Ryder thought. He knew Linkin was never far behind, and there was another security person keeping an eye out for Shareen. His fingers caught her arm and he said, "I don't think we should go back to your place. My apartment or the Gunn Spire would also be a problem. Do you know of a place we can go to investigate what's inside this dog?"

"My sister has an apartment in C35. It's empty and it's location is along the route back to my place."

Ryder gave her a tug, and they continued their trek to the railcars. "That'll work. I didn't know you had a sister."

"It just hasn't come up. She's two years older than me. She's in the middle of a vacation aboard the Rising Sun Cruise ship," Shareen explained. She quickened her pace as she now led the way to the correct railcar that would take them to their destination.

Lifting his interlink close to his lips, Ryder said, "Linkin, I won't need you for a while. Tell Ella to do the same. You can pick up our trail at the rail station at the corner of 145th Street and 55th Lane."

Shareen overheard as Linkin confirmed the orders. Of course, she knew who Linkin was, but she was curious about Ella. She had an idea, but thought it would be better not to ask. Her own theory was, *often, it was better not to ask the questions you don't want the answers to.*

Ryder was grateful Shareen didn't ask about Ella. She was one of two women assigned to keep an eye on her. He hadn't found a good time to tell her about the surveillance—and this certainly wasn't it.

Twenty minutes later, they arrived at a ten-story-high, brownstone building. As they walked the hallway to Shareen's sister's first-floor apartment, he saw the building wasn't overly lavish, but it was quaint and clean. Shareen pressed a four-digit code into the numeric pad on the door, allowing them entry inside.

"Lights on," Shareen said, resulting in several lights through the apartment illuminating. As Ryder plunked himself down on the couch, Shareen was returning from the kitchen with two glasses of water and a knife, thinking Ryder would need it to find what was hidden in the stuffed dog. However, as she came closer, she found her boyfriend, eyes closed, tongue hanging out the side of his mouth, with his index finger searching inside the bear.

She held back her laughter as she put the water and knife down on the table. Turning the metal band of her wrist interlink to the appropriate angle, she pressed a virtual button on the visible pad. The image of Ryder undertaking the delicate procedure appeared there. She adjusted the angle until the image was perfect, and she said, "Snap." There was a flash and the picture was taken, the image automatically saved to her private server space.

The flash surprised Ryder, who opened one glaring eye. "Really? A picture?"

She sat down beside him. "No worries. Your secret fetish for cute little dogs will stay only with me," she offered through a smirk.

Ryder ignored her as his finger touched a hard object in the dog. He pushed his finger in deeper and dug out a small capsule. It consisted of two halves which he separated, and a small roll of paper fell into his lap. Carefully unrolling it, he saw a written computer address, file name and password.

He tilted his gaze to Shareen. "I could look this up on my interlink, but that might create a path for my family security people to discover our activities."

Snapping her fingers, she replied, "My sister has a computer." Without waiting for a response, she rose and started down the hallway towards the back of the apartment. Ryder followed until he found himself in what looked like a small art studio. There were paintings filling all the wall space, and on an easel, was a half-finished painting. "Your sister is an artist, I see."

"Yes, and she is successful." Shareen gave the reply as she strode to a desk against the far wall. She pulled out the chair for Ryder and said, "C'mon."

Once seated, Ryder pressed the *power* button on the side of the computer, causing the screen to fill with light. All computers, servers and personal interlinks in Talus were on the same network. There were different levels of security and various enhancements a user could apply. Ryder did so now as he loaded a firewall and encryption software from his own personal storage space.

The location scrawled on the roll of paper was a location somewhere on the network. Ryder was able to access it, and there was only one video file stored there. He applied the password, and a moment later, a video began to play.

Wilam Fex was sitting at a desk. Ryder's eyes became moist, knowing his friend was now dead. He looked tired, and the creases of stress across his face definitely made him look older than his years. Wilam cleared his throat and began speaking.

> *"Hello Ryder. Unfortunately, if you're watching this, it means I'm dead. The first thing you're likely wondering is, why have I intended this video for you? The answer is simple. First, you're the most honest man I know. Even though you're the primor of a large family, you still believe in honesty and the requirement to do the right thing. You also have the resources many others do not. You'll need those to unearth a conspiracy—one causing the death of my father, and I assume now, me as well."*

Wilam sat back in his chair behind the desk.

> *"I'll give you a few minutes to consider that before I continue."*

Obviously, Wilam thought predicting Ryder's reaction to his video was hilarious, and he burst out laughing. Ryder cracked a smile as he saw the stress clear from Wilam's face. Now, he resembled the college friend he fondly remembered. It only lasted a few moments before Wilam's face once again returned to a stoic demeanour. He continued.

> *"You'll recall, my father was a scientist working for the Fex family. His duties included developing improved ammonia refinement processes. However, on the side, he and three other scientists decided to stretch their scope of work. As scientists, they couldn't understand the limitations of the gravity patches supplied by the Gunn family. As a group, they secretly investigated the patch formulation and were surprised how simple it was. Buoyed by this information, their confidence grew, and they looked at alternatives to the Gunn gravity patches."*

Ryder's brow furrowed with irritation. His friend's father had been investigating his own family's livelihood. His first thought was, *it would have been simpler for Wilam's father to come to him.* But, through a scowl, Ryder knew that wasn't realistic. He was the primor, and as such, any man holding that position was thought of as not always being objective. His thoughts were interrupted by Wilam's continued words.

109

"My father and his fellow scientists changed their direction as they searched for a vaccine to replace the patches. Can you imagine—a one-time injection that would supplant the need to constantly replace the thousands of patches used over one's lifetime?

Then, a problem arose. One of the scientists became greedy and approached a senior member of the Gunn family—your cousin, Gaylin. Some might call it blackmail, but on the other hand, my father and his group were hitting roadblocks. They needed better equipment to complete their research. That type of equipment was only available at Gunn Pharmaceutical."

Ryder paused the video. Tilting his face up to Shareen, he said, "I'm not sure you want to see more of this. I don't like where it's going, and the information here could put you at risk."

"What? So you might assign someone to follow me?" she answered through a smirk and a wink.

"Women," he mumbled as he turned the video back on.

"Gaylin convinced my father and the other scientists it would be to the betterment of Talus to find the vaccine. He even said, with the price they could offer as an option, there wouldn't be a loss of income for the Gunn family. He lied. My father finally discovered a successful vaccine, eliminating the need for patches, and it wouldn't have been expensive to produce.

However, one by one, my father's fellow scientists began to disappear. No one knew what happened to them. Then, my father was murdered. His body wasn't supposed to be found. Someone tried to pressurize him out of an airlock, but when he was being sucked out, his arm got caught in the grating of the outer door. He was found there by security, hours later. It gave them a good clue regarding the fate of his fellow scientists, but even with this evidence, the crimes remained unsolved."

The information truly saddened Ryder. Shareen saw this and put a comforting hand on his shoulder. Within the sadness was anger as the realization came that, although he knew Gaylin was capable of deceitful deeds, he was also capable of murder.

"As you know, I'm a scientist as well—one who also has sources. After my father's death, their Gunn Pharmaceutical laboratory was dismantled with every piece of equipment incinerated. All vaccine samples were also destroyed—except one. One sample was retained. I was close to finding it's location when I realized I was in over my head.

I've seen men following me in the shadows. That's why I'm making this video."

Wilam leaned forward, bringing his tired face closer to the camera.

"If I'm gone, someone needs to find that last sample of vaccine. My father has no legacy. His vaccine is for the people. That's why I need to find it. But I need you to back me up. You're the most honourable man I know. Even though you're part of the Gunn family, I know you'll do the right thing."

Wilam peered from side to side, then turned back to the camera.

"I have one clue I'm sharing with you now. It's the name of a woman who, apparently, has direct knowledge of the location of the last sample of vaccine. Her name is Nicola Edy."

In the video, Wilam stretched his arm forward, and just before he turned off the camera, with a sigh, he said,

"Find her. Goodbye, my friend."

Chapter 14: The Tour

Gaylin looked out from the floor to ceiling window of his office on the 40th floor in the Gunn Spire. His hands were clasped behind his back as he rocked back and forth on his feet. Looking down, he saw the first signs of people on the streets below, like insects scurrying to their tasks. He enjoyed the feeling of ever increased power as he looked down from on high—even through the gut-wrenching feeling—the one that gave him the urge to jump. He pushed on the thick, plate glass window and thought, *not today*.

Turning, long strides of his six-foot-six-inch frame took him to his desk. He lifted his wrist and checked the time on his interlink. It was just past the eighth hour. Pushing a virtual button on the link, he said, "Tala, can you please call Ryder and ask him if he can come down and see me for a few minutes?"

His assistant, just outside his office, replied, "Of course, Sir."

Gaylin lowered himself into his padded chair and grasped the bottle of water on his desk. Even though he drank from thousands of such bottles, he turned it and read the label – *Oro Pure Water*.

There were several sources of water servicing the residents of Talus. The Oro family who controlled water farming in space, mainly consisting of finding and hauling large water comets back to Talus, was a primary source. Most often, there was an abundance of water stored in many vast storage tanks running down the central axis in Talus. However, when water was in short supply and there were ample supplies of hydrogen and oxygen, they were used to make water.

The third source of water was the recycling process used throughout the population. It might sound crude, but urine and feces were diverted to one of the many recycling stations in Talus, maintained by the Hak family. The fecal material was dried and the moisture reclaimed. It, along with the purified urine, was then sent to the water storage containers. This water was of a high quality, perfectly acceptable for all purposes including drinking.

When the Oro family's water trawlers found ice comets in space, most often the water had impurities, requiring processing in a refinery. Less often, a trawler would find a comet of extremely pure ice, void of contamination. In these instances, the comet was sent to an off-asteroid ship specifically to bottle pure water. Since Gaylin couldn't cope with the thought of drinking processed urine, no matter how pure, he drank only the bottled water available from the Oro family at a hefty premium—one Gaylin was willing to, and did, pay.

Gaylin's door was open and there was a knock on the jamb. He looked up to see Ryder's face peeking around the corner.

"You wanted to see me, Cousin?"

Waving his hand towards a chair on the other side of his desk, Gaylin urged, "Come and sit. We haven't talked for a while."

Taking the offered seat, Ryder had a curious look on his face. It wasn't often Gaylin asked him for a personal one-on-one meeting like this. Ryder was almost always suspicious of his cousin's real motives, but especially this morning after the Wilam Fex video.

"It's been three weeks since you had your meeting with the Zaf family officials," Gaylin said. "Is there an update on the proposal you negotiated regarding the move of their family to our alliance?"

"Well, I spoke with the Zaf primor just yesterday, asking what the delay was. He said there was some other personal business needing attention first, but they would have an answer shortly."

"That's good."

"Actually, no, it's not," Ryder retorted. "A move from one alliance to another is a huge event, one that could not possibly be postponed by personal business of any kind. I am sure the Zaf family is playing us." He looked into Gaylin's eyes for some type of reaction, but there was none. Immediately, Ryder felt incredulous deceit, but that subsided quickly as he remembered how cold family business could be. "You already knew this…"

Gaylin leaned forward and wrung his fingers together on the desk. His head was bowed down, but his eyes lifted to Ryder. "Yes, I knew they were playing you. I only had confirmation of this late yesterday, but I'm impressed you figured it out without the technical advantages I have at my disposal."

Smirking, Ryder was impressed in a different way, one where Gaylin had it in him to provide a compliment, even though it contained a patronizing sentiment. "What should we do now?" Ryder asked.

"Certainly don't tell them we know. Let's see where this plays out." Gaylin leaned back in his chair and let out a long sigh. "Cousin, do you ever think back to when we were kids? We spent so much time together. Things were so much simpler."

Ryder wondered where his cousin was going with this. It was odd and made him feel uncomfortable. "Sure, I think back to what great friends we were, but we both grew up and life compelled us to change. I am the family primor, and you are the leader of the largest company in Talus. We both have other responsibilities now."

Gaylin looked down as he felt his eyes grow moist. All he heard was the past tense— "we were friends" —and it stung. He missed his friend. Even though he and Ryder were adversaries in many ways, deep down, Gaylin knew he loved his cousin. Things changed the day he pushed Ryder out of the tree. He tried many times to tell him he was guilty of the crime, but he couldn't. If only he'd been caught and punished appropriately, it's likely the entire incident would've been quickly forgotten, and he and Ryder would be the best of friends today. Instead, over the years, the guilt ate at him, fueling the cruelty he provided to many.

Giving his head a shake, Gaylin lifted his face. His eyes were not moist any longer, but his face was still sagging, showing his vulnerability with his aggressive persona lowered in a moment Ryder had not often seen. "I need to tell you something, Ryder." Gaylin's words stopped.

The pause became awkward and Ryder asked, "What is it?"

Gaylin opened his mouth. He wanted to confess his guilt. He tried to push the words out, but his lips clamped shut. He tried a second time with the same result. As hard as he tried, he couldn't tell Ryder he had pushed him out of the tree. He couldn't admit to his cousin he did something bad. Finally, his lips parted again; the softer persona was gone, replaced with his more typical, stoic demeanour. "Byron tells me you've been seeing a girl."

Gaylin's knowledge of his dating was not a surprise. Ryder knew Byron was Gaylin's man, but the knowledge did reinforce the fact—any information that went to Byron was passed directly to Gaylin. "Her name is Shareen Zaf." Looking at his wrist interlink, Ryder added, "I need to go. She is probably waiting for me downstairs. She wanted to see the Athletic club." Without waiting for a reply, Ryder rose and exited Gaylin's office.

As he took the elevator to the ground floor, he had a difficult time removing the thought of the strange meeting with his cousin out of his mind. In some ways, it was creepy, but in another, it was the first time in a long time—maybe forever—Ryder felt sorry for his cousin.

Shareen always seemed to look great, especially when she gave Ryder that beaming smile. They hugged in the main lobby, before he led her to the elevator and a straight shot up to the 89th floor. Knowing they were going to the Athletic Club, Shareen had a bag of running clothes with her. They both changed and met on the terrace facing the running bridge that was connected to the end support spire in the distance. Ryder was a good runner, using the facility often, and was impressed to see Shareen easily keep up with him as they made their second loop of the circuit.

As they passed the small restaurant on the cantilevered terrace hanging from the support column, Shareen grasped Ryder's arm and moaned, "You promised me an ice float."

Ryder frowned. He could not recall promising her any such thing, but it did sound like a great idea. They found a table with two seats near the railing, with the city almost 300 metres below. The waiter brought over two fruit ice floats, consisting of a ball of ice shards, covered in fruit syrup, surrounded by sweetened cream. They both dug their spoons in several times before either of them said a word.

Looking over the edge of the railing, Shareen confessed, "I've never been up this high. It's scary but amazing at the same time."

Waggling his finger at his girlfriend, Ryder countered, "Remember, you promised to give me a tour of the nuclear facility when we are done here—and lunch at your apartment. I'm sure, since I've never been in a nuclear plant, I'll find it just as exciting."

She waved her hand at him as she chuckled. "The plant isn't as exciting as this, and not as exciting as lunch will be."

"What are we having?"

"It's a surprise."

They finished their ice float, and as they rose from their chairs, Shareen said, "I'm surprised you have the time for me. We've been seeing each other almost every day for three weeks. I would think, as primor, you would have many other duties."

As they walked towards the running bridge, he replied, "I've told you I have no love for my position. I have delegated most of my duties to my cousin, Gaylin."

"I still find that odd. Gaylin isn't a nice person, and you've told me that's the reason you haven't completely abdicated your position as primor. I should remind you now, again, I have no desire to be a vidame. I'm happy living in the background, and in that way, I think I'm much like you."

Not being able to resist, Ryder leaned over and gave Shareen a lingering kiss on her lips. As he pulled away, he offered, "I had an unusual meeting with Gaylin this morning. He was strange."

"How strange?"

"Well, he didn't seem to have that cruel, selfish persona. He appeared vulnerable—giving me a reminder of the person I knew as a boy. Maybe there is some hope for him—after all."

Shareen cocked her head at him. "We should hope. Maybe you should spend more time with him. Just not today." As she finished her last word, she slapped him on the butt and ran off. Ahead of him, he could hear her shout, "There's a reason they call this a running track!"

After showering and changing, they were on their way back down in the elevator. However, Ryder pressed the button that would stop them on the 30th floor. He told Shareen he needed 20 minutes with his people, and then they would be on their way to the nuclear plant.

Once they exited the elevator, Ryder led her into a large room jammed with low cubicles, where 20 of them were filled with workers. As he led her towards the window, he said hello to each person he passed, even waving at a few who were farther away. She was impressed that, throughout the day, even when they were in the Athletic club, in a hallway or the elevator, he greeted everyone by name. He remembered them all.

She saw he had a large desk, but was surprised to see it in the same communal area as his workers. He didn't think himself deserving of any more than they had. He steered her into a glass-walled conference room beside his desk, and asked her to wait there for a few minutes.

Shareen, with more than a little interest, watched and listened to his interactions with his workers. One was giving him an update on an assignment that was not progressing well. In a firm voice, Ryder expressed his displeasure at the delay, but left him with a positive thought, reinforcing the man's competence and skills. Ryder told the man he had all the faith in his ability to complete the assignment successfully.

Shareen found it interesting, even though the man had been somewhat scolded, Ryder left him with a smile on his face and renewed energy to attack his work. In fact, every person Ryder talked to had a smile on their face when he left them.

She'd seen this over the last three weeks, in how he dealt with people, just as he dealt with his workers today. Ryder was a natural-born leader. He didn't know it, just as many natural leaders didn't. He had no desire to be primor, yet he was made to fill such a position. One day, he would realize it, and there would be decisions to be made.

An hour later, after taking the public Ctrain to C25, they arrived at the Rossnol Nuclear Plant. It was a large building, taking up several city blocks. Its outer layer was made of cubic metre sized, concrete blocks, extending five stories in the air. Further towards its center was a concrete dome, extending another thirty metres above the outer offices. The first guard at the main gate, seeing Shareen, just waved them through. There was a main entry to the building in a cut-out along the thick side wall. Here, there were no doors, just an opening with a long hallway running along the inside of the outer wall.

Ten metres from the opening was a guard. As Shareen came closer, the guard had a wide smile and said, "I thought this was your day off, Miss Shareen."

"It is, Titus. However, this is Primor Ryder Gunn." She pointed. "I promised him a quick tour."

Titus's eyes lit up when he heard the name, and he straightened his frame as best he could, but it just further revealed the pot belly he carried. Under the bill of his military style cap, he gave a sharp salute and said, "Pleasure to meet you, Sir."

Shareen slapped his elbow and scoffed, "Stop that and get him booked in."

Titus placed his fingers on a large tablet on the counter. As Ryder answered the questions Titus asked, the guard typed them into the system. Once this process was completed, a plastic visitor badge was produced from a machine under the counter. Titus handed the pass to Ryder along with a clip. "Make sure you keep this visible," the guard warned. He shrugged and lowered his thick, black brows. "Otherwise, someone might shoot you." After an awkward pause, stopped by another slap from Shareen, Titus burst out laughing.

Ryder, not as exuberantly, joined with his own half-hearted chuckle.

They left the guard post and were now inside the main facility. They took an elevator to the third floor, then entered Shareen's office. As she unlocked her desk, Ryder looked down through an interior window into a large three-story room. The walls were pale-green, and the floor area was covered with rows of desks and control panels. "What's this?" he asked.

There was a slam as she closed a drawer of a cabinet along the wall. "That's the main control room. It's where all the action is and where we're going next."

When Ryder turned, he saw Shareen wearing a white lab coat and a matching, white hardhat. In her hand was another hardhat, offered towards him. "You're kidding, right? A hardhat?"

"It's policy. If you go into the control room, you have to wear a hardhat."

Ryder laughed, then, emphasizing each word, said, "It's—a—nuclear—

plant. If something bad happens, the hat won't help."

Shoving the hat into Ryder's gut, she grumbled, "Just put it on."

They took the elevator down to the first floor and continued down a hallway towards the center of the complex. Here, there was another security guard, and behind him was a thick, metal double door. Having a business only attitude, this guard, Duggan Zaf, was not as jovial with Shareen. At his request, she ran her wrist interlink over a scanner on the counter in front of him. A light above the double doors turned green, and the guard turned his attention to Ryder and his visitor pass. Duggan lifted his interlink to his lips and connected to the main security room. After giving the control room Ryder's name and badge number, a positive verification came back. Duggan almost cracked a smile as he stepped aside, telling them they could proceed.

After moving through a metal detector, there was another scanner on the wall beside the double doors. Shareen passed her interlink over it, and the two heavy pocket doors slid into the walls on either side. Once inside, she pressed a blue button, and the doors closed behind them. They were in the main control room.

Shareen whispered, "Stay close to me. Don't wander, and whatever you do, don't push any buttons."

Ryder had a comical look on his face. They had only been dating for three weeks. As such, he kept the thought, *why the fuck would I push any buttons in a nuclear plant,* to himself.

Shareen gave a detailed explanation of the nuclear plant's operation to Ryder. They began at one row of electrical cabinets with many computer monitors built into them. "These are our interface to the nuclear portion of the core. We use enriched uranium as the fuel for the reactor. Centuries ago, we only used uranium enriched by five per cent. Anything more than that was considered unstable and typically used in atomic bombs. However, our technological advances allow us to use uranium enriched to 50 per cent."

"How do you keep it stable?"

Curling a finger at him, Shareen said, "Follow me." She led him to a second row of cabinets. Here, she pointed to a large monitor where a representation of the core was shown. As she pointed to different areas of the view, she explained, "The uranium at the inner core is 50 per cent enriched. The molecules move at a tremendous rate of speed; in fact, at a rate considered an explosion. But as the molecules expand outwards, we apply a modified electromagnetic containment field that slows the molecules."

"So you're controlling a nuclear explosion?"

"In a manner of speaking, yes. We flow water over the core to take advantage of the heat. The energy transfers to the water, creating steam that runs several turbines, creating electricity." Shareen raised one hand, palm up, on either side of her shoulders. "It's really quite simple."

Ryder responded with a nervous chuckle. "What if the containment field fails?"

Again, Shareen's curled finger drew Ryder forward. She led him past several workers in white shop coats and hats, through a wide doorway, into a second room. In the center was a glass dome made of large glass plates. After walking towards the dome, she pointed down and said, "That's the core. There are many redundant systems to control the reaction, including a second, completely redundant magnetic field."

"It just sounds like more things that could fail."

Shareen, standing beside him, gripped his shoulder, giving it a reassuring shake. "As a last resort, in the case of an imminent explosion or a melt down, the core can be ejected into space. There's a three-hundred-metre-long channel cut in the crust under the core. If the core exceeds specific conditions for a specified period of time, the core will automatically eject, or it can be manually jettisoned with the correct passwords."

Ryder realized what she was saying and somberly replied, "You have a lot of responsibility."

She laughed, then gazed about to make sure no one was watching. She twisted her mouth into a sneer and lifted her hands beside her face. Pointing her fingers at Ryder, she waggled them as she said, "The Bringer of Fire."

It was the second time today he gave a nervous laugh. He had learned enough for one day, and Shareen led them out of the complex back to the public railcar, where it was a short run to her apartment. The train was 12 cars long. At their destination, Shareen and Ryder exited from the first car. It was somewhat comical since Linkin exited the second car, keeping a short distance away. Ella Sny exited the seventh car—the woman who Byron assigned to keep an eye on Shareen.

From the tenth car, another man exited and followed Ryder and Shareen through the throng of people exiting the station. Soren Pym had been following Ryder and Shareen for three weeks, ever since his pretense of piano lessons at Shareen's apartment. He knew about Linkin as well as the woman following Shareen. He also knew the woman was part of a two-woman team, and the other woman would be waiting at a small café opposite from Shareen's apartment.

Once they reached ground level, there were quite a few people on the sidewalks. Soren followed at a discrete distance behind until he saw Ryder and Shareen turn a corner, moving down the street she lived on. Having waited at the street prior to Shareen's, he jogged down it to a point in line with the location of her apartment. He ran up the side laneway, to the back of the apartment across from Shareen's home. He raced up the stairs to the third floor, to the empty apartment he was borrowing in his elicit activities. He threw off his coat and strode over to the window where the long-barreled rifle was lying on the table.

He shifted his position and looked through the scope out the open window. He saw Ryder and Shareen walking along the far side of the sidewalk towards his location, followed a short distance behind by Linkin, and just after that, by the woman. He took his eye from the scope and stuck his head out the window. Yes, the second woman was sitting outside the café as predicted.

Soren moved his gaze through the eyepiece back to Ryder and Shareen. There was a group of people walking past them in the opposite direction. He didn't have a shot. Once the group passed, he slowed his breathing. For a moment, he thought he had an opening. His finger came in contact with the trigger, but a man—someone who must have been from Shareen's apartment—came up beside the pair. Soren's shot was blocked. He tracked them with the scope, but the newcomer kept bobbing around, continuing to interrupt a kill shot.

Hoping the man would leave, Soren was disappointed when the man went up the stairs to the apartment building entrance with Ryder and Shareen. They ducked inside the building, but Soren was not deterred. Shareen had the apartment against the near wall, facing the street. There was a hallway window and the window to her living area, where the curtains were always open. Both were backup options.

He pointed the air rifle at the hallway window across the road. His finger was again at the trigger as the pair came into sight. He shifted the rifle back and forth as the two were in a playful mood, bobbing down the hallway. They kissed and Soren thought he had a shot, but Ryder spun Shareen around and she stumbled towards the door. He aimed through the scope, but just as he was about to pull the trigger, they both tumbled inside. "Shit," Soren whispered. "Just one more chance."

Inside the apartment, Ryder chuckled as he pulled Shareen into his arms. He kissed her passionately, lips parted, as Shareen gave a light moan. Ryder, pulling away, grinned as he gave her a smart slap on her butt. "I'm hungry. Where's lunch?"

Through a scowl, she said, "Lunch? Really?"

Ryder had a playful look on his face. "Aren't you hungry?"

Still scowling, Shareen replied, "It's in the fridge. You can take it out. Oh, can you close the curtains. It's too bright in here. I'll be back in a minute."

Ryder backed towards the living room window while watching Shareen go into her bedroom. He reached back and closed the curtain.

Across the road, Soren saw the curtain shift. He slapped the table and growled, "Shit!" again.

Walking to the fridge in the kitchen, Ryder pulled the door open. He bent over and peered into it and was immediately confused. There were a few simple items in the fridge, but nothing prepared. He scratched his head and then moved the few items around, but still there was nothing he could find resembling lunch.

He pulled his head from the fridge and lifted himself to his full height. The only word he managed to get out of his mouth was, "hey," before he took notice of Shareen. She was standing in the doorway of her bedroom, leaning with one hand on the jamb and one foot crossed over the other—and she was almost naked. The only item of clothing she wore was a thin robe with a tie at the waist. Its length went only half-way down her butt and the front was open well past her navel. Since the material was sheer, there was little left to Ryder's imagination. He gulped and said, "There is no lunch, is there?"

She smiled coyly and whispered, "Nope."

He closed the fridge, walked to her and brought her into his arms. He felt her shiver as he backed her into her bedroom. He growled, kissing her while his heel kicked back and closed the door.

Chapter 15: That'll Leave a Mark

"Excuse me, Boss. I have something that can't wait."

Gaylin glared at Byron's face poking in through his doorway. Byron never interrupted him unless it was really important. He shifted his gaze to Tala, sitting across from him. "We'll pick this up later."

Without a word, Tala rose and scooted out the door towards her desk. Byron, having stepped aside, closed the door behind her. Byron was nervous, peering from side to side, even though he was in a secure office swept weekly for listening devices. He leaned over Gaylin's desk, his palms supporting his large frame. In a low voice he said, "We have a meeting and need to leave right now."

Gaylin's face glowed from the flush sweeping over it. He thought Byron had lost his mind, forgetting who worked for who. "I have no idea what you're talking about," Gaylin retorted.

Gaylin's eyes widened when Byron strode around the desk and leaned over with his face close to Gaylin's ear. Byron whispered, "Matteo contacted me. We need to go—now."

With his heart rate jumping, Gaylin rose to his feet. "Now?"

As Byron walked towards the door, he repeated, "We need to go now."

Gaylin followed and saw Byron with his hand stalled on the door lever. "Is there more?"

"Tell Tala we're going for a meeting at the pharmaceutical factory in C34. It's best we leave some breadcrumbs."

Gaylin did just that. He spoke momentarily to Tala, then he and Byron went down in the elevator. Gaylin was about to push the button that would take them to the basement, when Byron pushed his hand away. As Byron pressed the button for the main lobby, he muttered. "It's best we take public transit."

It took them 35 minutes to arrive at their destination. Along the way, Byron explained they were to go to the medical building at 344 62nd Lane. "There's a coffee shop on the tenth floor where Matteo told me we would receive further instructions," Byron explained.

Once they entered the lobby, Gaylin headed straight for the elevator.

Byron wrapped his fingers around Gaylin's arm and tugged him in the opposite direction. Byron led him down a short hallway and into a room located just off of it. Seeing it was a public locker room, Gaylin gave his head of security a curious look.

"Put a token in the locker," Byron requested.

As Gaylin complied, he asked, "Why?"

"We're leaving our jackets here. First, we'll look less formal, and especially for you, less recognizable. Second, without jackets, it'll look like we work in this building."

"Ah, more bread crumbs."

Byron gave a quick nod before he folded his jacket and placed it in the locker. Gaylin did likewise, and they retraced their steps towards the elevator. Once they arrived at the tenth floor, amongst the many medical offices, they found the entrance to the café shop halfway down the hallway. Gaylin, seeing there was a serving counter but no sitting area, was about to say, *what the fuck*, when a pretty brunette waitress said, "Right this way." She led them through a second doorway, out onto a wide patio area. Although it was an outdoor veranda, it seemed dark due to the oxygen-vine beams running overtop at one metre intervals.

The pretty waitress led them to a table in the middle of the sitting area and told them she would return with menus. As soon as she left, Byron's wrist interlink beeped. He answered it and listened to the voice at the other end of the connection. It was a low voice, but still loud enough for Gaylin to also hear. "Move to the corner table—the one beside the fake plant." With a click, the connection was terminated.

As they rose, the waitress returned with the menus and a dumbfounded look on her face. "Is something wrong?"

Byron cracked a smile. "We'd like to sit in the corner, so we can look out over the city."

A smile returned to her face as she led them to the table they wanted. As the two men sat, she put the menus between them and explained the daily special.

As soon as she left, Byron's interlink buzzed again. The voice said, "Tell Gaylin to put a five-token piece on the table.

Gaylin once again heard and asked, "Why?" His eyes searched out the dining area. There were two other couples on the far side of the veranda, and then he saw a single man slouched back in a chair in the far corner opposite them. The man looked scruffy, with brown pants and a black sweater. The attached hood was pulled up over his head. As he brought his wrist interlink up to his lips, Gaylin saw a momentary flash of white hair within the shadow of the hood.

It was Matteo. "The money is for the girl's tip."

"But we haven't even ordered our food, and I'm hungry," Gaylin insisted. Leaning on his elbow, Byron had moved his wrist forward, so both he and Gaylin could communicate with the killer. Since a response wasn't forthcoming, Gaylin slapped the five-token piece down on the table.

Matteo then continued, "You won't have time for lunch. Gaylin, reach your hand under the table."

With a quizzical look on his face, Gaylin did so. He felt a metal object taped to the underside of the table.

"Remove it," Matteo hissed.

Gaylin complied and pulled off the tape. It was a small electrical magnifying eyepiece. He glanced at Matteo in the far corner, and the assassin's voice came across the interlink again. "Don't look at me! Look on the far side of the road, four buildings down. Do you recognize it?"

Putting the eyepiece to his eye, Gaylin looked over the concrete railing and found the fourth building. He muttered, "Shit." In their haste to travel to their destination, Gaylin hadn't realized the medical building they were in was so close to the Krl family estate. When he pulled his gaze away from the building, he saw Matteo with his own eyepiece looking down the street perpendicular to the building they were in.

Matteo mumbled, "Right on time. Look down the street. What do you see at the far end?"

Once again, Gaylin was looking through the eyepiece. At first, he panned the eyepiece up and down the road, not really knowing what he was looking for. Then, a flash of silver caught his eye. It was a beautiful silver family car. On the front was a round, blue insignia. He snickered as he recognized the emblem of the Zaf family. Everyone in Talus knew only Vidame Marta Zaf used the silver family car—and only when on official business.

The waitress was heading towards their table. Gaylin slipped the eyepiece under the table as Byron told her they would need more time. When she left, Gaylin whispered to Byron, "It's that fat bitch, Marta, coming to visit the Krl. You told me she was playing Ryder, and now, here she is."

From behind a stoic face, Byron dryly replied, "Awesome."

When Gaylin brought the eyepiece back up, it was just in time to see the large double gates in front of the Krl residence, opening. There was a wide semi-circle, stone driveway curling in front of a large entryway. Two Krl guards waited on the veranda at the top of the few stairs to the door. The side door of the family car was pushed open, and a bodyguard stepped from the vehicle. He waited a few steps away as a second man, in a crisp suit, stepped out. It was the family lawyer carrying his briefcase. He took a position at the top of the stairs as Gaylin saw the booted foot of the vidame press out from the car door opening. "Here comes the fat bitch," Gaylin muttered.

As her foot hit the stone driveway, there was a flash and a second later a loud *crack*. Gaylin bobbled the eyepiece, almost dropping it, but recovered. When he put it back to his eye, the driveway was covered with smoke. He couldn't see a thing, but when he heard a shrill, female scream, Gaylin cracked a smile.

Matteo wasn't watching. He knew exactly what happened. Five nights ago, using a drone with a specialized paint adapter, he coated the stones in front of the entryway with acetaldehyde, a chemical if exposed to air for a prolonged time, was known to react violently with certain peroxides. Specifically, a reaction dubbed a *vigorous condensation* would cause a spontaneous explosion. Although it took a little more effort, it was within Matteo's skill set to break into the vidame's house and inject hydrogen peroxide into her shoes—the ones Matteo had observed were her favorite, especially for formal family business. Matteo knew, when she stepped out onto the coated stone driveway with her saturated boots, chaos would be the result.

Gaylin was trying to hold back his snickers as he watched the smoke clear. Every few seconds there was another scream. He was impressed the woman could swear with the best of them. Finally, the smoke thinned, and Gaylin saw Marta Zaf lying on her back, her head cradled in the lap of one of her bodyguards. There had to be 20 Krl family members packed on the veranda just outside the main door, horrified, yet not able to look away from the carnage.

Gaylin chuckled. "Wow, that's her boot about ten metres from her." Gaylin adjusted the focus and looked from the boot to the vidame, through the people surrounding her. He looked back and forth several times. He bounced on the chair and slapped the table. "Holy fuck, Byron. There's a bloody stump in the boot. Her foot's there and she's *way* over there." Gaylin pulled himself from the eyepiece, and with his face holding an evil look of astonishment, said, "Her foot is blown off."

Byron snatched the eyepiece and rose to his feet. "We better go. They'll be shutting down the trains shortly."

As Gaylin rose, he said to Byron, "I guess they won't be joining the Krl alliance anytime soon."

"Of course. You need to pay the man."

Gaylin led the way past the two couples who were looking over the railing, engrossed by the carnage. The waitress had joined them, and even the cook came out from the kitchen.

When they had met Matteo in Joyville, Gaylin paid the man half up front, the remainder to be paid when the job was complete. Matteo was slouched back in his chair against the railing with his face in the shadow of the hood.

Gaylin flipped a disc across the table. On it was a credit of 125 quadtokens. Without stopping, Gaylin muttered, "A little harsh, but quite effective."

Chapter 16: A Council for Peace

The Sholite Buffalo-class battleship, *Tobarra*, was travelling at its full speed, 20 per cent SOL. The massive space vessel was fully armed, as were the two Sholite Tiger-class destroyers running alongside it. The three military spaceships were escorting the Sholite presidential frigate, *Sovereign*, to Talus.

Vidame Timo Jez had announced, at the Council of Nine meeting, five days ago, she had approached the Sholite president regarding a possible truce between the Sholites and Korians. It was only the council delegates from the Fyr box who vehemently objected. The other families didn't mind that the Jez, a powerful secondary family, had bushwhacked the Fyr clan. However, they were irritated the Jez family had circumvented the council in proceeding without their collective approval. At times, the ends do justify the means, and irritation was as far as the general council's reprimand went.

The turmoil at the council meeting called by the Sholite president was more intense. The president's health was deteriorating quickly, but he found the strength to lead the impromptu meeting. Without any previous notice, citing his failing health, he announced I'lish Mann to the position of vice-president with full authority to act in his stead.

Not including I'lish, of the 11 ministers around the table, seven remained relatively calm. Only three jumped to their feet: Black Brighton, Admiral Merrick and Minister Jacob, a political minister who was also a religious minister representing the Sholite faithful. As the three men vigorously displayed their objections, President Balorian gave I'lish a sly wink. The ratio of ministers, for and against, was exactly as they forecasted.

Black Brighton was the first to come to his senses, realizing their objections, so far, appeared as wanton panic. He asked for a fifteen-minute recess, which was granted. When he returned with Merrick and Jacob, all three were calm, although the darkness of their eyes and the frowns on their faces, still revealed their unhappiness with the decision.

Having checked facts with his legal advisor, Black Brighton conceded the president did have the right to proclaim a vice-president, and that person could act on the president's behalf. Furthermore, if the president died or was mentally incapacitated, the vice president would take over the presidential duties.

Balorian smiled, seeing the three who he thought would put up a staunch fight, were oddly compliant now. The only statement made by Brighton, even remotely threatening, was the reminder to the president that the proclamation for vice president was only valid under certain conditions such as a president's failing health or another immediate issue sourced from a sudden and unforeseen event. Brighton also reminded the president the proclamation, under any circumstances, would last no more than one year. At that time, the position would fall to a general election of the people.

I'lish was astonished Brighton took the news so well. When President Balorian made the second part of his announcement, indicating he had begun peace negotiation with the Korians through the Jez family, again there was some disorder, but nothing terminally upsetting. I'lish Mann was to lead a peace delegation to Talus. Two ministers from the council would join her, along with the council lawyer and two technical specialists.

There was a quick round of nominations and two rounds of voting before Black Brighton and Jessica Furlong were successfully voted onto the delegation. Even though Black Brighton was now on the delegation, giving him some solace, I'lish thought the sequence of events transpired with less pain than expected, and Black Brighton's relatively timid behaviour was totally out of character. He was a man who usually fought his position tooth and nail. When she saw Merrick and Brighton glancing at each other, trying to hide their sarcastic smirks, she didn't know the two men were the only people who knew, in one month, the six sleeper agents would be turned loose, completing their deadly missions in Talus. In Brighton and Merrick's minds, who was vice-president would be completely inconsequential.

That was five days ago. Now, I'lish sat in the lounge of the Sovereign with Black Brighton and Jessica Furlong. I'lish hoped Jessica could be useful in some way, but she represented the academics of the Sholite population, so that would remain to be seen. Black Brighton had a previous history in the banking community. Even though I'lish despised the man, he might come in useful if there were monetary issues to be addressed.

Also in the lounge, sitting across from I'lish, were Jameson Crenna and Captain Brent Murdock. Jameson was a well-respected leader within the space farming community. It was expected the question of how space supplies would be shared, would be the most contentious issue in a proposed peace treaty. Captain Murdock was the only military man within the group. He was known to President Balorian, who trusted the man to speak on military articles within the broader agreement expected. Surprisingly, Admiral Merrick had also been favourable to the appointment of Murdock to the negotiating committee.

The last member of the committee was standing by a window, looking out into the blackness of space and the few stars in the distance. Bethany Raymond was the chief legal council for the President's Council. It was expected she would manage the difficult task of putting the thoughts and ideas, agreed to at the negotiations, to paper with concise yet easily understood wording.

"Miss Raymond, can you please join us for a few minutes?" The request came from Bandy Mal, a well-respected and highly educated Korian lawyer employed by the Jez family. A week ago, she had been nominated by the Council of Nine to be the Sholite delegation's liaison.

Once Bethany Raymond sat beside I'lish Mann on the wide couch, Ms. Mal said, "Well, we're well into Korian space. We've been travelling for almost two days, but we've been decelerating for the past hour. We are now close to Talus." She turned her gaze to Vice-President Mann. "Can you please make sure the ship's commander notifies the escort ships to hold a position 2,000 kilometres clear of Talus. At that point, a Korian military cruiser will continue the escort duties."

A Sholite officer in a traditional, dark-blue uniform stood by the long hallway leading to the command deck. I'lish gave him a nod, and he immediately saluted, then headed up the hallway to pass on the message. "Why do we need a Korian escort? Are you expecting trouble?" I'lish asked.

For a lawyer, Bandy Mal had a warm, reassuring smile. "We're not expecting trouble, but this meeting and, hopefully, the following negotiations, are extremely important. In Talus, we do have small pockets of fanatics and even a few terrorists. Our military is on high alert to foil any efforts these groups might have to disrupt the proceedings."

I'lish chuckled, leaving a confused look on Bandy's face. She didn't have the heart to tell the young woman, although she had a great smile, she spoke as a true professional of the legal community. "I'm assuming the plans have not changed. Our ship will stay off Talus tonight, and we'll dock with the asteroid first thing in the morning. Is that still the plan?" I'lish asked.

"Yes, that's the plan. But for now, everyone, please relax," Bandy Mal urged. "This could be a great moment in the history of both our races. I don't say that to apply undue pressure. It's a way to tell you—well—the bar is still open, and I've learned the Sholites have an excellent selection of wine."

Nervous laughter filled the lounge—all except Black Brighton. Although he put on a good façade, he really wasn't interested in peace with the Korians. It was bad for business. He was going along with this knowing, in less than a month, none of this would matter. He didn't care about the rest of the delegation. He just needed to ensure he was well away from Talus on the day the sleeper agents were activated. If the negotiation's duration lasted that long, he would ensure there was an emergency at the Sholite fleet requiring his immediate recall.

Brighton had moved to a position in front of the port side window. Fifteen minutes later, he saw the Sholite escorts peel off and slow their speed. They were easy to see in their silver and grey livery. A minute later, he almost jumped out of his skin. He saw a movement 100 metres off their port side. At first, he thought his eyes were deceiving him, but then he saw the subtle shift of blackness against the stars in the background for a second time. Brighton didn't know it, but he just had his first view of a Talus Dog's cruiser—a view few Sholites lived to tell about.

Twenty minutes later, a Sholite officer from the command deck stood beside his fellow officer in the hallway. The newcomer announced, "We're minutes away from Talus. It's visible in the distance. You can get an excellent view from the observation deck." He pointed to the stairs at the far corner of the lounge.

It was rare for Sholites to see Talus. A Sholite's close proximity to it usually ended in a hailstorm of firepower, resulting in death. This new experience was the case for all the members of the committee, except for I'lish. She had a long history of smuggling that often found her in places she wasn't supposed to be.

Once they were in the observation room above the lounge, they had a panoramic, breathtaking view in all directions. They saw Talus as a long grey cylinder in the distance, and the Sovereign was making a wide arc from behind to come in line with the asteroid's bearing. Even this maneuver—sounding simple—wasn't. Talus was moving through space at 6 per cent SOL. Although, relative to the frigate, this was slow, it was still a velocity of 70 million kilometres per hour. Their frigate slowed as it caught up to the rotating asteroid. The Talus Dog cruiser took up a position between the Sholite frigate and Talus, 50 kilometres clear of the asteroid.

The distance was necessary because of the nature of their drive systems. The modified electromagnetic drives Sholite and Korian spaceships used, warped space around their ships. The space in front of the ship was compressed, and the space behind was expanded, creating a warp bubble that was propelled through space at phenomenal speeds. The bubbles of two or more ships could be combined, but this was a sensitive operation, requiring the speed of each vessel to match perfectly. And only then could the ship's individual bubbles be slowly merged together. Failure to follow this procedure perfectly, could cause destruction of the ships. Considering this, the Sovereign, the Talus Dog cruiser and Talus, were far enough apart so there was no risk of their warp bubbles coming into contact.

I'lish did consume two large glasses of an excellent Sholite wine before she went to the presidential suite to retire for the night. She slept well until she was awakened by her early morning alarm.

After washing, she adjusted her hair. It had been in a long braid for as long as she could remember, but today, for the special occasion where she needed to make her best impression, she pulled her long, black ponytail out. As she combed her hair, it maintained its weave pattern. Placing a ring at shoulder height, her hair was pulled tight, only to fall loosely from the ring down to her waist.

Looking at her image in the full-length mirror, she thought her outfit looked casual—yet still classy. She wore white pants and a white shirt with a bright-blue jacket, short in the front but having a tail extending to mid-thigh. Knee length, black boots completed the ensemble.

She met the remainder of the group in the lounge where they had a light breakfast. Once again, it was suggested they move to the observation deck since they were going to dock with Talus. Through the thick windows they saw the black Korian military ship was nowhere in sight. Their own ship was firing side thrusters, and, little by little, the Sovereign was catching up to the rotation of the asteroid. This was something simply not possible by human control alone. The Sovereign's computers were talking to those within the Talus control tower, until finally, their rotations were matched.

Six large bay doors opened above them, revealing their destination dock. Again, the computers initiated the thrusters, pushing them upwards and into the large opening. It took critical timing to cut out the Sovereign's thrusters once they were fully inside the dock, otherwise they could easily ram into the walls of the docking area. Their docking was completed perfectly as the Sholite ship's docking hatch connected with the one above them. There was a slight jarring motion, and with the sound of the engines shutting down, they were the first Sholite ship to dock with Talus in 200 years.

The group followed a contingent of five Sholite marines out of the ship onto the loading deck in the hanger above the ship. Their marines were armed, but they didn't draw their weapons even though, across the hanger, they saw at least 100 armed Korian soldiers. In front of them was a receiving party, who were making their way towards the Sholites. Primor Dante Jez welcomed I'lish and her committee to Talus. After a brief exchange of pleasantries, the Korian primor led them across the hanger and through a set of double doors.

They were in the primary Fyr naval base. The Sovereign was docked in one of 17 bays available at that location. This specific bay had a fully functional private railcar station attached to it. I'lish saw they were being led to a series of six black vehicles—with even the windows tinted an impenetrable black. The Sholite party, along with their liaison, Bandy Mal, were ushered into the second car. The Jez primor, along with the remainder of his welcoming party, boarded the fourth car. The Sholite marines boarded the first car, while surprisingly, police officers from the Jez controlled force, looking resplendent in their silver, dress uniforms, boarded the other three cars.

Once the cars began to move along the monorail, I'lish asked Bandy about the police escort, and the liaison explained the police had jurisdiction within Talus, so once they left the military base, the police had responsibility for the group's safety.

All of Talus knew of the historic meeting. It had been declared a state holiday, and almost every citizen of Talus was ready and waiting in front of a video monitor. The private rail line between the Fyr military base in C24 to the Talus Government Center in C35 had been cleared of all traffic. Since the delegation's cars could proceed at full speed, the trip only took 15 minutes. Once they arrived at the station just below the government building, the entire group made their way up to the main floor. There were windows, three stories high, fronting the building, and as I'lish looked through them, she asked Primor Dante Jez, "Can we go outside for a moment?"

He hesitated, but after conferring with a leading police officer, he agreed. A contingent of ten officers, followed by the five Sholite marines, then I'lish with the remainder of the Sholite delegation, left the confines of the building. I'lish felt light headed. At first, she thought, *this must be some type of technically enhanced illusion.* After all, they were in an asteroid which, technically, made this a cave. But instead, she saw a wide-open space, the largest she'd ever been in, where she could not see the far wall she knew must be there, and she could barely see the ceiling 300 metres above. It wasn't dark and drab; rather, the space in front of her was filled with colour, people and light. She felt envious. The Sholite space station where she lived was nice, but nothing compared to this. In her mind, her resolve to come to a lasting peace grew. Only one other thing was held in higher regard, and that was to find a world where even this space would be considered confining.

She whispered to the primor, "Thank you. We can go back inside."

The Sholite group was led into an anteroom provided for their use during the proceedings. Bandy Mal informed them the meeting would begin in thirty minutes, after which she left the room.

Black Brighton said to the group, "We can still leave." He hadn't said a word during the trip, but it was clear he wasn't happy with the improved lifestyle the Korians appeared to have.

I'lish's eyes grew dark. She pointed to the door and said, "If you want to go, then leave. A replacement can be easily found."

Black Brighton lowered himself into a chair. He had a smug look on his face. He had no intention of leaving. He said what he did to ensure I'lish knew he had his own mind and would be watching her closely.

The back door of the room opened and Bandy returned. She looked from one to the other and asked, "Are you ready?" She saw enough nods in the group to feel she had a positive answer. Turning her focus to I'lish, she reminded her, "As we discussed earlier, there'll be formal introductions; then the Pym vidame will speak, then you."

I'lish nodded in response. By now the unofficial channels in both Talus and the Sholite fleet carried the rumour that the Jez and Pym families had been secretly collaborating on the secretive peace initiative. Both families could improve their status with a weakening of the military based Fyr family.

Taking a deep breath, Mandy led the contingent of five Sholites into the two-story-high council chamber. The families had already filled their boxes, both in the semi-circle of boxes for the nine primary families, and those for the secondary families in the tiers facing them. As the Korians saw I'lish, there was instant silence in the room. It was rare for Korians to come face to face with Sholites. Although, they knew they were similar to their own kind, they were still somewhat surprised when they saw the Sholite vice-president. She was stunning, and she walked in a manner exuding confidence.

Ryder and Gaylin Gunn sat behind Vidame Nola Gunn in the Gunn family box. Gaylin leaned over and whispered in Ryder's ear, "What's wrong with your mother. She's been acting nervous all morning, and now, when she caught sight of the Sholite delegation, she turned white as a ghost."

Ryder shrugged. "She's been acting strange ever since the announcement of this meeting with the Sholites."

Their discussion was interrupted by the sound of a bell rung by the council moderator. He stood and brought the meeting to order. Reading from a tablet, he made the necessary introductions, taking the time to introduce each of the members within the nine primary family boxes. After taking a deep breath, he continued, introducing I'lish and her team. He then gave the floor to Vidame Pym before he sat down behind his desk.

Vidame Pym, in a formal, black dress, rose to her feet. "Welcome to all.

Before we begin, I would like to send the Pym family's best wishes to Vidame Marta Zaf for a speedy recovery from the horrible attack she encountered. It's a shame she can't be here. I'm sure she'll soon be back on her feet—" She looked around awkwardly for a moment "—well, I mean to say she'll soon be here providing important advice to this council."

Vidame Clarice Pym looked out into the audience of secondary families, each box overflowing with many more family members than were usually in the council room. "Thank you all for coming to an important meeting that hopefully leads to a lasting peace between Korians and Sholites." There was a murmur from the tiers of people. Some enjoyed the thought of peace, while others did not. Vidame Pym raised her voice and said, "I'lish Mann, vice-president of the Sholite people will speak next."

I'lish rose to her feet, smiled at those in the Council of Nine boxes, then turned away and faced the larger audience in the tiers of secondary families—what some in the Council of Nine might see as an insult.

In the Gunn box, Gaylin slapped his thigh and almost choked. Through a grin, with only Ryder close enough to hear, he muttered, "This ought to be good."

I'lish took the time to make eye contact with many of the people in the audience. "Thank you for having me here to speak to you today. I understand the process is to see if a peace agreement is even feasible. If the answer is yes, then the Korian's will establish a negotiating committee, similar to the one you see here behind me."

She seemed to change before the eyes of the Korian people as she left the box and the microphone behind. She walked in front of the railing and leaned back on it. Without the microphone, she increased the tone of her voice, although she looked and sounded casual. "My grandfather was from Earth. His name was Lashkar Mann. Some of you might remember his name and the name of my grandmother, Nancy Tellman. Both were at the famous Battle of Fort Nelson on Earth, over 60 years ago."

Most within the boxes of the Council of Nine wondered where the Sholite vice-president was going with this.

As I'lish continued, she left the railing she was perched on and walked across the floor area. "We all know the story of the heroes of Fort Nelson, but did you know Rowan Gunn and my grandfather were great friends at Fort Nelson. After the battle, Lashkar Mann left Earth to live with the Korians, where he and Arlo Gunn also became great friends." She continued as she paced back and forth in front of the audience. "And of course, my grandfather was friends with former Vidame Natalie Gunn." I'lish turned around and pointed at Nola Gunn. "She used to sit right there."

With a warm smile on her face, I'lish turned back to the audience. She lifted her hand over her head, waving and spinning it. "I have to tell you a funny story."

Again Gaylin, with his fist covering his mouth, whispered to Ryder, "Shit, she's going to tell a funny story."

I'lish said, "I'm sure all Korians know, in great detail, the story of the Battle of Fort Nelson. But I bet you don't know your Vidame Natalie Gunn, while on Earth, broke my grandfather out of jail so he could help her. Can you believe it!" She gave out a loud guffaw. There were a few in the crowd who joined her. She froze with her finger lifted in the air. "Here is the real funny part. She knew he wouldn't do it. So she released my *great* grandfather, who was in a different jail, and then blackmailed Lashkar Mann for the help she needed. It's absolutely ridiculous!" Again, she laughed and almost everyone in the audience joined her. She was winning them over.

Ryder leaned forward and whispered in his mother's ear, "She's very good."

Nola Gunn tilted her head back and replied with a grin on her face, "She certainly is."

Now having a connection with the audience, I'lish returned to the railing of her box and crossed her arms in front of her. In a lower voice, she said, "Natalie Gunn killed Rowan Gunn. It was a tragic mistake, instigated by the Sholite people. A small group of overzealous Sholites tried to destroy this asteroid." The murmurs in the audience began again. She lifted off the railing and offered, "It's one thing to be at war, but what the Sholites of the time did was to try and exterminate your race." There was silence. "The Sholites have never apologized for that, but I do now. Officially, the Sholite people apologize for their actions on Earth."

The silence was maintained except for the sniffles of many who had lost loved ones. For many, the apology brought closure. For Black Brighton, he was fuming, his knuckles white from the pressure of his closed fists. *How dare she,* he thought.

"My grandfather eventually left Talus to live with the Sholites. His love for my grandmother was greater than his place in this or any society—or the ongoing war. We should all think on that. There are things greater than this senseless war." She returned to her seat in the Sholite box as she heard the clapping from most of the audience.

The appreciative atmosphere was interrupted by Vidame Anne Fyr. Her voice, loud through the microphone, drowned out the clapping. "That's a nice speech, but these are just words. Actions speak louder, and the only

Sholite actions I know of are the destruction of Korian ships by Sholites!"

"There is more!" The interruption came from Vidame Pym. "I'lish Mann has an offering to show their sincerity in pursuing peace."

I'lish rose and pulled a data disc from her inside pocket. As she held it over her head for all to see, she said, "There are six Sholite sleeper agents in Talus. Five years ago, our intelligence service brainwashed these six Korians. They were given missions that would destroy critical government facilities or would result in the death of high-ranking Talus officials."

There was an unruly roar from the crowd. Every person was on their feet in protest.

I'lish spoke into the microphone. "The six Korians have no idea they have been programmed. On this disc are the six names and also the code phrase that will stop their missions."

As the audience heard this news with relief, a member of the Jez family, who was also the head of the police service, walked from the Jez box and took the disc. He turned to the moderator and suggested, "It's important we deal with this immediately. Please announce a recess until we have these people detained."

Everyone rose with many leaving the council room to stretch their legs. Ninety minutes later, bells were heard throughout the building, indicating the council meeting was being called back to order. Vidame Pym rose and stated, "The Jez family has an update to share. I will now defer to Vidame Jez."

From her front row, secondary box, Vidame Jez also rose. "Our police force has acted quickly. We have found and detained four of the six people on the list provided by the Sholites. We have verified the other two have died in the war. We will not release the names at this time, but we will say there were three women and three men on the list. The four remaining are two women and two men. The four are presently being escorted to a hospital where they will be debriefed by Bli family psychologists." She took a deep breath and added, "A disaster has been averted, and we thank the Sholite delegation for that."

"Thank them!" The words had been blurted out by Admiral Milton Fyr, sitting behind his vidame. He burst to his feet and thrust a finger towards I'lish Mann. "These people are our enemy! Thank them? It's tantamount to a man breaking into your house and pointing a gun at you. He tells you he's going to kill you, but ultimately, he decided against it. Do you thank him for not killing you? After all, burglary and threatening your life are both crimes. Since when do we thank people for not committing crimes?"

Beginning as a murmur, in no time, there was a raucous scene in the tiers of secondary families. Some realized there was some truth to the admiral's words. Others thought it was not that simple. If something wasn't done soon, the moderator would lose control of the proceedings.

To the surprise of his mother and cousin, Ryder Gunn rose to his feet and tapped the microphone. He caught the moderator's gaze, in whose eyes was a desperate cry for help. Ryder asked, "Can I have the floor please?"

A few heard the request over the din, and they stared with surprise at the Gunn family primor. They elbowed their neighbours and whispered to others near them. If anyone else had asked to be heard, it was likely the audience wouldn't react, but Ryder Gunn never spoke at council meetings—ever. He was known as the *quiet* primor, the one who didn't care to be primor. So when he asked to be heard, it piqued the interest of everyone in the audience.

The moderator, nodded and said, "You have the floor, Sir."

Ryder took a moment to survey the audience. He took the time to look Vidame Fyr and her admiral in the eye. Making sure not to yell, Ryder still spoke in a firm voice. "We are a little people."

Murmurs began in the audience again, but Ryder raised his finger in the air as a request for their silence. "Vengeance is an unusual act. Typically, it's an act from a single person or a small group. Vengeance is purely looking in the past and reacting to it. It has nothing to do with looking forward to our future. I understand the emotion within vengeance as many of you do, but it's typically putting the needs of a few over the needs of the many." He looked directly at the delegates in the Fyr box. "That makes vengeance a selfish act."

Ryder turned back to the audience and asked, "If I asked you the question, 'Why do you dislike the Sholites?' most of you could give me an answer immediately, with many of those based in a need for vengeance. However, if I asked you, 'Why are we at war with the Sholites?' does anyone know the answer?" He chuckled as his gaze across the families was visibly mocking. "I understand the war began 2,500 years ago in a solar system many light years from this location. I have no idea what happened the day the war began, and honestly, by the looks on your faces, I see neither do you."

Admiral Fyr interrupted, "What's your point?"

Ryder returned the admiral's cold gaze, then shifted it to Vidame Fyr. "Madam, can you please tell me how many military ships Talus has in her navy? If you don't know, you can lean back, and I'm sure the admiral has the number at his fingertips."

The vidame did lean back, and then returned after the admiral whispered in her ear. She said, "We have 205 military spaceships."

Looking around her, Ryder asked the admiral, "How many ships do we have in the Exploratory Corp.?"

"Twelve ships."

Ryder turned towards the Sholite box. "I'lish Mann, I will assume you have approximately the same number of military ships we have. But, can you tell me how many exploratory ships you have?"

"Eighteen," came the reply.

Ryder rubbed his chin as his gaze panned the audience. "Hmm, so collectively we have around 400 military ships and 30 exploratory ships." He laughed. "We certainly are a little people."

Ryder's voice took on a lower tone. "I have a son. He is six years old. He lives in an apartment with me, here in this rock." Holding his arms out, Ryder spun in a slow circle until he faced the audience once again. "Don't get me wrong, if we have to live in a rock, this is a nice rock—but there is no question—it's still a rock! My hope is, one day, my son will feel wind on his face that doesn't come from a circulation fan, and water droplets that don't come from a shower head, or even beads of sweat that do come from a hot sun beating down on him."

Ryder sighed. "Four hundred ships focused on vengeance from our past, and only 30 ships looking towards our future. If we vote for peace, we can afford to shift some of those military ships to exploration. If we don't, we will remain—a little people." Ryder sat down. He was exhausted and the protruding blood vessel on his forehead showed his stress, as did the tingling in his fingers.

The room was silent. The moderator finally broke it. "It seems the time for a vote is here. I would ask for the Council of Nine to vote with a hand raised in favour of a truce with the Sholites. The truce would be for one month, over which time a longer peace will be negotiated. Vote now, please."

In each of the nine boxes, the dignitaries of each family huddled together. The Pym were the first family to raise a hand, followed by the Gunn then the Oro and Sny. There was a hand raised in every box except the Krl who maintained their stubborn support of a lasting war.

The moderator went through the motions of counting the raised hands. With a smile on his face, he announced, "The 'yeahs' have it. We have a truce." This was followed by a cheer from the audience. The moderator interrupted as he spoke into his microphone. "We still have a task to select a Korian negotiating committee. This will occur over the next five days."

Gaylin Gunn was never one to miss an opportunity. He knew he would never be accepted to lead the Korian negotiating committee, but he had someone in mind who was suddenly in high favour with the people, and it was a person he had a close reign on. He jumped to his feet and cried into the microphone, "Sir, why waste five days when we can be negotiating immediately. It's clear we have a leader in our midst who can well represent the people of Talus. To lead the Korian peace committee, I nominate my cousin, Ryder Gunn."

Ryder moved to rise, but Gaylin held his hand on his cousin's shoulder. He whispered, "Don't ruin this. It's going so much better than expected."

The moderator saw there were no objections from the families, so he put it to a vote. This time, even the Fyr family voted favourably, and the nomination was unanimous.

Ryder's head was spinning. He finally managed to rise. He opened his mouth to object, but he was interrupted by clapping—a single man clapping in the back tier. He was joined by all the members of a family in the front row. They all rose to their feet and clapped. Row by row, more people rose and clapped. Ryder heard clapping from closer by. He turned to see Vidame Pym clapping, soon joined by the Oro and Edy families. Leading the secondary families, Vidame Jez had a smug look on her face. In a matter of minutes, the entire room was clapping, and to Ryder's amazement, they were all looking at him.

Even the dignitaries within the Sholite box rose to their feet, led by I'lish Mann. She clapped as fervently as anyone. There was a wide, proud smile on her face, while she could barely hide the tears filling her eyes.

Chapter 17: Explorers

The Explorer spaceship, *Constellation*, had already matched Talus's rotation as the frigate-sized vessel approached from the rear of the asteroid. Ryder watched through the thick glass of the observation post, with his fingers interlaced behind his back.

Of course, the asteroid didn't have a smooth skin; rather, there were many undulations with valleys and protrusions up to 100 metres in height. This observation post took advantage of one such 50-metre rise of rock, allowing the occupants within to see out over the Explorer Corp. space docks. Eight huge bay doors, four on each side, were already open. The lights in the hanger bay were off, leaving the target area lit by red strobing lights flashing around the perimeter of the opening itself.

Ryder was fascinated by space and the exploration of it. Many saw it as a vast void of nothing, but he saw it as a wealth of minerals, gases and infinite possibilities. There were black holes, ice comets, suns and planets. That's where their future was, not here in this rock.

The Explorer Corp. consisted solely of volunteers. Not many citizens were brave enough or able to make the sacrifices these men and women made. Explorer ships left from Talus once a month. Their ships were large, but stripped down, having few luxuries. They didn't have weapons, and they carried just enough oxygen for their tour—a tour typically taking them away from Talus for 180 days.

Once they left Talus, they would move ahead of the asteroid's path at 35 per cent SOL for three months, a distance of 800 billion kilometres. At that point, they would stop and wait for the next explorer ship that was one month behind them. Their time was filled with experiments and observation of the space around them, utilizing the powerful, long-range telescope integrated into each Explorer ship. Once the next Explorer Corp. ship arrived, the first ship would begin their return flight. Since Talus was now moving towards them, their return voyage was only a little over 60 days.

The *Constellation* was just now returning after their 183-day tour. Before each expedition, Ryder asked, so he knew there were 28 men and 12 women on the spaceship. As well as sacrificing their time, there was another peculiarity coming with extended time flying at high speed, due to the fact speed and time are closely related. The faster a person moves towards the speed of light, the slower his relative time moves. So a person returning after five months of travel at 35 per cent SOL, is three months younger than if he would have remained in Talus. Since, typically, these space explorers spend their six months in space, then furlough for the next three months before repeating the process, many of the veterans had aged significantly less than their wives, brothers and sisters.

The 200-metre-long ship, painted red from tip to stern, was now directly over the docking bay. The space dock computers were communicating with and controlling the vessel. Even a small error now would cause the ship to crash into the asteroid, something having happened only three times in the last 200 years. The ship slowly lowered until it was lost from sight in the darkness of the hanger bay. Large mechanical arms groaned as they pulled the massive hanger doors closed. The ship had successfully returned.

Ryder turned away from the window. In front of him, tied securely to a chair, was a heavyset man in the maroon uniform of the Explorer Corp. There was a sack over his head, and his head snapped from side to side as the bag sucked in violently every time a panicked breath was inhaled.

Ryder flicked his chin towards another man in the shadows behind the seated man. Linkin stepped forward and pulled the sack from the man's head. Admiral Janus Rok sucked in a deep breath as his eyes tried to adjust to the dark room, with the only light coming from the steady beat of the red, strobing target lights. The admiral was confused by the lights, but they put an eerie glow on a face he recognized. "Ryder? Ryder Gunn!" the admiral screamed. "What are you doing?"

Ryder grinned. He thought, that was a good question. *What am I doing?* Ryder didn't care for family business and politics. In reality, it wasn't that he didn't care, he just cared vastly more about finding a new world for the Korians to live on—and that meant he cared more about the Explorer Corp. His concern was deep enough that, several years ago, he hand-picked a team of 15 Explorer Corp. soldiers. These men and women were selected by he and Linkin, and they were truly loyal to Ryder— and only Ryder. That's why Ryder knew Admiral Rok was involved in some activities that insulted the fibre of the Explorer Corp. and created barriers towards space exploration.

The strobe lit again and Ryder saw the beads of sweat on the Admiral's brow. "I know you've been working for my cousin, Gaylin."

The admiral's eyes were seen as large as saucers when the red strobes lit again. He stuttered, "I—I have no idea what you're talking about."

Linkin's hand appeared from the shadows, handing Ryder an envelope. Ryder spilled the pictures from the envelope into the admiral's lap. "These are pictures of the meetings you have once a month with Gaylin, or at times, with his chief of security, Byron Gunn."

141

Admiral Rok tilted his head down, but between the awkward angle and the strobing light, he was having difficulty. Ryder nodded his chin again. A second later, the admiral's hands, secured behind his back, were cut free. Now, the admiral grasped one picture after the next. His shoulders slumped as the photographs fell to his lap before they finally slipped to the floor.

"The hotel room you meet in has been monitored by my people for a long time," Ryder explained. "I have audio tapes you can listen to if you think to continue your disavowment of the knowledge of your indiscretions."

The admiral took a deep breath, then just shook his head from side to side.

Squatting beside Admiral Rok, Ryder summarized what they both knew. "Admiral, you're in the top echelon of the Explorer Corp. It's an important position whereby, if corrupted, you could have a significant influence on the future of this society. That's why my cousin pays you five thousand tokens a month for you to disrupt the activities of the Corp." Ryder kept his pent-up emotion at bay as he continued. "The best thing that could happen to our people is the discovery of a habitable world, yet it is the worse thing that could happen to Gaylin Gunn. As the CEO of a company making most of its fortune on the sale of gravity patches, what place would he have in a world where gravity patches were not required?"

Ryder stretched himself to his feet. The admiral took the opportunity to blurt out the words, "What do you want from me?"

Ryder, who had taken two steps towards the window, spun on his heel. The strobes outside lit up, highlighting the fire in his eyes. "I want you to do your fucking job!" Ryder saw the admiral shrink back while his hands began to shake on the arms of the chair. The admiral was 60 years old and, apparently, fragile. A *dead* admiral would do him no good at all. In a softer voice, Ryder said, "You will not tell anyone about our meeting this evening. You will continue to have your meetings with my cousin, and you can continue to take his money. Tell him whatever stories you want, but you will no longer disrupt the Corp. Is that understood?"

The admiral nodded his chin in acknowledgment.

"Good," Ryder said. "The exploratory missions are coming close to a three-star solar system. My grandmother, Natalie Gunn, told us on Earth it was called *Alpha Centauri*. Since we didn't have a name for the system, we Korians adopted the same name for the system we've been heading towards for 64 years. Through our long-range telescopes on our explorer ships, we've known for some time there are planets orbiting around each of the stars. If and when we find one that's habitable, you will immediately bring the message to my intermediary in the Corp. communications office. Is that understood?"

"Who?"

Curling his finger towards the back of the room, another figure was coaxed forward into the strobing light. The general looked up and saw a woman in a maroon Explorer Corp. uniform. Her hair was cropped short—almost shaved. For many the look would not work, but for her, it accentuated her attractive features. "Lieutenant Fyr!" the admiral blurted. Zena Fyr's desk was outside his office, three desks away. *Flaming shit*, he thought.

"You will provide Lieutenant Zena with a weekly update, and of course, she will be the first to know if a habitable planet is found."

Seeing his subordinate as part of this mini-coupe, the admiral grew a momentary backbone. "What if I don't?"

Once again, Ryder held out a hand, and Linkin handed him a second envelope. Removing the single picture, Ryder tossed it in the admiral's lap. Admiral Rok twisted his neck as he lifted the photograph into the strobing light. When the older man's jaw dropped, Ryder gave an explanation. "Do you know what a masking party is?"

The admiral's voice was subdued. "Vaguely."

Ryder shrugged. "Your son is more familiar with them." He took slow steps around the admiral as he continued. "There are a few underground organizations throughout the city that plan these events on a regular basis. The attendees are typically those with few inhibitions. They are called masking parties because the attendees are required to wear a mask, but as the night goes on, it's expected the mask would be the *only* thing anyone is wearing."

The admiral was crying. "Why? Why my son?"

Ryder felt his own momentary pang of sympathy. However, if there was one thing most important to all Korians, it was finding a home planet. This was not negotiable. "Get up!" Ryder snapped at the older man.

Admiral Rok jumped to his feet. Ryder pointed a finger at him. "I didn't force your son to go to the masking parties. I didn't ask him to pose for the picture on the bed with—what is it—three naked men and two women. For most people, it wouldn't be a big deal if this was leaked to the media. However, your son is an up-and-coming superstar within the Krl military. He is a *chosen one* who is being groomed for a lofty position. For him, this picture would end all that."

"I understand," the admiral muttered.

Ryder came closer, face to face with the admiral. In a soft voice, he said, "Do you? I think you might leave this room thinking, *who am I more fearful of, Gaylin or Ryder—Ryder the quiet primor?* You should know my thoughts on the topic. I have heard there are many people who talk up a storm, but are much like an empty bag of wind, ultimately, capable of little action. Then again, I hear it's the quiet ones people need to worry about. They are the ones who don't just say—*they do.* Yes, I am the quiet primor, chief negotiator of the peace treaty and also now, apparently, the darling of the people."

Ryder was a good actor. This wasn't who he was, but he had to make the admiral understand he was. "So are you sure you understand?"

Feebly, the older man replied, "Yes."

Ryder pointed to the door of the observation room. "Good. Then, get out."

Chapter 18: The Necklace

Ryder trembled as his face contorted from the large yawn. He only managed three hours of sleep after his meeting with Admiral Janus Rok of the Explorer Corp. It was now midmorning, and the Council of Nine were in deliberations in the council chamber. The purpose was to select five Korians to join Ryder on the negotiating team; however, the vidames and their advisors were finding difficulty coming to a consensus.

At first, several vidames nominated themselves, but this wouldn't work for two reasons. First, there were nine vidames and only five positions available. Second, the Sholite team only had two council members on their committee. In one sense, the Sholites might have difficulty coming to an agreement if they felt they were outranked and outnumbered. At the same time, the vidames would likely feel the Sholite members were beneath them and not worthy of their time.

Many of the advisors were relieved when the vidames didn't pursue their desire to be on the committee, since they knew the vidames were really nothing more than figureheads. Even the primors weren't as qualified as some of the other advisors available.

Quinlan Zaf was the first to be successfully nominated. Some of this was due to sympathy for the Zaf family after the vidame's foot had been blown off. However, Quinlan, second son of the primor, was extremely competent and had an excellent ability to express his views in a convincing manner. Poe Krl and Alora Oro, respectively from the powerful construction family and the family controlling space farming, were both young, up-and-coming women, who were well respected but also aggressive.

The Council of Nine knew they needed a legal advisor on the team, and that meant a member of the Mal family would need to be nominated, even though they weren't one of the nine families on the council. A quick recess was announced and calls were sent out for Vidame Bella Mal and her advisors, to hasten to the council.

The Mal family were not stupid people—after all, they were lawyers, judges and the like. They were waiting nearby since they knew the call would come. When they arrived in the council chamber, they brought Bandy Mal with them. Bandy had been selected over many others to escort the Sholite negotiating committee to Talus, and Vidame Mal saw no reason to withhold her nomination to the committee.

With Bandy Mal acclaimed, the negotiating committee, including Ryder, now stood at five members with one still to be elected. The Jez clan, even though they were a secondary family, pushed for someone from their family. They were adamant, since they initiated the peace talks, they should be there to finish them. The thought process backfired on the Jez family as their nominee was voted down. Although it wasn't said aloud, everyone knew the negative result was because the Jez family acted without the approval of the Council of Nine when they initiated peace discussions with the Sholites.

A few minutes later, Ryder wished the Jez family member had been accepted. The Fyr vidame rose to her feet and said, "I nominate Admiral Milton Fyr to the negotiating committee." To Ryder's chagrin, he was accepted to fill the final position. Milton Fyr was the admiral who had sat behind the vidame the day before. He seemed to disagree with anything and everything to do with peace between the Sholites and Korians. It would be a challenge for Ryder, as leader of the committee, to dissuade the man's negativity.

After a brief lunch, the next two hours were filled with logistical decisions that were mundane to Ryder. He was tired and couldn't help but continue to yawn through the proceedings. He hoped this wasn't misinterpreted as a lack of interest in the peace process. In fact, Ryder fully expected the days ahead to be intense and filled with tension.

Two important decisions came from this discussion. It was decided the entire building would be shut down of all activity except that pertaining to the negotiations. All entrances would be guarded by the police, along with the small contingent of Sholite marines travelling with their committee members. The third and fourth floors would be allocated to the negotiations. This included a large conference room, a dining room and a lounge on the third floor. On the fourth floor, a modest bedroom was assigned to each member of the Korian and Sholite committees. Although the Sholites planned to return to their spaceship every night, the available rooms gave them the option of taking a short respite within the negotiations, or spending the night, if they should so choose. The only exception to the complete lockdown of the building was a kitchen crew and a small housekeeping staff.

The vidames of the Krl and Fyr families asked for one added concession. They requested a small group of advisors from each family of the negotiating committee members be allowed to be nearby.

When Ryder heard this, he rose to his feet and, as leader of the committee, answered. "This is acceptable as long as the advisors are a *small* group, and they aren't disruptive to the process."

On that note, the day's proceedings were called to an end. Knowing he wouldn't soon have a shred of free time, Ryder decided he would spend his last night with Romy and Shareen. After that, he would stay in the bedroom provided during the negotiation period he estimated would last about a week. He would encourage the other Korians to do the same. With that in mind, he was looking forward to seeing Romy and Shareen—one who had always been the most important person in his life, and another who he now put in that same category. He and Shareen had spent much of their time together. They hadn't yet professed their undying love to each other, but they both knew it was there—in the way they touched each other and the way they looked into each other's eyes.

When Ryder arrived home, he was immediately drawn into another version of the *Battle of Fort Nelson*. Romy was playing Josh Harris. This time, Ryder played Nick Anderson and Linkin, to his disgust, had to play Natalie Gunn. That left Fehyr to once again play the evil Sholite leader, Adrian—the one who always had to die a horrible death. Fehyr had done it so many times, with ever-improving theatrical improvisation, he was reaching superior levels of excellence in the final, dramatic death scene.

It was late by the time he arrived at Shareen's apartment. As it often happened when she threw her arms around Ryder and gave him a passionate kiss, all his worries disappeared. She prepared a light snack for the two of them. He grinned as he thought, *she was getting to know him very well*. She was correct in her assumption he hadn't eaten since the early morning hours. She also sensed he was exhausted, and even though she knew they would not see each other for several days, she just held him in her arms as he quickly fell asleep in her bed.

He was awake early the following morning and the first to arrive at the Talus government building. He checked his bedroom on the fourth floor. In the closet were several suits of clothes he had delivered from his home. He showered, then changed into a blue outfit, intentionally avoiding his family colours, hoping it would impress a point on his fellow Korians.

When he came out of his assigned room, he heard another door open at the far end of the hallway. There, he saw I'lish Mann. She smiled as she walked towards him. He thought she was attractive, and he liked her long hair in the braided ponytail.

"Mister Gunn, it seems I should know you well by now, but in reality, we've never met." She held her hand out to him. "Hi there."

He chuckled as he shook her hand. "Hi backatcha."

She lowered an eyebrow as she released his hand. "Backatcha?"

He waved his arm across his chest. "Oh, it's just a saying my grandmother used to say—something from Earth."

"Funny, my grandfather was from Earth, and I don't remember him saying that one."

Ryder instantly liked the woman. With mirth filling his eyes, he replied, "Funny haha, or funny unusual?"

It surprised Ryder, even though I'lish was laughing, when she punched him in the shoulder. "You're too much, especially for a Korian."

Ryder opened his mouth to object as he thought she hit him pretty hard, but she interrupted, "Let's get down to the meeting."

They were the first to arrive in the large conference room. Shortly thereafter, the Sholite delegates arrived followed by the remaining Korians. It seemed unavoidable that the Korians sat on one side of the table, while the Sholites were seated on the other. Introductions were made and the first order of business was to create an agenda. This was done with the first discussion item being the length of time for the truce and the timing of reviews by this committee.

Recommendations were made. Both Poe Krl and Bandy Mal indicated they needed to see their advisors for a few minutes. The family advisors were in the vidame chambers on the first floor. When they returned, 30 minutes had passed. Ryder didn't appreciate the interruption, but at least they did come to a consensus.

The next agenda item dealt with the sovereign space to be allocated around Talus and the Sholite fleet. This was easily agreed to, but when the topic of who could pass through this space and for what purpose, once again Bandy Mal needed to see her advisors. The same was the case for Quinlan Zaf and Alora Oro.

Ryder was frustrated. Holding back his emotions, he just snapped at them, "Make it quick."

They weren't. Forty minutes later, the Sholite delegates were fidgeting. Three of them had moved next-door to the lounge, and I'lish Mann, one leg casually crossed over the other, was whistling some silly song as she stared at Ryder.

When Ryder could take no more, he took the elevator down to the first floor. The first door he came to was the one reserved for the Mal family advisors. He burst it open and was shocked to see 20 advisors packed into the small room. *No wonder this is taking so long,* he thought. Ryder's eyes narrowed as he hissed, "What the fuck is this?"

One of the advisors smiled and offered, "Hello, Mister Gunn…"

Ryder's arm sprung up as he pointed at the man. "Shut up!"

The man did, and Ryder snapped his fingers at Bandy. "Go back upstairs—now." Once she left, Ryder faced the remaining occupants. "You can all go home now. She won't be coming back down."

Another advisor rose to his feet. "But we're here to advise her."

"Not anymore!" Ryder yelled. "She was selected to be on the council. Anyone else want to take her place? Put up your hand now!"

No one did. "I thought so," Ryder scoffed. "Now, all of you get out of the building before I have the guards throw you out."

They didn't need more convincing. They cleared the room and hastily left the building. Hearing the commotion, the doors to the other advisor rooms were open and a few heads were peaking out. Ryder saw these rooms were also overflowing with advisors. He made a roundhouse wave with his arm, abruptly ended with his finger pointing at the exit. "What are you waiting for? Everyone out!"

There were grumblings, but they didn't need to be asked a second time. Ryder stood by with his feet spread and his fists pressed into his waist. He watched them follow the Mal family advisors out. At the end of the line, a woman on crutches, assisted by two men, was hobbling to the exit. When she lifted her head, Ryder eyebrows shot up as he recognized Vidame Marta Zaf. He didn't know what to say, but he felt he needed to have some words for the high-ranking official. Ultimately, as she walked by, all he managed was, "Sorry about the foot."

It was awkward and a good time to head for the elevator. When he brought his gaze up, he saw I'lish leaning against the wall, one leg crossed over the other. As he came closer, he also saw the smirk on her face. He pushed the button that would open the elevator door, hoping she didn't have a comment to add to the smug look on her face. He was disappointed when he heard her say, "I think I'm getting to like you."

He shrugged, thinking, *maybe that's not a bad thing.*

They worked late into the night with productive results. The next four days were the same. There were a multitude of issues to work through, but now, without the interference of advisors, the delegates were able to make their own decisions.

Surprisingly, Admiral Milton Fyr was more than helpful. Early on the second day of negotiations, Ryder saw the admiral highly engaged in the discussions. Rather than the expected dissension and roadblocks from the older man, Ryder saw his tendency was to strongly support the peace process.

After lunch, Ryder couldn't help himself and pulled the admiral aside. "I have to admit, Sir, you're not at all what I expected."

"Ah, you were expecting the admiral you saw in the council meeting a few days ago—the one who is a war monger."

"To be blunt, yes. That is who I expected."

When the admiral smiled, only one corner of his mouth rose, and it did so now. "That's the persona I put on when I have to, especially when I'm in the presence of the vidame. But that's not really who I am. Now that we have an opportunity to stop this infernal war, I will help."

Confused, Ryder asked, "Why the change?"

Admiral Fyr nodded as he understood Ryder's confusion. He reached into his back pocket and retrieved a wallet. Turning to stand beside Ryder, he opened it and began to flip the flaps within. "This is my granddaughter Millie. She is nine. This is Martin. He's 11. This is Vera. She is only two." His eyes met Ryder's as he whispered. "I do it for them."

The negotiations moved along quickly. I'lish kept her crew in check, although the only one who needed to be pulled back often was Black Brighton. He always seemed to find the bad in things, no matter how insignificant, especially when compared to the magnitude of good. More than a few times, I'lish had to take him out of the meeting. When he returned, he was always compliant, at least for a time. As such, progress continued to move forward.

On the afternoon of the fifth day of negotiations, the group had a detailed framework. The Council of Nine was notified that the following morning the details would be presented and simultaneously videocast to the Sholite council. Unfortunately, I'lish was notified the president wouldn't be in attendance. He had fallen into a coma, without an expectation for him to awaken.

Having been cooped up in the building for five days, the delegates were happy to leave its confines. The Korians went to their homes, and the Sholites returned to their spaceship. However, I'lish and Ryder were not so lucky. In the morning, they would be required to present the treaty to the councils. They decided to arrange for a lavish dinner for the two of them, over which, they would decide the details of the presentation.

A four-course dinner was made by the kitchen staff and brought up to the small, third-floor dining room. It was an informal setting where they worked through the details of the presentation. When Ryder finished eating, he leaned back and patted his stomach. "I think that's more food than I've eaten all week."

I'lish agreed with him as she put the last forkful of cake in her mouth. That's when an unfortunate sequence of events occurred. When she tried to put the fork down, the end of it hit her glass of wine, and the silver utensil flipped onto the floor, a metre away. She leaned sideways and down, but when she did, the lapel of her blouse caught the corner of the table, causing the top button of the blouse to pop off. Her necklace slid out from underneath it and hung down. As she quickly retrieved the fork, her other hand was even quicker, covering the light-blue and black pendant hanging from the bail of the necklace.

When she was once again upright, her face was flushed, but not only from her previously inverted position. "Well, that certainly wasn't lady-like," she offered.

Ryder was as white as a ghost. His eyes were wide, but they slowly narrowed to suspicious slits. "Can I see your necklace, please?"

She hesitated as her gaze met his. Finally, she mumbled, "what the fuck," as she pulled the long platinum chain from the confines of her blouse. The pendant at the end was cradled in her palm.

Leaning closer, Ryder inspected it, verifying what he saw when the pendant flashed out from the blouse the first time. The pendant was, in fact, not a pendant at all. It was a wide black ring with tendrils of light-blue scattered through it. It looked like lightning. He sat back and I'lish quickly pushed the necklace back into it's hiding place.

Over the last five days, he had come to like I'lish. He trusted her, but now, something was wrong. "Why do you have a copy of the Gunn family ring around your neck?" Ryder asked in as calm a voice as he could manage.

She sighed. "It's not a copy."

Ryder blurted, "Ha! I am Primor Gunn. I have held my family ring in my hand many times. I know it very well, and I know it sits on my mother's finger!"

"I have the original. Your mother wears an excellent reproduction."

Ryder rolled his eyes. "Why would a Sholite have my mother's ring?"

"I'm not a Sholite."

Ryder paused. He was speechless. Finally, he blurted out, "You're talking in riddles. Have you gone mad?"

"You're not as smart as I thought you were. You should have figured this out by now," I'lish whispered.

"I have no idea what you're talking about," Ryder responded, incredulity in his eyes.

I'lish rose to her feet. The chair behind her toppled over. She threw the napkin from her hand at Ryder. "Your mother is my mother, you idiot! I am your sister, Emmaril."

As his jaw dropped, once again speechless, Ryder saw tears streaming down her cheeks. He tried to say a word to stop her, but there was nothing as she ran from the room, sobbing.

Chapter 19: A New World

Vidame Nola Gunn looked spectacular. She was wearing a dark-green, flowing gown with gold trim. Her matching, gold earrings were long and hung down, almost hitting her shoulders. She, Gaylin and Ryder were sitting in the Gunn family anteroom, adjoined to the main council chamber.

"Well, Cousin, you've really done it this time," Gaylin uttered. "A peace treaty brokered by you. Who would've thought it possible?"

Ryder enjoyed seeing the playful look on Gaylin's face. It brought back the memories of their youth. He shook a finger at his cousin and said, "Remember what our Grandmother Natalie used to say in these situations—don't count your chickens until they've hatched."

Gaylin roared with laughter. "I remember that well. When we first heard her say that phrase, we asked her, 'What is a chicken?' She tried to explain it, and we were almost at a point of understanding when she explained the concept of an egg coming out of the chicken's butt."

Ryder burst out a guffaw as he pointed a finger at Gaylin. "And then she lost us altogether when she explained people on Earth ate those ass-extruded eggs!"

Nola Gunn leaned over and slapped her son on the knee. "Grow up, both of you! Here we are, about to go into the council chamber where you have the most important speech of your life."

Gaylin interrupted, "Yes, you need to behave yourself."

Vidame Gunn's eyes narrowed as she scolded her nephew. "I know you well, Gaylin Gunn. You started this whole thing. It stops now."

Ryder let loose a last chuckle before he calmed himself. He turned to his mother and asked, "Can I see your ring?"

From time to time, Ryder had done this in the past, so Nola Gunn was not surprised, even though the request seemed to come from nowhere. She removed the ring and handed it to her son. Ryder pulled it up close to his eye, turning it under the light. He inspected both the inside and outside surfaces. Satisfied, he handed it back to his mother.

"What's that about?" Vidame Gunn asked.

"It's nothing," Ryder replied.

Nola Gunn was about to continue the line of questioning when the inner door to the anteroom opened. The council moderator poked his head in and said, "We're about to start. Best you find your seats."

The three Gunn family members entered the council chamber and were surprised to see it crowded from one end to the other. Every box was stuffed to overflowing with secondary family members, and the wide, standing room only gallery at the back of the room was packed with additional people. In addition, several media personnel were situated along the side aisle with their video equipment and microphones.

The moderator brought the room to order. From the Gunn family box, Ryder looked towards I'lish in the Sholite box across the room. She was smiling for the audience, and her appearance showed nothing of the emotion from the night before. After inspecting the family ring on his mother's finger, Ryder felt reassured it was the original. It still begged the question, *why did I'lish have a copy?*

A large video screen behind the Council of Nine boxes crackled then roared to life. Pictured there was the Sholite Council anxiously awaiting the reading of the proposed peace treaty. Ryder knew, for the radio waves to reach the Sholite council spaceship on anything close to a real time basis, it must be relatively close to Talus.

The moderator introduced Ryder who began by explaining the process of negotiations undertaken over the past five days and then a summary of the treaty. Next, I'lish rose and joined Ryder at the podium where the speakers could be seen by all interested parties. As I'lish came towards Ryder, she gave him a warm smile, but he questioned if it was just part of her act—one he didn't yet fully understand. However, he was surprised to not see the platinum chain of the necklace around her neck. She had removed it.

I'lish, in detail, explained the first two articles of the treaty, then Ryder continued with the next two. The back-and-forth process continued until, two hours later, all 20 articles had been explained. After that, the next 90 minutes were filled with questions from the nine families and also the Sholite council. Ryder and I'lish could answer most of the questions, but on more than one instance, they referred the question to either the Sholite or Korian legal council.

When there were no further questions, the moderator explained the voting process. The Council of Nine families would move to their private anterooms to discuss their position. This deliberation would be allowed for only thirty minutes, and the Sholite council would have the same time to come to their decision. In this way, the vote would be simultaneous.

Furthermore, I'lish, Black Brighton and Jessica Furlong were members of the Sholite council. As such, a separate room with a radio link was setup, so they could participate in the Sholite council's deliberation.

Surprisingly, considering the magnitude of the decision, it didn't take long for all nine families to return to the council chamber. As directed, each of the vidames passed a piece of folded paper to the moderator. On each would be their vote—yes for peace, or no for a continuing war. The moderator then asked the senior member of the Sholite council to read out their result. Within the chamber, there was total silence. This was the most important moment for both races in the past 200 years.

On the video screen, Admiral Zane Merrick rose to his feet. He had a sour look on his face, making most believe the announcement would be negative. However, he gruffly said, "The Sholite council accepts the terms of the proposed peace treaty."

I'lish Mann had a satisfied smile on her face. Admiral Merrick had, predictably, voted against the treaty, but when all votes were counted, he was alone. I'lish, as vice-president, gave the admiral the honour of announcing the result. She knew it would be considered dishonourable for him to refuse. So when he did make the announcement, in the eyes of the Sholite people, his face would be forever locked to the peace agreement. Consequently, it would be difficult for he and the Sholite military to break the treaty he agreed to with his own words.

Vidame Pym was given the honour of announcing the Korian result. She rose to her feet, turned towards the cameras of the media and said, "The Council of Nine approves the peace treaty."

There was a momentary silence—until the audience's shock wore off. Then, there was a loud roar permeating around the acoustically-perfect council chamber. Everyone was shaking the hands of those around them. I'lish turned to Ryder and shook his hand. She then put one hand on the microphone, muffling it, while she leaned close to his ear. "Congratulations, Brother," she said.

"When time permits, we need to discuss your odd views of *my* family," he responded.

"Of course," I'lish replied. When she pulled away from Ryder, he was troubled by the unexpected honesty in her dark eyes. He felt more uncomfortable when her soothing voice added, "Let's make the time."

They were interrupted by a media reporter who poked a microphone between them. She asked one question after another and demanded a picture of I'lish and Ryder together. Other media reporters crowded around, taking picture after picture. The odd pair, a Sholite vice-president and an unmarried Korian primor, were going to be the talk of the day. Ryder sensed the rumours were already beginning. It made him think of Shareen. He wished she was here.

Beginning with the Council of Nine and the Sholite committee, the occupants of the council chamber were herded out into the large atrium between the chamber and the outer doors of the building. With the expectation of a favourable result, the floor area had been set up with tables, topped with many bottles of the best wine and wonderful appetizers. Every time I'lish or Ryder tried to remove themselves from their pairing, someone or other would pull them back together for some unnecessary political bravado, or to continue the onslaught of pictures.

In the middle of another picture request, I'lish's interlink beeped. Now having a good reason, she excused herself from the group. Sliding her way through the crowd, now numbering at least three hundred people, she made her way to their assigned Sholite anteroom. Ryder frowned when he noticed the reporters disperse once I'lish left. *I guess we know who the darling is*, he thought.

Ten minutes later, when I'lish returned, she grabbed Ryder by the arm. She whispered in his ear, "Come with me. I need to make an announcement."

He could barely hear her above the general din in the room. Leaning in, he whispered back. "Are you crazy? Things are just fine. We don't need any more attention."

She pursed her lips together and pulled hard on his arm. "Come with me," she demanded.

Having no choice, Ryder was dragged along behind her as she strode towards a small stage that had been set up in the event speeches were required. I'lish skipped up the three stairs to the raised platform. She moved in front of the microphone with Ryder standing beside her. He tried to shuffle further away, but she gave him a stern look while pulling him closer. "You're going to want to be part of this," she said.

Ryder rolled his eyes as I'lish tapped the microphone. Many of the people turned towards the podium when they saw the pair move onto it. The remainder now did the same as they heard I'lish say, "Excuse me, I have an important announcement to make."

After a few seconds, the audience was silent. The Council of Nine vidames were surprised since speeches weren't planned. They wondered what the upstart Sholite vice-president had to say.

"I've just received an urgent message from the Sholite council," I'lish explained. "On a historic day for Sholite and Korian alike, I have additional, wonderful news."

There was a murmur through the crowd. They all wondered, *what possibly could make this day better?*

I'lish continued while her voice quivered with emotion. "We have a verified report that one of our explorer ships has been in what you call the Alpha Centauri system, for a month. They have discovered a large, habitable planet."

There was complete, utter silence in the large atrium. Then, a murmur began. Many in the audience thought this must be a cruel Sholite trick.

"A Sholite expeditionary group has been on the surface of the planet for three days. The surface has a 60 per cent coverage of clean, drinkable water. Of the land mass, 25 per cent is temperate and comfortable with a dense coverage of vegetation over much of it."

The audience was silent once again. If this was a Sholite trick, there was no reason for details. Now, as the truth settled in, many of the people began to cry with joy.

"This new world is large enough for all Sholites and Korians. One of your Explorer class ships was in the neighbouring system. We have sent them a communication, and they're on their way to the new planet as I speak to you now. They'll be there within the week, and they can verify what I'm telling you."

The sound of joyous crying was quickly drowned out by clapping, and then this was drowned out by roaring cheers. Ryder grasped I'lish's arm and pulled her to face him. He had a suspicious look on his face, but she alleviated it when he heard the honesty in her voice. "It's true—every word."

The last two days had been more than emotional for Ryder. First, there was the mysterious family ring I'lish carried, and now the news of a new world. No one seemed to any longer be focused on I'lish and Ryder. It was like they were suddenly *old news*. With his fingers still wrapped around her arm, he coaxed I'lish off the stage. He saw his mother and Gaylin not far away and headed directly for them.

Gaylin and Nola Gunn were the mirror image of emotions. Nola's face was filled with joy while Gaylin had a huge frown. The last thing Gaylin needed was a new world where gravity patches weren't required. Their family would be severely weakened, and he would no longer have a lofty position of power.

When Ryder arrived at his mother, the fingers of his free hand grasped around her upper arm. He gave a quick, "excuse me," to his cousin before he pulled her away. He coaxed the two women towards the Gunn family anteroom.

Once inside, Nola Gunn demanded, "Ryder, what's the meaning of this?"

Leaning back against a table edge, I'lish nonchalantly said to Vidame Gunn, "There's no need to act. He knows."

The vidame gazed at the younger woman and took a deep gulp of air. "He knows?"

Through clenched teeth, Ryder said in an exasperated tone, "This is crazy. What exactly is it I'm supposed to know?"

"As I told you last night, I have the family ring because I'm your sister, Emmaril," I'lish answered.

"Please tell her she's wrong," Ryder implored his mother.

"I can't because she's right," his mother offered in a soft voice. "She is your sister."

Narrowing his eyes to slits, Ryder said, "I get it. You two are in some kind of alliance with the goal to drive me mad. My sister died in child birth."

In a louder, berating tone, Nola Gunn said, "Ryder, stop it. I'm not lying to you. This *is* your sister."

Ryder recognized the tone in his mother's voice. It was one she didn't use often, but when she did, it meant she was serious and truthful. His shoulders slumped and he said, "Explain it to me."

"Sit down," Vidame Gunn said. "This will take a few minutes." Ryder slumped into a chair, and I'lish sat next to her mother. Nola Gunn leaned over and gave her a kiss on her cheek. "I have missed you, my dear."

From the words, Ryder realized this was not the first time his mother had met I'lish. Rather than asking questions, he waited for his mother to explain.

"I'lish was born two years before you. We knew well into the pregnancy things weren't normal. The irregularities were known only to the doctor, your father and I. You see, Emmaril, or the woman you know as I'lish, has *red* blood."

Trying to be patient, Ryder crossed his arms. "How can that be if she is your daughter? Korians have blue blood."

"Remember, your grandmother was from Earth, and she had red blood. Our Korian blue blood has been predominant in our lineage, except for

I'lish. In her, her Earthen DNA is dominant."

Ryder nodded, knowing there was more to come.

"Up until a week ago, we've been at war with the Sholites, another race with red blood. Although our people are liberal minded, they wouldn't have been accommodating to a Korian baby with red blood. Emmaril would never have survived in Talus," Nola Gunn said in a nonnegotiable tone.

Although he didn't like the thought, Ryder knew his mother's views were correct. "So you sent her to live with the Sholites?"

"Yes," came the response. "Only days after she was born, I contacted an old friend, Lashkar Mann. Seeing it was important to her father, Lashkar's daughter took Emmaril in, raising her as her own."

Diverting his eyes to I'lish, he asked, "How long have you known?"

"My foster father and mother told me when I was 18. At first, it wasn't difficult, but as I grew older, it ate at me to a point where I had to meet my birth mother." I'lish put her hand on her mother's knee. "When I turned 30, I could wait no longer, so I surprised your mother with a visit."

Ryder was still in shock. "How?" was all he could manage.

"It was at a time when I was a well-established smuggler, having connections both in the Sholite and Korian spheres of influence. I came to learn your mother would visit a Korian Spa Ship every month."

Ryder interrupted, "So you crashed the Spa Ship?"

"The first time she presented herself to me there, it was quite a shock," their mother added.

"What did you do?" Ryder asked.

His mother was quick to respond, "I had a facial and a hot stone massage." She looked at her daughter, and asked, "I think you had the same, or did you have the hot-cold sauna package?"

"I don't recall, mother. I might have had the pedicure as well." came the reply.

"That's not what I meant!" Ryder yelled.

"I'm sorry, son," their mother replied while her hand covered the laughter that followed. "What I did is I continued to go to the Spa Ship every month. I'lish meets me there every third month, and we spend two days together. That's been the schedule for the last 12 years."

Ryder turned back to I'lish. "And what do you have to say for yourself?

You're my sister, yet you let me go through five days of negotiations before you told me."

"I wouldn't have told you at all, except you accidentally saw the ring," I'lish qualified.

"Yes, and how do you get the family ring? I never received anything like that from my mother!"

"I guess she loves me more." I'lish lifted her chin as she said the words.

"But I'm the primor, and the family ring is supposed to come to me. Not the copy, but the real one."

Nola Gunn clapped her hands together with glee. "You don't know how wonderful this is—seeing my children bickering for the first time. I wish I was recording this!"

Both Ryder and I'lish couldn't help but burst out in laughter. When it subsided, Ryder said to his mother. "Can you leave us? I would like to speak to my sister alone."

"Of course," she replied. She rose along with I'lish, and the two Gunn women gave each other a loving hug. When Nola Gunn was about to turn the door knob, she looked back over her shoulder. "Remember, the Gunn family seems to have a penchant for doing the right thing, even though it might not be the most popular. Rowan Gunn did the right thing at Fort Nelson, and he gave his life for it. Natalie Gunn took Rowan's life and thought she was doing the right thing for the people of Earth. I did the right thing for Emmaril, but also for our family." She let out a sigh that had been held back for a long time. "Both of you are political leaders now. I suspect both of you might have to make sacrifices in the future to keep this peace. I have confidence in both of you." The click of the door knob broke the momentary silence, and then she left the room.

Ryder rose to his feet and stood across from his sister. As he looked at her, he could see the resemblance to his mother. "You have her nose," he said.

"Oh, great. Now you notice my worst feature."

When Ryder stopped chuckling, he said to her, "She's right. This peace is fragile. We might have to make sacrifices to keep it. Are you prepared to do whatever it takes?"

Without hesitation, I'lish nodded her chin up and down. "I will. I am Korian born, but Sholite at heart. I have friends and family in both places."

Ryder stepped forward. "Here, you also have a brother." He opened his arms and wrapped them around her. He whispered in her ear, "One that loves you."

That was all it took for a stream of tears to flow from I'lish. She embraced her brother. Through the sobs, she said, "Some brother—this is the second time—in two days—you've made me cry."

Chapter 20: A Vaccine

The week following the Council of Nine meeting was like one not having been seen for many years. Although the day after the momentous meeting was declared a holiday, the festivities lasted the better part of a week. For some Korians it was the thought of peace with the Sholites; for others, it was the news that a new planetary home would soon potentially be within reach. In either case, based on the many people with varied levels of intoxication on the streets of Talus, it was not clear who was happier, the citizens drinking the alcohol, or the vendors who were filling their pockets with tokens from the sale thereof.

The morning after the Council of Nine meeting, as Ryder was leaving the Talus government building, I'lish hurried after him. Catching him on the sidewalk just outside the main doors, she pulled her brother aside. She said she had to leave quickly. In confidence, she told him she had received a message from the Sholite Council. The president's health was failing, and the only thing keeping him alive was a life support machine. Clinically, he was dead, but the Sholite doctors were waiting for I'lish to return before they removed him from it.

As the Sholite ship, Constellation, left, Ryder wondered when he would see his sister again. Circumstances had provided an unusual twist to his life. He could not reveal the real identity of I'lish Mann, who was about to become the interim president of the Sholite people—no more than his mother could have revealed her identity at any time over the last 42 years.

Even though there were many Korians who were focused on the festive atmosphere in Talus, there was a group hard at work preparing for the new world the Sholites had found. The Council of Nine and the Sholite presiding council, had agreed on a larger joint expedition to Alpha Centauri. For three days, workers in the Explorer Corp and the Fyr-led military service, worked day and night to prepare a fleet of Korian ships. Five explorer ships were being retrofitted, while an extensive team of scientists, engineers and construction experts, were selected to be the first colonists. The large telescopes of the explorer-class ships were removed, with the exception of that on one ship. In their place, the ships were filled with both scientific and construction equipment. The construction equipment and the associated experts, were of paramount importance towards building the initial colony from which the many tests and experiments would be conducted.

Notwithstanding the recent peace treaty with the Sholites, two Tiger-class destroyers would be sent with the Korian fleet. The Krl admirals reminded the council vidames they were sending the expedition to an unknown galaxy. There could be inhabited planets, and if so, they might not see the colonizing ships as friendly. The vidames agreed as did the Sholite council, who were also sending five explorer ships and two of their own destroyers to rendezvous with the Korian expeditionary fleet. Four days after the council meeting, the expedition group was ready. The seven Korian ships left and met the Sholite fleet at the predetermined coordinates. From there, it would take four months for the joint fleet to reach Alpha Centauri.

With I'lish and the Sholite delegates now back with the Sholite fleet and the joint fleet on its way, Ryder had much of his time once again under his own control. He took a few days away from both the business and the politics that went with it. He enjoyed spending more time with both Romy and Shareen. As much as he was smitten with his girlfriend, Romy seemed to share the sentiment. He loved spending time with her.

However, whereas Ryder could adjust his own routine as he saw fit, Shareen had a regular work schedule she had to maintain at the nuclear plant. In addition, Ryder hadn't forgotten about the message in the stuffed dog received at the Galactic Fair. With some time to himself, Ryder decided it was time to find Nicola Edy, the person who supposedly knew the location of the vaccine for the gravity bends.

With so much for Ryder to do in the previous two weeks, he had given the task of narrowing the list of Nicola Edy's down, to Linkin. His bodyguard initially found 15 Nicola Edy's in the main Talus directory. Digging deeper into the identity of the women on the list, there were ten he pushed to the back of the list immediately. That left five candidates with the highest potential of being the Nicola Edy who might have an association with a vaccine. With actual surveillance of the first three on the list, he dismissed them as well, leaving only two persons of interest.

It was the morning of the fifth day since the Council of Nine meeting when Linkin rose from the breakfast table in Ryder's apartment. Having enjoyed some sweet biscuits, he wiped the corners of his mouth, and rose to his feet.

Ryder asked, "Where are you off to?"

A sudden worry crossed Linkin's mind, evident from the three furrows appearing on his brow. "I thought you were staying home today, so I was going to investigate the last two names on the list."

"I'm going with you," Ryder offered. He gave his goodbyes to Fehyr and Romy, and a few moments later, he and Linkin were out the door.

Outside, or at least what the inhabitants of the chambers called outside,

Linkin led the way to the public railcar line. The overflow of celebrating Korians had subsided, and Talus had returned to normal, daily life. Ryder took a deep breath of the recirculated air and wondered how different it would be on the new planet.

Since Talus was travelling at six per cent SOL, they wouldn't arrive at Alpha Centauri for 16 months. However, they should receive confirmation back from the expeditionary force within seven months, and if positive, it's likely additional fleets of ships would move to the settlement planet in advance of Talus.

It was now the tenth hour of the Talus day. Ryder lifted his wrist interlink up and pressed a virtual button. He saw Shareen's code come up on the surface of his skin. He heard the audible beep six times before Shareen's answering message was heard. Ryder left a short message as Linkin noticed the look of concern on Ryder's face.

"Is there a problem, Sir," Linkin asked.

"I'm sure it's nothing, but it's a bit odd. Shareen goes into work early and usually has a break at the top of the tenth hour. It's become a thing between the two of us, for me to call her at that time. This is the first call she's ever missed."

"She has an important job at the nuclear plant," Linkin offered. "I'm surprised this is only the first time your call has been deferred."

Once they were on the Etrain from chamber C21 to chamber C31, Linkin explained the most likely Nicola Edy was a chemist working for the Fex family, and she knew Wilam Fex's father. Ryder agreed with Linkin's determination this had a high probability of being the Nicola Edy who might well have information about the location of the last sample of vaccine.

There was a large nitrogen processing plant in C31. The railcar stop was conveniently located right under the office area, so they only needed to proceed up two flights of steps to arrive at the large reception area. They asked the young man behind the reception desk if they could speak with Nicola Edy.

"Do you have an appointment with her?" the man asked as he scanned through a visitors list on his computer screen. His head began to motion slightly from side to side, and it was replaced by an all out shake as he determined, "I don't see any appointments here for Nicola Edy."

Ryder didn't like to pull rank, but he did this time. Pulling out a thin wallet and flipping it open in front of the receptionist, he said, "I'm Primor Ryder Gunn. I wouldn't insist if this wasn't of extreme importance."

The young man's eyes lit up. "Of course! Now I recognize you. You're the quiet primor who has saved us from the war and will lead us to the new world."

Is that really what the people of Talus thought of him? Ryder blushed as he ignored the idolizing look coming over the receptionist's face.

The young man offered, "You'll have to excuse me this morning. First with the commotion in C25 and now an unexpected visit from a Council of Nine primor."

"What's going on in C25?"

The young receptionist rolled his eyes. "Who really knows? There's an evacuation order for the chamber, but it's likely just another drill." His voice trailed off as he printed off two passes. "One drill after another—a course correction—take cover—now an evacuation. It's so predictable"

Linkin and Ryder looked at each other, but only for a moment before they returned their inquisitive gaze to the receptionist. The young man pointed to a door along the wall of the atrium they were in and said, "I'll call Nicola right away. If you wait in that room, she'll be there in a few moments." The young man already had his wrist interlink close to his lips as he waited for a response from Nicola Edy.

It was five minutes later when the door to the small conference room opened, and an older woman with pulled-back white hair and sharp, dark eyes, entered and joined the two men at the table they sat behind. "How can I help you Mister—" She looked from Linkin to Ryder until Ryder lifted his hand. "—Gunn," she said as she focused on Ryder.

Ryder leaned forward on his forearms, and with a slight tilt of his head, answered, "We're assisting the Talus police on an investigation."

Nicola's thin lips turned down in a frown. "Talus police. Oh, my."

"Do you know a Wilam Fex?"

She slowly shook her head from side to side. "Can't say I do."

"How about Calvin Fex? He was Wilam's father."

Her face scrunched up as she thought for a moment. "I knew a Calvin Fex many years ago, but only from a distance. For a time, we worked in the same building but different departments. I had no idea he had a son. I just didn't know him that well."

Ryder continued to ask questions. He asked about any association she might have with Gunn Pharmaceutical, or any other work she might have done outside her present scope of nitrogen refinement. The woman seemed honestly perplexed, and after twenty minutes, Ryder indicated he was satisfied with her answers.

As they left the building, Linkin said, "It's not the right Nicola Edy. I would've been able to tell if she was lying."

Ryder chuckled. "And she was at least 70 years old. Don't get me wrong, she seemed adept for her age, but I'm not sure it's the age to get involved in bootlegging medication."

Linkin led them back to the railcar line where they boarded a Ftrain headed to C11 at the very front of the asteroid. "This is the last Nicola Edy on your short list," Ryder reminded Linkin. "If this isn't the right one, you'll have to start all over."

"This Nicola Edy has good possibilities, but then, I thought the same of the woman we just met."

"Tell me about this next woman," Ryder urged.

"She's 29 years old, and she's a veterinarian…"

"A veterinarian!" Ryder blurted. "What could a veterinarian possibly have to do with a vaccine?"

Linkin had worked for Ryder for a long time, so he could afford to give his boss a scathing look. "Relax. She used to be a doctor, having finished that degree first, but she seems to like animals better than people, so she changed her specialty. Also, she was married to a woman by the name of Melinda Gunn who is a chemist at Gunn Pharmaceutical."

"Well, your evaluation actually makes sense."

With his chin elevated, Linkin replied in a matter-of-fact tone, "Yes—it does."

When they arrived at the veterinary clinic, they were met by a woman wearing a white lab coat. She told the two men Nicola was off for the day, and she needlessly added a comment about people not caring enough about their animals now that they were distracted by a peace treaty and a possible world for them to live on. They both just smiled in response, knowing even a single word would likely set the woman off in a long drawn-out lecture on the importance of pets in Talus. Instead, they quietly backed out the same way they came in, avoiding the potential barrage.

"That was close," Ryder said as he rubbed his chin. He checked his interlink and frowned, seeing he hadn't received a message from Shareen. "Do you have the veterinarian's home address?"

"It's within walking distance," Linkin muttered as he led the way down the laneway they were on. Twenty minutes later, Linkin stood in front of a large home in a posh neighbourhood. He looked from the ground level surrounded by colourful flowerbeds, to the third floor where a large balcony teetered over the sidewalk. "Wow! They must pay veterinarians a lot of money—surely more than I make."

Standing beside Linkin, the comment was not lost on Ryder, nor the fact, although it sounded hypothetical, that it was purposely intended for him. He gave Linkin a backhanded flick in the gut and said, "Let's go."

At the top of the three wide stairs was an impressive veranda. Ryder pulled the tassel hanging from a chain by the door. They could hear the corresponding bell chime inside the house. A moment later, the heavy door was pulled open.

When he saw the familiar face topped with platinum-blonde hair, the inner edges of Ryder's brows tilted down in confusion? "Dana—Dana Bli? What are you doing here? Are you also Nicola Edy's doctor?"

The woman who opened the door froze. When she saw Ryder, her face lightened until its hue matched the colour of the white flour coating the spoon she held. Her voice came feebly. "Ryder—what are you doing here?"

Ryder tried his best to smile through the confusion clouding his mind. "It's odd that you answered my question with a question."

Colour returned to the woman's face—the woman who was Ryder's doctor and had been tending to him for the past three years. She let out a sigh before saying, "It's best you two come in. There's some explaining I need to do."

Dana Bli led them down a wide hallway to a large communal room consisting of a comfortable living area, a large dining table and a well-appointed kitchen. Dana scooted behind the large kitchen island, turned off the oven and placed the spoon down beside the bowl of flour. She pulled off the apron, and as she placed it on the counter, pointed to the dining table. "Why don't you two sit down?" Dana moved to a cabinet in the living area and poured two glasses of fruit liquor, placing one in front of Linkin and the other in front of Ryder.

"I don't need a drink," Ryder offered.

With a long blink and a slight tilt of her head, Dana said, "You might when you hear what I have to tell you."

Swivelling his head from side to side, Ryder asked, "Where's Nicola? We're here to see her."

Leaning back against the island, the woman confessed, "I *am* Nicola

167

Edy."

Ryder let out a jolt of nervous laughter, but couldn't think of a response. He glanced at Linkin, hoping he didn't look as dumbfounded as his bodyguard.

"I am indeed Nicola Edy, even though you have known me as Dana Bli."

"Are you telling me I have been treated for the last three years by a—veterinarian?"

"It's not that bad," Nicola responded. "I do have a medical degree…"

Ryder's voice took on a deeper tone as his words came through clenched teeth. "This has my cousin, Gaylin Gunn, written all over it. Am I correct?"

"Yes, he hired me to act as your doctor."

Ryder gave his head a shake, trying to clear his mind of the confusion. "I need some answers Dana—or Nicola—or whoever you really are. Start by telling me about the vaccine."

Once again, Nicola's face went white. Her eyes turned moist and her response came in quivering words. "Ryder, I can tell you your cousin paid me well to look after you. And I have done so. You're in perfect health, but, as for the vaccine, I cannot tell you more other than the answer to that question must come from Gaylin himself."

Seeing Nicola purse her lips together, indicating nothing more would pass them, Ryder reached down and tilted the glass to his lips, letting the fruit liquor slide down his throat. As he passed by Nicola on the way back to the hallway, he whispered, "You were right about the drink."

Back out on the sidewalk, Linkin asked Ryder, "Where are we going?

With a grim look on his face, Ryder replied, "We're going to the Gunn Spire to see my cousin, Gaylin."

There were no words spoken between the two men as they took the public railcar to the Gunn Spire. Once they left the elevator on the Spire's executive level, Ryder told Linkin to wait outside the office. As Ryder passed Gaylin's assistant, Tala, she smiled and was about to stop him. He raised a finger and whispered, "Don't bother." He burst open the door of Gaylin's office and found his cousin gazing out the large picture window filling the far wall.

Gaylin jumped and flattened his back against the glass. When he saw it was Ryder, his body relaxed. But as he saw the stern look on Ryder's face, Gaylin's sphincter tightened. As Ryder walked towards him, Gaylin managed, "Hello, Cousin. Is everything okay?"

Ryder took the last few strides across the vast office and was now face to face with Gaylin. "No, everything is not okay—Cousin." The last word was drawn out in a sarcastic drawl. "I know about Dana Bli and Nicola Edy and Wilam Fex and Calvin Fex."

Gaylin shrank back against the glass and gulped. "You've been busy."

Gaylin flinched as Ryder brought his finger up quickly, only a centimeter from the tip of Gaylin's nose. "I know about the vaccine. Tell me about the location of the last sample and what Nicola Edy has to do with all this."

The shock of Ryder's abrupt entrance had worn off. Gaylin raised both hands and gently pressed back on Ryder's chest until there was a metre between them. The look on his cousin's face was now one Ryder recognized as the smug, corporate Gaylin he despised. Gaylin said, "Fine. It's about time you knew. There is a vaccine for the gravity bends. A one-time dose would provide relief for a person's lifetime."

"Why are you hiding it?"

Standing taller than Ryder, Gaylin looked down at his cousin, and it was now his turn to press a finger in front of Ryder's face. "Are you kidding? Our family is the most powerful one in Talus, and most of that is because of the gravity patches we provide. If we replaced them with a vaccine, our family status would plummet from Talus society, both socially and financially."

A low growl came from behind Ryder's pursed lips. As much as he didn't like Gaylin's version of logic, he was correct. But Ryder was still confused. "Where is this last sample of the vaccine hidden?"

Gaylin's eyes took on a playful look as he held back his impending laughter. "Why, It's inside you." Then the laughter finally let loose.

Ryder's face turned red and the only word he managed was, "How?"

"I hired Nicola to be your doctor. Three years ago, when she was administering your annual inoculation, she added the vaccine."

Ryder knew his cousin had a cruel, self-serving tendency, but he didn't know how low he could go—until now. In a low voice, holding back his building anger, he asked, "How do you know it works?"

Gaylin shrugged. "How do you feel?"

"Fine, but I take the gravity patches every week."

"No, the patches Nicola Edy has been giving you for the last three years are just placebos." Gaylin let out another cackle.

Ryder could hold back his anger no longer. He grasped the front of Gaylin's shirt in a tight fist. His other hand, also balled into a fist, was pulled back and about to be administered to his cousin's chin, when the room shook violently. Both men were thrown to the ground. Ryder fell backwards while Gaylin rolled and thumped against his desk, leaving a cut on the corner of his forehead. When they both rose to their feet, they peered out the picture window and were speechless. The remnants of the running bridge were on the road below, and the building down the street had collapsed.

As Ryder gazed further into the distance, there were other collapsed buildings and signs of smoke in the distance. Ryder turned to Gaylin, and even though he didn't think his cousin would understand, he said, "The evacuation order—It's real!"

Chapter 21: Sleeper

The alarm in Shareen's bedroom activated as it did every workday morning. As she heard the *beep*, she stretched her arms up over her head. She made the effort to open her eyes, but they fluttered before closing once again. The voice from her alarm said, "Good Morning. It's the top of the eighth hour, day four in the week and the fifth day of the tenth month of the Talus calendar."

As her mind processed the information, her arms relaxed down onto the bed, and her eyes fully opened. They didn't blink, nor did her body move for a good half minute, as if her mind was contemplating the day ahead. Once she finally rolled onto her feet, she walked directly to the bathroom. This was odd, since Shareen was a creature of habit, and skipping a light breakfast was something she just didn't do.

She pulled one arm out of the night shirt, then the other, letting it fall to the bathroom floor. Her shower followed the typical sequence, first cleaning her teeth, then her hair and finally the rest of her body. However, when she came out of the steaming shower enclosure, she only towel dried her hair, whereas normally she would have used the hair dryer to straighten the natural curls.

The night before, she put out a dress to wear, but she bypassed it now, instead moving to her cupboard where she pulled out a casual, royal-blue pant suit. She also claimed a white blouse to wear under the zip-up jacket. After dressing, she pulled on her athletic shoes, looking every bit as if she was going to the gym instead of work at the nuclear plant. It was odd.

As she did every morning, she walked the eight blocks from her apartment to the nuclear plant, but this morning, with three blocks left to traverse to her destination, she made a detour. Entering the train station, she walked down one flight of stairs to a locker room. For the last 20 minutes since she left her apartment, she paid no attention to the many morning commuters. Her head didn't shift and her eyes remained locked on a point somewhere in the distance. Between two rows of lockers, she turned and entered a four-digit code into the locking mechanism. The door popped open and she reached in, pulling out an air pistol. After checking the charge level, she pressed it inside her jacket and pulled the zipper halfway closed.

Soren Pym sat on the padded seat cushion of the metal-frame chair in the café on the second floor of the building opposite the Rossnol nuclear power plant. He was seated by the railing of a wide balcony where his position gave him a clear view of the plant and the intersection almost directly below him. He was waiting.

Soren had been following Shareen Zaf in Talus for almost a month. It was awkward, since much of that time she spent with Ryder Gunn. He made Soren's task more difficult; it was distracting from the task he had to complete—the one he had waffled back and forth on since his arrival. Shareen needed to die today. Many lives depended on the completion of his task, yet even more lives could possibly be lost if he was successful. There had been more than a few opportunities for him to kill the woman, yet each time he hesitated.

The waitress came to his table with two narrow jugs of milk. "Would you like a refill? Hot or cold?"

"Hot please," Soren replied.

After refilling his mug, she placed one jug on the table and fumbled in the pocket of her apron. "I assume you want another cocoa pod?"

Soren smiled from under his blue eyes and swept-back, brown hair as he nodded.

She placed the wrapped pod on the table and continued to the next table. Soren placed a spoonful of sugar in the mug, then ripped open the pod's paper covering before dropping it into the hot milk. As he performed the task, he darted his gaze back and forth from the mug to the street below. His hand froze as he saw a woman in a blue pant suit cross the intersection towards the power plant's entrance.

As Shareen crossed the road, Soren took two items from his pocket. One was a magnifying scope. His position at this exact table at this exact café was not random. He lifted the scope to his eye. Turning the small wheel on the side, the main security gate to the complex came into view. More importantly, he could see down the hallway behind it. It was the hallway eventually leading to the main control room.

Soren pulled the second item from his pocket. It was a small, black detonator, and integrated into it was a toggle switch and a small pushbutton. He picked up the mug and took a deep drink of the hot cocoa milk. As long as he remembered, it was the cocoa flavour he preferred. With his thumb, he flicked the toggle switch to the active position. The pushbutton turned green. The detonator was live.

Three nights earlier, Soren had placed a half-kilogram package of plastic explosives against the exterior side wall of the complex, well hidden behind two large bushes. The concrete wall running along the exterior of the long hallway he expected Shareen to walk down, was thick. If Soren pressed the green button as she walked by the deadly package, the explosion would blast through the wall. She would be killed. It was an excellent plan.

Glancing down, Soren saw Shareen was across the road and walking down the sidewalk used to reach the main building. She still had another 30 metres to walk, so he took another deep drink of the flavoured milk before lifting the scope to his eye.

Shareen kept a constant pace as she reached the main gate, where the guard she saw every morning had a wide smile on his face. "Hello Miss Shareen," he said.

There was no response—just the blank look on her face. He shuffled his feet, turning as she walked by him, her eyes still fixed on that point somewhere in the distance. Now looking at her back, he tilted his cap back on his head, scratching under the bill. He thought, *why's her hair wet?"*

Soren's hand shook as his thumb was close to the pushbutton trigger. Through the scope, he saw Shareen pass through the gate and walk directly towards the hallway leading to the control room. The last three mornings, he had sat here in the same position with his thumb on the trigger, but he hadn't been able to complete the kill. This was his last opportunity. *He had to do it!* His thumb came a hair closer as Shareen was moving down the hallway. She was almost there. He could hear his teeth grinding as sweat beaded on his forehead. *What should he do?*

He saw her a metre from the sweet spot directly across from the plastic explosive. His thumb came closer, but he let out an audible growl as his thumb pulled back. He pushed the toggle switch down, deactivating the device. He sighed as if a great weight was lifted off his shoulders, then mumbled, "Fuck—that's that." He relaxed back in the chair and took another drink of the cocoa milk. He had two hours.

Shareen was walking down the long hallway towards the control room. Halfway down, she veered right and continued to the last security guard station directly in front of the control room. Duggan rose from his desk as he saw her approaching. He thought her casual appearance unusual as was the badge not hanging in front of the jacket. "Ma'am. I'll need to see your security badge."

Shareen kept walking as she reached inside the jacket, pulling out the air pistol. As it slid by her face she whispered, "Full power." Once her arm extended, she pulled the trigger. The bubble of compressed air shot forward, hitting Duggan just off center in his forehead. She kept the gun in her hand as she walked through the metal detector. A red light above the detector flashed, and a local buzzer began to honk. It didn't matter to Duggan. He was dead.

Security was set up such that when the detector recognized a threat, the guard had 30 seconds to clear the alarm. If it wasn't cleared, the main doors to the control room would lock internally, making it inaccessible from the hallway. Shareen knew this, so she continued to the doors without delay and pressed her wrist interlink to the sensor. The door cracked open and Shareen slid in.

At any time, there were always three engineers in the control room. Shareen walked down the ends of the rows of control cabinets until she saw one of the men, in his white lab coat, at the far end of the row she was looking down. He was looking at a series of gauges on a control cabinet and entering values into a tablet. He heard the footsteps behind him and turned. "Miss Shareen, you know you're not allowed in here without a hardhat..."

The compressed air bubble hit him in the chest. At this close range, it ripped right through him, leaving a clean hole through his heart. Shareen heard a scream from her left. A woman had both hands in front of her mouth. Calmly, Shareen lifted the pistol and made a good long-range shot, dropping the engineer to the floor. As she walked by her, she was moaning until Shareen tilted the gun and put another shot through the back of her head.

Hearing the sound of shuffling feet to her left, she saw the last engineer fumbling with his interlink at the inside door sensor. The light above the door flashed green and the door slid open. As the man rushed through, Shareen fired another shot. However, as he bolted through the opening towards the safety of the hallway, the bubble hit his upper arm just before the door closed behind him.

Putting the pistol back inside her jacket, she coolly walked to the door. Beside it was a glass case. Above it was a small hammer which she used to break the glass, allowing her to press the red palm button within. The light above the door immediately flashed red, and five seconds later, two 30-centimetre-thick, metal doors began to slide inwards from within the metre-thick concrete containment wall. Once they closed, she could hear the internal locks engaging. Far behind her, from the other side of the control room, she could hear the emergency doors close at the secondary entrance. The red palm button was to be used in the event of an outside terrorist or

Sholite attack. In such an event, the security door could only be opened with a password—one known only to Shareen, the facility director and the Zaf family vidame.

Shareen moved over to a long computer table with three computer screens on it. This was the room's primary computer station. Logging in, Shareen's fingers skipped over the keys as she transferred several files from the server in her office. Her wrist interlink beeped. She lifted her arm and saw the name, *Ryder Gunn*. Above the incoming name, she saw the time. It was the top of the tenth hour. Glossy-eyed, she ignored the call, returning her fingers to the keyboard and the task at hand which, it appeared, she didn't have the will to stop.

Alarms had been sounding throughout the facility. Zane Zaf, the director of the facility, and Kern Zaf, the head of security, arrived at the buzzing metal detector at the same time, along with ten security guards just behind them. They saw Duggan's body in a pool of blood and the wounded engineer leaning back against the wall. Blood was oozing through his fingers clutching his arm.

"What the fuck is going on?" the director said to the wounded engineer.

The engineer's eyes showed the pain he felt as he turned them to the director. "It's Shareen Zaf. She's gone crazy! She killed the other two engineers and I barely escaped!"

"Shareen!" Chief Kern exclaimed.

"Chief, get your men ready at the door. I'm going to open it with my override."

The chief waved his hand over his head, motioning his guards forward. "Pull your guns and shoot to kill if you have to!" he ordered.

There was a small office just off the side of the hallway, and the director entered it, moving to one of the two computer terminals within. He logged in and was at the screen used to unlock the security door. He said to Chief Kern who waited by the door, "Make sure your men are ready." As he input his password, on the last letter, he yelled, "Now!"

The security chief, who was intently watching the control room door, turned to the director. "Nothing!"

Director Zaf thought he made a mistake and entered his password again. Once again, the message, *Access Denied*, came across the screen. There was panic in his eyes as he blurted, "She's changed the password!"

"What now?" As the chief asked his question, the tone of the alarm changed to a faster paced rhythm and the colour of the alarm lights through the facility changed to a strobing cadence. "And what does that mean?" the chief asked as he looked from side to side at the lights above him.

"No—no," Director Zane whispered. His fingers flashed over the keys and a window filled the corner of the screen. Within it, in red was, *98 per cent.* The director tilted up to his full height and turned to the security chief. He slapped his palm into his forehead as he said, "She's turned off the electromagnetic containment field."

The chief gulped, "How long do we have?"

"Even with the field turned off, it takes time for it to dissipate. In an hour, when the field strength gets to 15 per cent, the resulting explosion will incinerate everything within a five-kilometre radius from the core. The radiation will get everyone else."

"Can't you restart the containment field from here?"

"Usually, yes, but she's deleted the program and also the backup."

"She's good," the chief grimly said.

"Too good." The director lifted his wrist interlink to his lips and made a call. Three minutes later, they heard two sets of footsteps running towards the office. Two men burst into the office, and the director said to the chief, "I think you know, Ben and Trent. They're the best software guys we have." He didn't wait for a response as he looked at the two young men. After giving them an explanation of their situation, he said, "I don't care who, but one of you needs to hack into the door lock and open it. The other needs to rewrite the program so we can dump the core, if need be."

Ben sat in a chair in front of one terminal, while Trent took the terminal on the other side of the room. As their fingers sped over the keys, Director Zane said to the chief. "Make sure the facility is evacuated. Also call the Talus police, and apprise them of the situation. The chamber needs to be evacuated as well. Tell them they have 45 minutes; then they need to close the isolation doors."

"They can't get all that done in 45 minutes!"

"I know," the director bleakly replied. "But that's all the time they have."

The chief left the room to make the arrangements. Director Zane knew it was highly unlikely he would survive the day. Looking at the computer screen, in the corner, he saw the containment field was at 87 per cent.

Soren looked down at the crowded street below the café, then his interlink, checking the time. He had 40 minutes left. It was time for him to leave. He walked out onto the sidewalk where there was shear panic. The alarms were blaring from the power plant, joining the evacuation alarm echoing throughout the chamber. People were running in one direction, others moving opposite to them, while still others just stood frozen in shock. He felt a bump at his shoulder, where a woman bounced off him. It was the waitress from the café, with her apron still tied around her waist. She screamed, "What are you doing just standing there? We need to evacuate!"

Soren grasped her arm and pulled her close. "You won't make it in time. They're going to close the doors. Go to the take cover pods at the top of the spires."

"But it's an evacuation alarm—not take-cover!"

"I know. Please, trust me. Two of the take-cover pods will survive." He released her arm.

She backed away from Soren; her eyes were calmer. For some reason, she trusted him. She ran towards the spire and the take cover pod at the top of it."

Soren sighed, thinking, *maybe she will be one of the lucky ones*. He walked through the chaos as panicked people continued to bump into him until he turned down a busy lane, where he vanished into the crowd.

Inside the control room, Shareen lifted her fingers from the keys. She had completed her tasks just as the program in her head willed her to do. There was nothing more for her to do but wait. She was the last sleeper agent, and now that her work was done, it made sense the program in her head told her to do exactly that—go to sleep. She leaned back in the chair and closed her eyes for the last time.

Sitting at his computer screen, Ben pulled at his curly hair. He spun the chair around and yelled, "Director! This is impossible. Not only has she initiated the terrorist protocol from inside the control room, but somehow she has also initiated the reactor meltdown lockdown."

"That's impossible!" the director replied. "Both security programs can't be initiated at the same time."

"She must have prepared this in advance. It'll take weeks to get through this," came the grim reply.

With his hands pressed into his hips, Director Zane said, "Well, you have 32 minutes left, so get to it." He walked over to Trent who was working on rewriting the program so they could dump the core before it exploded. He glanced at the corner of the screen. The countdown was at 54 per cent. He whispered to Trent, "I think this is going to be up to you."

Trent kept typing. "You know if I am successful and we eject the core, we're still likely to die."

Director Zaf gave a reassuring shake to Trent's shoulder. "It's a shame. You're young. Since I'm older, let me tell you, at least going out as a hero is a good way to go."

"Yes, Sir," Trent managed.

Both young men continued to work feverishly. Director Zaf paced back and forth between them. Each time he turned to Trent, he checked the countdown—40—30—20. "We're almost out of time," the director urged.

"I'm almost there!" Trent replied.

The countdown was at 18 per cent. Having just slammed his finger into the *enter* key, Trent pushed his chair away from the desk and yelled, "It's done. Core ejection process is initiated."

The three men looked at each other. Finally, the director sat down and said to the two of them, "Great job guys."

There was a loud roar from the direction of the control room. It became overwhelming, and the floor shook violently. Then, the roaring sound dissipated and Trent said, "I think we might make it."

If the ejection would have been initiated 30 seconds earlier, they would have. However, unfortunately, the result of the ejection was worse than if the core would have exploded in the chamber. If it had, everyone in the chamber would have died, but it is likely the damage would have been contained to only one chamber. Instead, the containment field hit 15 per cent as the core was rushing through the asteroid's crust, still 100 metres from space. Here, the explosion shot back up the ejection tunnel, but also pressed outwards on its walls. Near the surface, where it was weakest, a huge crack was created. It was five kilometres long in each direction around the circumference of Talus—and growing.

Chapter 22: Escape

Ryder and Gaylin looked down from Gaylin's office in the Gunn Spire. Below them was chaos. Forty floors below, they saw people streaming out into the street—or at least what was left of it. As quickly as they exited the buildings, once in the open space, confused people stopped and looked to each other, not knowing what to do next. There were also bodies, some mixed in with the rubble of the collapsed running bridge, and some lying on the open roadway where they had fallen to their death.

Ryder turned from the window and pressed the virtual button on his interlink. There was sweat on his brow as he waited for Shareen to answer. He angrily disconnected the call when he heard the beginning of her voice message. Next, he called Fehyr, and when he heard the older man's voice, he exhaled with relief. "Is Romy okay?" Ryder asked.

"Yes, we are both fine."

"You know the drill. Get to the evacuation ship at the Gunn space dock. Do it quickly and I will meet you there."

"Yes, Sir."

Ryder disconnected the call. Talus was a city of continuous drills, but this was no drill. The senior Gunn family members had practiced for this eventuality, and even without knowing the scope of the present emergency, they knew the safest place was off the asteroid.

Ryder initiated a third call on his wrist interlink.

"Yes, Sir," came the reply.

"Byron, get in Gaylin's office—now."

Almost immediately, the sound of running footsteps down the hallway could be heard. They came closer until Byron Gunn burst into the office. Gaylin was still transfixed at the window with his hands pressed against the glass and his gaze tilted downwards at the carnage below.

Ryder grabbed Gaylin's shoulder and spun him around. He pressed his finger into his cousin's chest and said, "Get it together! This is no time to shit your pants!" Ryder turned to Byron. "Do you have an agent surveilling his wife and daughter?"

"Yes, Sir."

Ryder placed his hand on Byron's shoulder. "Get Gaylin to the evacuation ship. Do you have your air pistol?"

Byron nodded in the affirmative.

Narrowing his eyes, Ryder added, "Get him to safety. Use the gun if you have to. Don't take a car because you'll never make it. The space field is only a few blocks away, so run if you have to—just get there."

"You can count on me, Sir."

Ryder gave the security chief a reassuring smile and in a comforting tone, said, "I know you can." Without thought, Ryder's voice shifted to a deeper tone as he added, "Take the stairs. The elevator might not work. Once you are clear of the building, call your agent and give direction for Gaylin's family to be immediately taken to the Gunn space field."

"Aren't you coming with us?" Gaylin asked.

"I will be right behind you, but I need to get my mother," Ryder replied.

When the three men exited the room, they saw Linkin as the only person who hadn't fled. The four men rushed down the forty flights of stairs and ran out onto the sidewalk just as a flash in the distance blinded them. A second later, as they turned towards it, the sound of the explosion swept over them. Ten kilometres away, on the roof of the chamber, a large fireball had exploded out of the rock. Huge chunks of the asteroid could be seen in the distance, falling to the floor of the cavern.

Ryder turned back to Gaylin and Byron. "Thankfully, that's not in the direction we need to go."

"What was it?" Gaylin asked.

"I suspect one of the hydrogen tanks along the central axis exploded." Ryder explained. "More will follow, so hurry." With that said, Ryder and Linkin turned and bolted down the street. Ryder's mother's house was seven blocks away.

Byron and Gaylin pressed through the throng of shocked Korians, then turned up the next laneway. The Gunn space field was six blocks away. After four blocks, Byron's wrist interlink beeped. Normally, he wouldn't have answered it, but the specific cadence and tone indicated it was a priority one call. His fingers wrapped around Gaylin's arm, pulling him to a stop.

The air above the laneway was hazy with the smoke drifting from the fires. A few of the overhead light banks had gone out—a few more were flickering. Byron hissed into the interlink, "What is it!"

"Commander Gunn, this is Ella Sny. I have important news."

Byron lifted his wrist to a position where Gaylin could hear the discussion. "Where are you Ella?"

The woman was one of the pair assigned to follow Shareen Zaf. Her voice was haggard, and it sounded like she was having trouble breathing. "Sir, I'm in C25."

"But C25 is locked down."

The woman replied through a nervous laugh. "I know. I'm as far from the reactor as I can be, along with thousands of other Korians."

"The reactor—what happened?" Byron asked.

"Sabotage—that's what happened. The reactor went critical. I think they tried to eject the core, but somewhere along the way, it exploded. There are many people with burns coming from that direction. I'm certain there's a radiation leak."

Byron and Gaylin both knew the woman was as good as dead. Even if the radiation didn't kill them right away, protocol for an evacuation was for all chamber exits to be sealed and the air filtration systems to be shut off. In no time, the survivors would have no air. The protocol was set in place to sacrifice a single chamber to save the rest of the asteroid. "I'm sorry," was all Byron could manage.

"There's something I need to tell you," Ella added. "I heard an engineer run from the reactor facility. He was holding his wounded arm and screaming gibberish as he ran, but I think I understood what he was yelling."

"Yes, Ella."

"Sir, he was yelling, 'Shareen Zaf was the person who blew up the reactor.'"

Both men were shocked and had very few words they could think to respond. Byron said, "Thank you. Thank you for everything." There was a click as he disengaged the call. His eyes turned to Gaylin and said, "We have wasted enough time. Now, we really need to run!"

Ryder Gunn was panting. He was in great shape, so he was able to run the seven blocks to his mother's house at a good clip. A block away, he saw two houses toppled over. His heart, beating at a ridiculous pace, came up into his throat as he caught sight of his mother's house—or at least what was left of it. Most of the back wall was still standing, but the other three walls had fallen in on themselves. Ryder dropped to a squat and closed his eyes. Although, he hoped his mother had escaped before the collapse, something deep within told him this was not the case.

Another explosion from down the street and the subsequent yelling, brought Ryder shooting up to his feet. There was nothing more he could do here. His thoughts were of Romy, but especially, Shareen. He knew Fehyr would do everything in his power to get Romy to the escape ship. Since Ryder considered Shareen part of his family, he had told her of their family's evacuation plan. His hope was for her to be waiting for him at the space dock.

Gaylin and Byron made it to the last corner and bolted down the laneway. Thankfully, at the end of it they saw the two-story hanger building still standing. As they moved closer, Byron saw five of his security personnel guarding the heavy, metal, double-doors that were slung open. The men looked menacing, with each carrying an air, assault rifle. There were three bodies strewn across the street in front of them—a sure sign the security personnel were not hesitant to use the weapons if unauthorized people tried to storm the dock below them. The guards recognized Byron and Gaylin right away and ushered them through the opening.

Gaylin stopped and put a hand against Byron's chest. "You wait here with your men for Ryder. Don't close these doors until he's come through. Is that understood?"

"Yes, Sir."

Gaylin skipped down the two flights of stairs to the boarding platform. There were two more security personnel there along with at least thirty family members who appeared directionless. Gaylin ran to the guards and told them to get everyone down the stairs and into the ship, with the understanding they would be leaving momentarily. Everyone followed Gaylin's direction except for one older man who stood on the boarding platform with his fingers intertwined behind his back.

Gaylin approached him and said, "Fehyr, where's Romy?"

Fehyr answered without taking his eyes off the entrance to the lower level at the far side of the hanger, "He is on board along with your wife and daughter."

"You need to join them."

"Not until Ryder arrives. I will not leave without him."

Gaylin raised an eyebrow as he thought, *good for you.* He turned and stood beside Fehyr, with his own fingers intertwined behind his back. "Then, we shall wait together."

Ryder and Linkin had a good ten blocks to traverse. They needed to run down several streets and lanes in a zig-zag pattern before they would arrive at the space dock. They passed bodies in the street and families, crying as they hovered over their loved one. Ryder knew he could not help these people other than yelling at them, "Follow your evacuation plan!"

Many of them looked at Ryder dumbfounded. The general population had often been told to have an evacuation point with a ship at a dock with their name on the manifest. But many assumed a real evacuation would never be needed. It explained the look Ryder saw on many of their faces.

Side by side, Ryder and Linkin rounded the last corner and bolted up the laneway. The heavy, metal, double-doors of the Gunn space field were open. Guarding it, they saw Byron and five of his people. They also saw the bodies across the road and grimaced at the reality of the events unfolding. *Many more Korians would die on this day.*

Ryder was almost at the double-doors, when a flash of metal caught his eye. He skidded to a stop and looked down a side alley where the flash of light originated. Cowering behind two large crates, he saw a family: a mother, father and three young children. One of them, a young girl, held a doll and the light played off it's necklace for a second time. He heard Byron call for them to hurry, but he hesitated. Ryder looked towards Byron, then back to the family.

He made a decision and urgently waved towards the family. "Hurry!" was all he said.

The family bolted out into the street, but behind the safety of Ryder. They were fearful of the armed guards. Ryder encouraged them and grasped the young girl's hand as they sped through the guards. Byron ordered the doors closed, and they followed Ryder down the stairs.

Fehyr smiled and Gaylin gave out a more boisterous whoop when they saw Linkin and Ryder running towards them along with the unknown family in tow. Running just behind them were Byron and the guards. As soon as Ryder was close enough, Gaylin said, "It's okay, Cousin. Romy is safely on board."

Between deep breaths, Ryder said to Linkin, "Please check on Romy."

Ryder turned back to Gaylin. "My mother?"

Gaylin gave his head a slight shake.

Ryder took a deep gulp of air before his fingers dug into Gaylin's arm. "Is Shareen here?"

Gaylin took Ryder aside, a few steps away from the others. "Ryder. She didn't make it. She was in C25 and the nuclear plant has blown up."

"No, that can't be…"

"C25 has been locked down, and everyone in the chamber is dead."

"No!" Ryder yelled as he took a step backwards. Ryder turned to run for the exit, but he ran headlong into Byron who had moved into a strategic blocking position. Ryder struggled to slip out of the security chief's grasp until he felt a pinch in his neck. Gaylin had pressed his ring into Ryder's skin, releasing a tiny needle. The ring was one quite a few of the Talus elite wore in case they were ever attacked or kidnapped. A small amount of solution was injected into Ryder's bloodstream, rendering him instantly unconscious.

Gaylin turned and yelled at the guards. "Get everyone on board. Tell the pilot we'll be leaving in five minutes." They complied—all except, as expected, Fehyr, who would not leave without Ryder.

With Ryder cradled in Byron's arm, Gaylin whispered, "I need you to do two things for me."

Worry overcame Byron's face. "You're not coming with us?"

Gaylin grinned. He knew there was no place for him on this new world; nor was there a place for him on the ships that would survive. This was his home and always would be. He said, "First, tell Ryder I'm sorry I pushed him out of the tree."

Byron's face looked confused.

"Don't worry. He'll know what that means," Gaylin added.

Byron nodded.

"Second, I need you to take an oath and promise you'll never tell Ryder what Shareen has done. It is likely the secret will die in C25."

Again, Byron nodded and then turned, dragging Ryder towards the ship entry. After two steps he turned his head back and said, "Mister Gunn."

"Yes."

"I just wanted to say, Sir, you're a *good* man."

A wide smile covered Gaylin's face. It wasn't the typical pretentious one he usually put on; rather, it was one filled with pure joy. Through it, he replied, "Yes, I think I am."

Both men turned. Byron dragged Ryder down the stairs towards the ship while Gaylin walked towards the exit. Fehyr watched curiously. First, he heard Gaylin hum. Then, it turned into a boisterous song. At the same time, he started to skip awkwardly with his arms moving in uncoordinated gyrations. If Fehyr knew Gaylin better, he would know he was seeing a last performance of the classic, Gunn family crazy dance, with Gaylin happier than he had ever been in his life.

Chapter 23: Taking Charge

Fernand Rok gripped the railing of the raised platform within the command deck. He thought, *I shouldn't even be here. It wasn't my shift. Keyon Oro was supposed to be on shift as Talus ship master, but he needed the day off. I owed him a shift, so here I am in the middle of the biggest disaster this asteroid ship has ever seen.*

The command center was a spheroid with a short diameter of 30 metres and a long diameter of 100. It was a module attached to the front of the Talus asteroid via eight heavy clamp arms and a boarding tunnel. One level below, Fernand viewed the main deck. On the left was a row of cabinets and computer terminals. These were only monitoring stations, with one specified to control the asteroid's stability, one was a radar station and the last controlled guidance.

Below, and on the right, was a similar row of controls. However, these monitored the environmental systems within each chamber, including, air movement, air quality, temperature, humidity, and lighting. Behind the main cabinets were row upon row of supporting electrical cabinets and computers, along with another twenty engineers who performed the legwork.

On the left, behind the monitoring stations, the same array of cabinets and engineers were working feverishly to deal with the emergency. Beside him, the Talus first mate, Ayo Fyr, sat in the chair behind her work station, white as a ghost. Fernand thought, *she'll be of no use at all.* Thankfully, at the end of the narrow catwalk sat Ebba Krl, the most experienced asteroid pilot in the military. At least she was keeping her cool, notwithstanding the holographic image across the front of the command deck, depicting the carnage escalating further down the asteroid.

Fernand turned to his left and yelled, "Radar, tell me what's going on out there!"

Vera Tor, the senior radar officer, replied, "Ship master, there are at least ten ships docked and taking evacuees away. There are another 50 ships behind Talus. As soon as one ship leaves a dock, another comes in to take it's place."

"Mister Jose Fex, keep this ship stable. Let me know as soon as you have issues with rotation or alignment."

Jose was the stability control officer. He snapped his head around and said, "Sir, rotation is stable, but I can only maintain 60 per cent rotational speed. That means gravity is at 60 per cent as well. But axial alignment is good, even though we have lost 28 of the 400 side thrusters."

Turning his head to the right, Fernand bellowed at the environmental control officers. "What are the atmospheric conditions in chamber C25?"

Viola Jez turned on her stool. Her face was drawn and her words were breaking with sorrow or fear—both were understandable in the present circumstances. "Ship master, there are *no* atmospheric conditions because there is *no* atmosphere in C25. The same can be said for C24. If anyone is left in either chamber, they're dead."

As soon as the evacuation alarm was sent out from C25, Ship master Fernand Rok had received a communique informing him of the events. He was continuing to receive updates every 15 minutes since that first call. He knew there was an asteroid-wide evacuation underway, even though there were nowhere near enough ships to remove even 10 per cent of the population. However, if they made a mistake on the command deck, absolutely no one would be leaving.

He and most of the people working under him had family in Talus. He needed to keep them focused. He yelled out, "Your attention please— everyone." They stopped their tasks and all eyes were upon him. It allowed him to continue in a softer voice. "Many of you have family in Talus. Some might want to go find them and help them evacuate—as do I." He paced up and down the narrow catwalk as he spoke, looking both left and right, trying to look into the eyes of each and every one of his crew. "But the highest probability of success for our friends and family to escape this rock, is for us to do our jobs—and to do it better than we have ever done it in the past. There are many ships waiting to take citizens off. To help them, we need to keep this asteroid together for as long as possible." He didn't think he saw much relief in many faces, but at least he did his best. "Everyone back to work."

Fernand glanced at Ayo Fyr, his first mate, and said, "Ayo, change the holographic view. I want to see the view from camera 23-A. let's see what that hole looks like."

There was no response.

Fernand turned his head and saw Ayo still seated, blank faced. Three strides put Fernand beside her, and he clenched his fingers into her shoulder, almost tearing a hole in the jacket. Through clenched teeth, he hissed, "You're second in command. Get it together." He shook her until her eyes came to look into his. The colour returned to her face. "Is that understood?" he asked. Without waiting for a response, he came to his full height. "Camera 23-A. Bring up the image now," he grumbled.

On board the Gunn family evacuation ship, *Rendezvous*, Byron Gunn looked out the glass bubble window. He was looking at the same scene Fernand Rok was looking at through camera C23-A. There was a massive, jagged hole in the side of the asteroid. As Talus spun, it came into view on each rotation whereby he could discern the large rift emanating from each side of the jagged hole. Byron had been watching for ten minutes—since the glow of a fireball caught his attention. It had burst from the hole, but lasted only a few minutes. The flame from the hydrogen tank explosion needed oxygen for sustainment, so once the oxygen was gone—so was the fire.

Byron heard a groan from behind him. Thirty minutes had passed since the ship left Talus, and Ryder was only now awakening from his drug-induced slumber. Linkin was standing over him and handed Ryder a glass of water. "Drink this. It'll help clear your head."

Ryder took a drink, and then names began to blurt from his lips. "Romy—Shareen—my mother."

As Byron walked towards the couch in the stately quarters usually reserved for the vidame, Linkin answered, "Romy is fine and sitting out in the common room. There's no word on Shareen or your mother."

Ryder pointed to the window. "Help me to see."

Linkin and Byron each took one arm and helped a still groggy Ryder to his feet. They helped him stumble to the window, where Ryder grasped the lower sill to help his stability. The three men peered out. Talus's rotation seemed stable, but it was slower. Covering the surface, like pockmarks, were hundreds of sets of open dock doors. To all who saw it, it meant there were people there waiting to be evacuated. To the rear of Talus, they saw a growing armada of ships. Many were military, but there were cargo ships, mining ships— anything that had a place for the citizens needing evacuation.

Ryder marvelled at the bravery of the men who manned the many control towers across the surface. They stayed at their stations, knowing at any moment the asteroid could come apart, leaving them to die in their towers.

Without looking at Byron, Ryder said, "I take it Gaylin did not come with us."

"No, Sir. Talus was his home. He felt he needed to stay there."

"You were loyal to my cousin. You are aware, he didn't particularly like me?"

A half smile came across the big man's face. "No, although his actions most often did not show it, he actually *loved* you. For those close to him, it was easy to see."

Ryder nodded. "I would like you to continue as head of family security and intelligence, but you will work for me."

"It would be an honour, Sir."

"Very good," Ryder said. "I have two assignments for you. The first priority is for you to find Shareen Zaf. Check all the ships. If she is alive, I want her brought to me. Second, it appears I am the senior Gunn family member. Let's verify that and also take a head count. I want to know how many Gunn family members have evacuated."

"I will begin immediately, Mister Gunn," Byron smartly replied as he turned to leave the quarters. *He felt bad.* He was in Ryder's employ for less than a few seconds, and already he was deceiving the man. He knew Shareen was the cause of the catastrophe in Talus, just as he knew she was dead. He'd sworn to Gaylin he would not tell Ryder, and it was a last task he would fulfill for his previous employer.

Turning to Linkin, Ryder said, "I also have a task for you. I want you to initiate a similar search throughout the fleet for my mother. I want to know if she escaped."

Linkin replied, "Of course. I will begin…"

Linkin's words were interrupted by a flash from the direction of Talus. They just caught the end of an explosion. A cargo ship was lowering into a docking bay. The ship must have hit the front of the dock opening and the front had been ripped off. The remainder of the ship spun on an angle until it crashed into the surface of the asteroid, half a kilometer away from the dock.

"Do you see it?" Linkin asked.

"Yes." They could both see the asteroid's spin had developed an irregularity. The front was beginning to wobble off center. "They're having trouble controlling the stability."

In Talus's command center, Jose Fex yelled out, "Ship master, we're having issues controlling the rotation! It's going to become difficult for the ships to dock."

Fernand Rok walked halfway down the catwalk and looked down at his stability officer. "Suggestions?"

"We need to stop Talus, or at least slow it down," Jose recommended.

Fuck, Fernand thought. Talus had never been stopped or slowed down—ever, as far as he knew. He knew the procedure. It just had never been done before.

Vera Tor, manning the radar station, yelled out, "Sir, we just lost a cargo transport! It exploded while trying to dock!"

Fernand had no choice. He strode to the end of the raised catwalk, to a position beside pilot Ebba Krl. He put his hand on her shoulder. "Send out a bulletin to all ships. Tell them we're going to stop. Tell them to abort all docking efforts until further notice." He gave Ebba a few minutes to coordinate the task, then he said, "Let's start the deceleration. Drop the electromagnetic drive by 10 per cent every ten minutes. Begin now."

The pilot had a dust-covered, glass plate overtop the far-left side of her control desk. She slid a lever to the side and opened it. Within, there was a lever with per cent graduations marked on it. She pulled it back to 90 per cent. The command center received a slight jostle but there were no apparent ill effects.

"Jose! Keep the ship stable. Manually adjust the side thrusters if you have to," Fernand bellowed.

Fifty minutes later, the drive lever was at zero per cent. Fernand said to Ebba, "Now comes the tricky part. The drive is off, and we have slowed significantly, but now we need to use the forward thrusters. It's all manual. Can you handle it?"

"Of course, Ship master," she replied, even as she thought, *how the fuck do I know. No one has ever done it, other than in the monthly tests in the simulation facility—and this was far from a simulation.* On the right side of her console was another glass enclosed system. She flipped the glass open and saw a multitude of levers, with a larger one in the middle. As soon as the glass had opened, additional gauges popped up on her monitor. She would need these to monitor their attitude to an incrementally finer level. These gauges monitored yaw, pitch and roll which, when first considered, didn't really matter in space. However, their rate of change was. As long as a change in their attitude was uniform, and most certainly not alternating, the asteroid would slow and finally stop.

Ebba placed her finger on the larger central lever and gave it a slight bump forward. The command center jerked forward along with Fernand Rok. He almost fell off the catwalk.

"A little less brake, please, Miss Krl," he offered as his fingers tugged downwards on the bottom of his jacket.

Ryder watched in amazement from the common area of the *Rendezvous*. Talus had come to a stop, as had the entire fleet. The only movement was the rotation of the asteroid and the now constant movement of ships in and out of Talus's space docks. Ryder had been listening to the military channels used in space and the police channel used in Talus. There were fires in many of the chambers along with explosions, typically from above, as tanks of hydrogen or oxygen were compromised. Five of the chambers were now reported as having zero atmosphere. Ryder didn't need the radio channels to understand the greatest risk. He just had to look out the observation port and see the rift around Talus had grown—now halfway around the asteroid.

Linkin was sitting beside Romy who had found a new friend. Romy was laughing in the middle of a silly game with the young girl with the doll, who Ryder saved at the entrance to the Gunn docks.

Ryder motioned for Linkin to come to him. Once close by, Ryder whispered to Linkin. "Get on the military channel. Find Admiral Milton Fyr."

"The admiral who was on the peace negotiating team with you?"

"Yes, the same. The one who is also the senior advisor to Vidame Fyr. Tell him I need to speak with him."

As Ryder turned back to the observation port, he saw a large chunk of the asteroid burst out from Talus. Just behind it was a large concrete structure, spinning as it left the rock structure. When it was ten kilometres from the asteroid, it exploded. Ryder knew it was a second nuclear core that had been jettisoned. That meant there was only one left to power the ventilation fans and the heating system. Once it failed, the hope of survivors would be gone.

Fernand Rok gripped the railing in front of him as the asteroid rocked from another explosion. First mate, Ayo Fyr, jumped to her feet. Her eyes were wild as she grasped the lapels of the ship master's jacket. "Sir, we can escape! The command center can separate from Talus! We must save ourselves!"

With one hand, Fernand grasped her jacket, pushing her to arms length. His other hand came around in a roundhouse slap to her face. With a trickle of blood dribbling from the corner of her mouth, Fernand threw her back into her chair. He pointed accusingly and, through clenched teeth, said, "I was wrong. I don't need your help. Just sit there, and don't say a fucking word!"

As she put her forehead on top of her desk and started to sob, Fernand considered her words. *She did have a point. The command center was a ship unto itself and had the capability to separate from the asteroid. However, it was a last resort he would consider only after there was no hope of more survivors.* He strode up the catwalk and stood beside pilot Ebba Krl. "Ebba, go through the process of preparing the command center for detachment." They'd all been through the process in the simulation facility many times, but again, there had never been a reason to undertake it in reality. When Fernand returned to his command station, a palm button in the corner was flashing red. He knew, once it was pressed, the command center would separate within five seconds.

For the next 18 hours, more and more survivors were evacuated from Talus. The evacuation ships transferred the Korians to nearby fleet ships such as the casino and spa ships. These other ships, not being used to waiting at a stand still, circled Talus at a distance of 500 kilometres. Ryder was surprised how well the recovery operation was progressing, when the inevitable occurred. Not having the option to jettison the final nuclear core, its reactor exploded in chamber C43. The massive force was too much for Talus. The stresses created by the explosion completed the fissure, and the front third of the asteroid separated from the remainder. This started a chain reaction explosion of all the remaining hydrogen and oxygen tanks running down the central axis of Talus. In the larger, rear portion of the asteroid, a massive fireball shot out from the separated end. Ryder saw several ships escape from their docks just in time. For others, they exploded while making the effort.

When the exploding tanks ripped through the front third of the asteroid, with a smaller mass, the force ripped it apart. From Ryder's position, the many sections looked like small pieces of rubble, but in reality, these were huge chunks—kilometres long. Within the chunks of dangerous rock, a spheroid shaped ship navigated through the carnage. Fernand Rok had pressed the disengage palm button just in time. They were safe.

The mining trawlers had been waiting for this. They swooped in and looked for sections of rock that might have take-cover pods within them. Since each pod had an emergency beacon, if there were survivors and they activated the beacon, the trawlers would know.

Eight hours later, there was no sign of the front third of Talus. The spinning remnants of rock were far out of view. The fleet—some 582 ships—for some reason, still felt the need to circle the remaining section of the asteroid, even though everyone within was dead.

Ryder had made contact with Admiral Milton Fyr. The admiral had been successful in finding the senior members of the families constituting the council of nine and several other secondary families with surviving vidames. As Ryder looked around the large meeting room within the *Rendezvous*, he was disappointed to see those seated at the table were absent vidames from the council of nine. Including himself, there were five primors. The other four leading families were represented by lower-level men—either the second or even the third in line. There were also three secondary families who's vidame had survived, and now felt they deserved a voice at the bastardized council meeting.

Ryder had come to the realization both Shareen and his mother hadn't survived. He felt lost and in no mood to chair the meeting. He had given his great uncle, Alton Gunn, some direction, and he was now bringing the meeting to order. First, Alton took a head count, identifying who was representing each family and identified the secondary families who now made a claim to the council of nine. Next, he turned to Admiral Milton Fyr who sat in front of three other fleet admirals. Alton asked, "Admiral Fyr, how many survivors are accounted for?

Admiral Fyr rose and reported, "We have not registered all the names, but we have a preliminary head count. Right now, there are 889,342 survivors."

Ryder's chin sagged. There were eight million inhabitants in Talus. *We have saved only 11 per cent.* Ryder asked, "Is there any hope in finding more take-cover pods?"

"The mining trawlers discovered 24 pods with live beacons. Only two weren't compromised and had survivors. Ironically, they were pods from chamber C25, the chamber where all this began."

Alton recorded the numbers and said, "Admiral, where are we on critical supplies?"

"It could have been worse," the admiral admitted. "We have 23 water tankers, 20 oxygen tankers, and we have several oxygen and water factory ships in full operation. It seems our critical supplies are food and space. We've redistributed the survivors, but still the ships are overcrowded."

"We need to start rationing food," Ryder determined.

Vidame Blaire Fex from the secondary Fex family rose to her feet. "Who put the Gunn family in charge? Who has given them the authority to run the meeting and give orders? I'm the senior vidame here, and I say, 'I'm in charge!'"

Primor Guthrie of the Vad family thrust back his chair as he rose to his feet. "Senior vidame—your family isn't even on the Council of Nine. You'll be in charge of nothing!"

For the next 30 minutes, the group around the table argued as they jockeyed for positions of power. They all seemed to have a reason why they should be in charge. They all had a point, but they also each had a fault; either they were a lower family or their vidame didn't survive.

Most of the meeting members didn't notice the *beep* from Admiral Milton Fyr's wrist interlink. He moved to the corner of the room and took the call. Ryder saw the stern look come over his face as he returned to the table. He called for order, with no response. He slammed his fist onto the table once—then a second time—finally resulting in silence. "I have just received a communication you must all hear."

Alton connected the speaker console on the table to the admiral's interlink. The admiral said to the group, "I have several ships patrolling space around the fleet. Commander Holden Fyr has spotted something."

The admiral pressed a virtual button on his wrist and transferred the connection. "Holden, please repeat your report," the admiral requested.

A frantic voice came from the speaker system. "Admiral, there's a massive Sholite fleet moving towards you. Our sensors show 15 battleships, 31 destroyers, even more, less powerful military ships and an armada of supply ships behind them."

Vidame Fex shouted out, "You see! It is true! Everyone in the fleet knows Talus was destroyed by the Sholites. Now they're coming to clean up the rest of us!"

The admiral looked to the group. "We Don't need panic. We need some dir…"

The words were interrupted by Commander Holden Fyr. "Admiral, we're receiving a communication from the Sholite fleet. I'm transferring the connection to the council."

A new voice came over the link. "This is Commander Sumi Ornesco aboard the Sholite battleship, Cordoba. Please provide your status."

The group sitting around the table looked at each other, confused. They all thought—*status—what does that mean?* Finally, the primor of the Fyr family rose and said, "I think they want to know if we surrender. What do we do?"

Admiral Fyr spoke over the murmurs in the room. "I need to know who's in charge. I need an order from this council to either surrender, or to prepare for battle, but if it's battle, we need to move our forces—now."

Ryder smirked. A few moments ago, the families were clamouring for power and the right to be the voice of the council. Now, as a battle was on the horizon and likely one that would be lost, there was complete silence in the room. After a few moments of the awkward pause, Ryder rose to his feet. "I'm in charge," he announced as his eyes strayed over the other makeshift council members.

There was only one person who disagreed. Langdon Zaf, third in line for primor of the Zaf family, rose to his feet. He was an upstart, looking for recognition. He scowled and said, "Says who?"

Admiral Milton Fyr walked over to Ryder and saluted. "What are your orders, Sir?" If that alone didn't answer Langdon Zaf's question, when the other three admirals rose and stood at attention, that did.

Ryder replied, "Admiral, tell your naval vessels to stay in place. I don't want to appear aggressive. But make sure they are on the highest level of alert and ready to attack at a moments notice."

Admiral Fyr answered with an, "of course," before crisply turning and returning to the other fleet admirals.

Ryder pressed a button on the console and said, "Commander Ornesco, this is Ryder Gunn. I am speaking for the Korian council and demand you stand down."

"What has happened to Talus? Have you been attacked?"

Under his breath, Langdon Zaf said, "They're trying to fool us—catch us off guard."

Tilting his eyes up, Ryder glared at the young upstart and thought, *he just might be right.* Ryder said, "What are your intentions, Commander Ornesco?"

A different female voice came over the speaker. Ryder was relieved when he heard his sister's voice. "This is I'lish Mann, acting president of the Sholite council. We see a catastrophe and are here on a humanitarian mission. Our weapons are not active—just tell us how we can help."

Chapter 24: Final Illusion

It was a challenge to coordinate the movements of 582 Korian and 700 Sholite spaceships. First, the task of coordinating the placement of this number of ships was daunting in itself. But, even though the truce was holding and moving towards an alliance, the two races didn't particularly like each other. This added to the complexity.

Some captains just wouldn't allow their ships to be placed alongside another ship from the opposite race. Ultimately, forming the vast flotilla into four smaller fleets, with each separated in a diamond shape, allowed the two ruling councils to accommodate almost everyone. In particular, many Korians were still suspicious of the circumstances resulting in the destruction of Talus. No one had come up with a plausible explanation. Was it an accident, or was it sabotage? No one knew.

The second problem was the Korian ships were overloaded with Korians. I'lish Mann offered accommodations within the Sholite ships to alleviate the crowded conditions the Korians were enduring. Some accepted, thinking being aboard a Sholite spaceship was better than the suffocating conditions on some of the Korian ships, while others, within the suspicious group of Korians, would rather die than live among the enemy.

Consequently, this task of moving almost 1,300 spaceships from a circular holding pattern to the diamond shape over an area of 250,000 square kilometres, took eight days. It couldn't be said everyone was happy, but at least shots hadn't yet been fired. Both Ryder, directing the Korian plan, and I'lish, doing the same for the Sholites, required all their efforts to maintain the fragile peace. The almost 900,000 surviving Korians and over two million Sholites, only had one option now; that was to continue to Alpha Centauri—a journey that would take four months.

A temporary Korian council, now increased from nine to twelve, was in place. Since the vidames from the Talus Council of Nine were now considered lost with no hope of rescue, advisors or primors, such as Ryder, temporarily replaced them. However, to keep the peace, the three surviving vidames from the secondary families were allowed to join the group.

One of the first motions passed by the new Council of Twelve was to designate a neutral spaceship for council meetings and other administrative duties. Ryder knew this was because, even though they agreed to let him lead the group until they arrived at Alpha Centauri, they didn't want the council to appear a dictatorship propped up by the Gunn family. That's why Ryder was on a shuttle along with Fehyr, Linkin and Byron. They were on their way to the council ship for their third council meeting in the last three days.

Ryder was happy to leave the Gunn family ship. Urslla's mourning of her husband didn't last more than a day before her romantic pursuit of Ryder began in earnest. She all but threw herself at him, at one point even slinking into his bed in the middle of the night. The woman just wouldn't take *no* for an answer. She was extremely attractive, but Ryder knew, considering his present position, an association with Urslla wouldn't provide an advantage for the Gunn family, nor the fragile alliance with the Sholites.

Ryder Gunn, Byron and Fehyr deboarded from the shuttle. When Linkin was about to follow, Ryder put a hand on his chest. "As we discussed, stay here for now. Take care of our guests until they are called for."

Linkin answered with a nod and watched the three men walk down the tunnel towards the makeshift council chamber.

The large room was simply organized with 12 tables in a square, so the delegates faced each other. Ryder, having been allowed to lead the group, sat at the head of the configuration of tables. Fortunately, the moderator from the Talus Council of Nine had survived, and he presided over the meeting. He had an agenda and read out the first item on the list. "The council members have asked for verification of our departure schedule for Alpha Centauri."

Ryder looked across the tables to Admiral Milton Fyr and gave him a nod. The admiral rose to his feet and reported, "Final preparations are being completed. The fleet will get underway at the top of the 23rd hour, tonight."

The acting primor of the Edy family posed a question. "Will we be sending word to the expeditionary group already on their way to Alpha Centauri?"

Ryder tried to hold back his grin. The Edy family was at a disadvantage since, in Talus, they controlled all leisure activities including sports, entertainment and the arts. In the present emergency conditions, these were the furthest things from the Korian's minds. Ryder knew the question was asked so the other delegates would realize the Edy family still had a voice at the table, albeit an impotent one.

Still, it was a valid question and deserved an answer. Ryder replied, "It really doesn't make sense to send a frigate ahead to notify them. It would make no difference, other than perhaps adversely affecting their mission which is now more important than ever."

Seeing the question satisfied, the moderator said, "The council has requested confirmation of the status of the Sholite leadership."

Again, Ryder answered the question. "I have confirmation former president Balorian has indeed died. I'lish Mann is the acting president and the council has agreed an election won't occur until after they arrive at Alpha Centauri."

Langdon Zaf, third in line but nevertheless the acting primor for the family, said, "Mister Gunn, I have heard there's some turmoil within the Sholite council. Two members are missing."

Remembering the communication from I'lish two days ago, he knew both Black Brighton and General Zane Merrick were the two members young Langdon spoke of. I'lish told him not to ask her questions, but he should know the two ministers would have been a problem in keeping the peace while on their journey to Alpha Centauri. She advised the problem was taken care of, and no one would know any better—as long as they didn't look too carefully in the waste disposal stream.

"There were some internal issues within the council, but the new president has assured me they have been resolved," Ryder answered.

The moderator moved to the third line item on the list. "This is specifically for Ryder Gunn as leader of the Gunn family, not as the interim leader of our council. We will be in space without the advantage of artificial gravity for at least four months. Does Gunn Pharmaceutical have a sufficient supply of gravity patches for the duration of the voyage?"

For many years, all the families requiring production facilities had expanded their operations to remote space factories on ships. This was because the space within the Talus chambers was finite, so it made perfect sense to have supplementary manufacturing and production facilities on large spaceships. Gunn Pharmaceutical was no different with one quarter of their production capacity in space. Ryder told the council of the existing capacity and his assurance the Gunn family would maintain an adequate supply.

Several council members, led by Vidame Fex, were not convinced. This was not the time for dissention within the council, so Ryder dropped a bomb. "Council members, I have hesitated, wanting to wait until we were underway, but there is a breakthrough regarding gravity patches." The council member's curiosity was piqued, and they all leaned in. "Our scientists have discovered a vaccine. One of our ships, as we speak, is in full production, creating doses of the one-time vaccine."

Ryder was not lying. Three days ago, he called on the scientists from the

Gunn Pharmaceutical group. They were shocked when they analyzed Ryder's blood and discovered the antibodies it contained. After a thorough analysis, they told him they could replicate the vaccine within a couple of weeks.

There were very few faces lacking the drawn look of shock, including Langdon Zaf. The representative of the power generation family was young and outspoken, but Ryder actually liked him for that. Langdon said, "To be clear, we will no longer require patches?"

"That's correct. Distribution will begin in a month. We will get a head start, then share the innovation with the Sholites." Ryder saw the disagreement on most faces. He stopped their objections before they began. "Do you think we can keep it a secret? Of course, the Sholites will find out, and if we don't share, it will lead to the end of our alliance and even more likely—war."

There was an awkward silence and the moderator felt it was the perfect opportunity to fill it with the next item on the agenda. "Admiral Fyr, I understand you have an announcement."

Once again, the admiral rose to his feet. "Yes, and thank you. We have all heard of the outstanding job accomplished by the Talus command crew. There are several commendations and promotions, most notably, Fernand Rok, who is promoted to *Fleet master*. He will have the responsibility of guiding us to Alpha Centauri along with Ebba Krl, who is promoted to *Fleet pilot*."

The moderator had a wide smile on his face. "Well, if there are no more issues, I'll bring the meeting to a close." He was about to bang his small gavel on the table when he was interrupted.

"There is one more issue needing to be discussed," Vidame Fex said. The moderator's smile turned to a frown as the vidame looked directly at Ryder. "Mister Gunn, we appreciate all you have done in coordinating the fleet preparations, and we have accepted you as the temporary voice of this council, but there is an issue."

Ryder took a deep breath. He knew this was coming, so the words that followed were not a total surprise.

"Mister Gunn," Vidame Fex continued, "This is a *Korian* council and our way is for a *vidame* to lead each family. Each of the primors or acting primors are making arrangement for their wives to be ordained as vidames. They will soon sit at this table. Other's, who are not married, are actively and expeditiously seeking a wife." The woman looked down her nose at Ryder. "You need to do the same."

Ryder threw up his arms. "Our home was just blown to pieces! We are in a fragile alliance with our enemy of thousands of years, yet your priority is for me to find a wife! This is not the time for that," he exclaimed, emphasising his final words.

The vidame was not to be deterred. She said in a quiet but direct tone. "Sir, we discussed this prior to your arrival today. We're all in agreement. You must find a wife—now, without delay—or we will ask you to resign your position as the leader of this council."

Ryder took another deep breath. "What would you suggest I do?"

On cue, Primor Guthrie Vad rose to his feet and strode to Ryder. He placed a folder in front of the Gunn primor and opened it. "Each of the families here have put forth one candidate, so you have 11 to choose from. For each, there is a full profile: picture, measurements, IQ, education, preferences and almost everything else you could possibly need to know."

Ryder glanced through the pages, looking at each for a few moments as he mumbled, "When do you expect me to decide?"

Vidame Fex answered, "We are in the 10th hour. We would like a decision before we depart in the 23rd hour, tonight. It gives you enough time to narrow down the list and even have a few quick interviews."

Slapping the folder closed, Ryder said, "I will do this under one condition. I need each and every one of you to take an oath, that no matter which woman I select as my wife, you will follow the two of us, without question, at least until we arrive at Alpha Centauri."

"'Without question' is a lot to ask," young Langdon Zaf offered.

Ryder blurted, "This council asking me to pick a wife in the next few hours is a lot to ask!" He glared at each and every one of them. "However, I will comply if you take an oath to follow us—the wife I select and I— without question or debate, at least until we arrive at Alpha Centauri."

No one wanted to be the first to agree. It was the outspoken Langdon Zaf, followed by Vidame Fex. Then they all took the oath.

When they were complete, Ryder turned to the moderator, "Please record in the transcript the name of each representative who took the oath for their family."

As the moderator typed into his tablet, Vidame Fex reminded Ryder, "We have done as you asked. We expect a decision from you before the fleet departs."

Ryder, who had been flipping through the pages describing the prospective candidates for a second time, closed the folder and leaned back in his chair. "I don't need that long. I can tell you right now."

Vidame Fex could not hold back her chuckle. "But you haven't met any of the young women."

"No matter. I have decided."

Sensing something wasn't right, a look of dread came over Vidame Fex's face. "Who?"

Through a smug grin, Ryder announced, "I will marry I'lish Mann."

There was complete silence. Ryder looked at the white, pasty faces around the table. It was Langdon Zaf who first realized what just happened. He slapped his hand onto the table and was bent over laughing. "Haha—haha—haha!"

Vidame Fex's face turned from white to red. She could barely talk but managed to spit out the words, "No—no! You can't pick her. She isn't on the list! She is a—Sholite!"

Young Langdon, tears in his eyes, glanced at the vidame while a finger came up to point at her. Another burst of laughter exploded from his lips.

Turning to the moderator, Ryder asked, "Check the notes. Did Vidame Fex, as well as the other representatives of the council, take an oath to accept my selection without question?"

The moderator stuttered, "Well—yes—they did—but…"

Ryder interrupted. "Check your notes. Was there a specific requirement for my selection to be limited to the list provided?"

The moderator scrolled through the notes on the tablet. He lifted his eyes to Ryder and cracked a smile. "No, there is no such limitation."

Vidame Fex fell back into her chair and rolled her eyes.

Ryder knew he had them all. "I expect each of you to abide by our agreement. It would not go well, in your efforts to maintain your precarious positions on this newly formed council, if your supporters found out you broke your oath."

Langdon finally stopped laughing. Now he just mumbled, "Oh, my. That was good."

Ryder rose to his feet and nonchalantly added, "Oh, and I am naming my son, Romy Gunn, as the next primor of the Gunn family. He will take on the role officially when he comes of age, of course."

Now, Primor Guthrie Vad took issue. "Sir, the primor must be the son of the vidame. That is the way it has always been."

"Actually—no," Ryder replied as he pointed at Fehyr who had been quietly sitting at the back of the room.

Fehyr rose to his feet, pulling out his own folder. "Three hundred years ago, Talus year 3211, Hudson Oro, the adopted son of Primor Dante Oro, was successfully acclaimed as family primor. Talus year 2485, the same result for Toman Fyr, adopted son of Deacon Fyr. Talus year 1107—" Fehyr glared at Guthrie Vad. "—a descendant of yours, Ignacio Vad, bastard son of Colton Vad, was acclaimed as primor of your family. I have four more examples, if you would like me to continue."

Rather than replying, Guthrie Vad meekly sat in his chair.

Langdon Zaf, having just finished wiping the tears from his eyes, said, "Sir, does the Sholite president agree to adopt your son?"

Again, Ryder pointed at Fehyr who took the few steps to the chamber door. He opened it and in walked Linkin Gunn, I'lish Mann, and in her hand was the tiny hand of Romy Gunn. I'lish looked every bit the presidential persona, while young Romy had a smile on his face, growing wider once he saw his father.

Once they were beside Ryder, I'lish put a hand on his shoulder, while Romy climbed onto his lap. I'lish introduced herself, even though she assumed they knew who she was. "I have heard your conversation and want to let you know, once we're married, I *will* be adopting Romy." One finger lifted, tickling Ryder's earlobe. "Isn't that right, Darling?"

Ryder flicked her hand away and then rose to his feet. He looked at Admiral Milton Fyr. "There's still much to be done before we depart—you especially, my friend." He turned to the moderator, "I think you can bring the meeting to a close."

Five minutes prior to the massive flotilla of spaceships beginning their journey to Alpha Centauri, the Gunn family ship, *Rendezvous,* made its way through several ships until they were behind two large battleships at the front of the vast diamond formation. One was a Sholite vessel, and the other was Korian with Fernand Rok and Ebba Krl aboard. They were waiting for a final command from Ryder Gunn.

Ryder and I'lish were alone in the forward observation port of the *Rendezvous.* They gazed out at the two warships and the expanse of space beyond it—where they hoped the successful future of both their peoples laid.

Ryder said, "I think our mother would be proud of us."

I'lish nodded. "Yes, somehow, I think she suspected we would have to make sacrifices for the betterment of our people—Sholite and Korian alike."

"The people won't be happy if and when they find out we are brother and sister, and our upcoming marriage is a sham."

Turning and smiling warmly at her brother, I'lish said, "We need to make sure no one finds out for the four months it will take us to arrive at our destination. Even after that, we might need to continue the pretense for a few more months until settlements are well established on our new home."

Ryder mumbled, "I hope you won't be a nagging wife."

I'lish raised an eyebrow. "Don't you ever try to kiss me—not even at official functions or ceremonies."

Ryder couldn't help but imagine the vision, and was overcome with a need to wash his tongue. A *beep* emitted from his wrist interlink. It was the top of the 23rd hour. He pressed a red button on the console in front of him. Immediately, footsteps could be heard coming up from the deck below.

A young ensign appeared in front of them. He saluted and said, "Yes, Sir?"

The young man was Ensign Marcus Fyr, the nephew of Kriton Fyr, captain of the Korian destroyer, *Reliant*. Milton Fyr realized Ryder needed a communications attaché, and he knew Marcus was a fervent proponent for peace. Ryder would like him.

Ryder said, "Marcus, please contact Fernand Rok. Tell him we can depart."

As Marcus turned towards the stairs, I'lish added, "Please also contact Sumi Ornesco, commander of the *Cordoba*. Tell her we're ready to go as well."

With a confused look on his face, the young ensign gave a salute to Ryder, then another hasty one to I'lish. Finally, he shrugged and headed for the ship's radio room.

Alone again, Ryder chuckled. "You know, he understood, from my order, to tell your commander as well."

I'lish interlaced her fingers behind her back. "You do realize, once we're married, as vidame and president, I'm in charge of the Gunn family as well as the Sholite people."

"Ah, that's the way it's going to be, is it?" Ryder replied. "You do know, the vidame is just a figurehead."

Raising her chin, I'lish replied, "Yes, and I will be the best figurehead you've ever known. Outstanding, would be a word you might want to use."

"I just might," he whispered through a grin.

The two battleships in front of them began to move forward. Once a reasonable gap was achieved, they heard the hum of their own drives engage. They were on their way to their new home, where if their sacrifices allowed, both Sholites and Korians could begin a new life in peace.

Epilogue

The man who had been reading from the tablet turned off the power and placed it on the table in the lounge of the yacht. It had been a long day. The telling of the story of Talus 3—the asteroid I knew now was simply, Talus—enthralled me for many hours. We had a short break for a light lunch, then another hour at dinner where an excellent baked fish was served. As the sun began to set, a chill had set in, and we moved into the lounge where the mysterious man—one who I was hesitant to say was still my abductor—kept my interest more than captivated.

By now, I was under no pretense the man's announcement he was an alien, or the details in his story, were anything but the truth. Even though, earlier in the morning, he gave me proof of his blue blood, it wasn't until approximately halfway through his reading that I realized there wasn't a shred of a possibility his detailed and intricate recollection could be contrived. I thought, *what would be the purpose?* So I listened to the entire story until this moment when he placed the tablet down.

I said, "Now that the story is over, will you tell me your name?"

The man smiled under his flowing brown hair. "Yevgeni, the story is not over. I have only told you half the events. There is so much more."

I'm sure he saw my eyebrows tilt downwards as they tended to do when I was confused. "I assumed Ryder, I'lish and the rest of the fleet were successful in their voyage, arriving safely at Alpha Centauri."

My one-time abductor leaned forward as the second Korian on the yacht—a man I had learned was Pascoe—brought us each a hot coffee. After the storyteller brought the cup of coffee to his nose and inhaled deeply, he said, "At this time, my name is not important. I make a point of not telling you since it would detract from the story. In fact, it would cause you great confusion."

I thought his answer both odd and intriguing. Still, I took his word for it as I brought the coffee cup to my lips. It was strong and kept me momentarily alert through the fatigue I was feeling. "I don't think my grandfather, Luca, would be happy with this story. Gaylin Gunn was the grandson of his good friend—the man described to me as Logan Russell, and from the story, it is clear Gaylin Gunn was a notorious and devious person."

"In many ways, yes, but the Korian people remember him for his bravery.

Eventually, word leaked out Gaylin had saved Ryder Gunn. In addition, there were first hand accounts from survivors indicating Gaylin Gunn helped evacuees on the last ships to leave Talus. He died helping to save many lives. That is his legacy."

"With everything you've told me, even though I've travelled to the moon and we're just beginning to send manned flights to Mars, it seems to me we're a small and insignificant world in this universe."

The man let out a laugh. "You have no idea, but I will answer in more detail if you will bear with me for another day. We both need a good night's sleep, and then I can tell you the remainder of the story." He leaned forward and his eyes lit up. "If you think what you have heard so far is surreal, then you must hear what I have yet to reveal."

"I need to call my wife."

"Of course," he replied. After reaching into his pocket, he threw me my phone. I was a little surprised he was so easily forthcoming. Nevertheless, I pressed the speed dial number and talked briefly to my wife. I thought it better not to tell her of the day's events. Instead, I continued the little, white lie my abductor began, and told her, since I was exhausted, I would be sleeping on the couch in my office. She would see me tomorrow evening. She accepted this without question since this was a common occurrence.

As I disconnected the call, I couldn't control the wide yawn that came over me. The man across from me took this as a sign and rose to his feet. He led me to the lower level where a luxurious cabin awaited me. He pointed to the pajamas neatly folded on the bed and offered me a "goodnight" before he left. Closing the door, I quickly changed into the night clothes which, once again, fit perfectly.

I rolled onto the bed. My eyelids were heavy. I couldn't help but think of the detailed story. My grandfather, Luca Ivanov, would have listened in earnest. It's likely he would have been disappointed, knowing after saving the asteroid from destruction in 2020, that it was destroyed 64 years later. I shot up to a sitting position as I realized I didn't really know *when* Talus was destroyed; it could have been a month ago or ten years ago. As I fell back on the pillow, the story whirled through my mind. *What happened to Ryder and I'lish? I must know.* The whirling thoughts subsided as my weariness returned. Moments later, my breathing slowed until I was fast asleep.

The story continues in Forsaken Drifter, book 3 of the Talus 3 series.

Dear Reader:

Reviews are important to every author. We are thankful that many readers take a few moments to return to the purchasing website, in this case, Amazon, and leave a rating and a review.

If you could do so for this story, it would be much appreciated. Keep in mind, a Hollywood style review is not needed. Even a few simple words would be great.

Thanks again, and I hope you enjoyed the story.

Peter Sandor